"Think for a minute what you'd like to see when you return home in the evenings."

"What I would like to see when I return home is an orderly house, *kinner* who are well cared for, and a good meal on the stove." He waved a hand. "As for what I like and don't like, other than what we've already discussed, the rest is inconsequential."

"And what are you willing to provide for your *fraa* in exchange for this?"

"Exchange?"

"*Jah*. A marriage, even a businesslike one, is a partnership, ain't so?"

"Yes, of course."

"So, in exchange for providing you and your *kinner* with a well-kept, pleasant home, what can she expect from you?"

"I'll provide her with a safe and secure home and with whatever else she feels she needs from a marriage, within reason."

She smiled as if he'd passed some sort of test. "*Gut.*" Then she gave him a probing look. "Are you absolutely sure there's nothing else you want to add?"

Noah hesitated a moment, then added, **"Only that I'm most definitely not looking for a love match."**

Her Amish Wedding Quilt

A Hope's Haven Novel

Winnie Griggs

FOREVER

NEW YORK BOSTON

Copyright © 2020 by Winnie Griggs
Cover design by Daniela Medina
Cover photograph by Shirley Green Photography
Cover copyright © 2020 by Hachette Book Group, Inc.

Forever
Hachette Book Group
1290 Avenue of the Americas, New York, NY 10104
read-forever.com
twitter.com/readforeverpub

First Edition: December 2020

Forever is an imprint of Grand Central Publishing. The Forever name and logo are trademarks of Hachette Book Group, Inc.

The publisher is not responsible for websites (or their content) that are not owned by the publisher.

The Hachette Speakers Bureau provides a wide range of authors for speaking events. To find out more, go to www.hachettespeakersbureau.com or call (866) 376-6591.

ISBN: 978-1-5387-3578-7 (mass market), 978-1-5387-3580-0 (ebook)

Printed in the United States of America

OPM

10 9 8 7 6 5 4 3 2 1

To my husband, my love and my rock, who supports me through thick and thin. To my agent, Michelle, who is always, always in my corner. And to Renee, who is so much more than a brainstorming and critique partner, she is my very dear friend.

Her Amish Wedding Quilt

Prologue

Noah Stoll flung a rock into Miller's Pond and quickly reached down for another one. He repeated the action, over and over, until his throwing arm was too tired to continue.

He plopped down on the ground, knees bent, and dug his heels into the rocky soil. He tilted his hat back and rubbed an arm across his brow, clearing it of sweat. Realizing there were tears on his cheeks, he swiped roughly at them with his knuckles. He might be only twelve years old, but *Daed* had told him he was becoming a man and everybody knew crying wasn't something a man did.

A rustling in the brush behind him had him scrambling to his feet. But rather than an animal, he spied a little girl who couldn't have been older than six.

"Hello," she said with a smile. She held a pail in front of her with both hands on the handle. Her *kapp* was slightly crooked and her fingertips were stained purple.

He looked around but didn't see anyone else. "Are you alone?"

She nodded. "The others are lost." She didn't seem the least bit frightened or concerned. Rather she was studying him with a kind of bright curiosity.

Noah frowned. Just what he needed, a lost *kinner* to take care of. Then he sighed, this wasn't her fault. "You're one of the Eicher girls, aren't you?"

She nodded, twisting slightly from side to side at the waist. "I'm Greta. Who are you?"

"I'm Noah. What are you doing out here?" Strange how at ease and unconcerned she was.

"Picking blackberries." She held the pail out. "Want some?"

"No, *danke*." She was an odd one. With a freckled face and a gap between her front teeth, she had the look of a curious kitten. And with numerous strands of brown hair escaping her *kapp*, dark stains on her fingers and smudges on her dress, there was an untamed look about her as well.

She studied him for a minute and came closer. "You look sad. Is something wrong?"

Embarrassed she'd read him so well, Noah turned and sailed a rock across the surface of the pond. He counted four skips before it finally disappeared below the surface. "My little *bruder* hates me." He swallowed hard, remembering the look on Calvin's face and the six-year-old's pleading and crying.

"Why does he hate you?"

Her words pulled him back from that painful memory. "We found an injured fox cub in the woods a while back that we brought home. We named it Kit and even taught it a few tricks. Calvin loved that fox and treated him like a pet." Noah had grown fond of the frisky, intelligent creature too.

"Once Kit got better, though, *Daed* told us we had to release it back in the woods where we'd found it." It was the first time he'd wanted to protest against something his *daed* had said. Not only because he liked Kit, but because he knew how it would affect his little *bruder*. But his *daed* had told him that the mark of a man was how he handled things when duty interfered with desire.

"So why is your *bruder* mad at you and not your *daed*?"

"*Daed* sent me and Calvin out on our own to set the fox free. Calvin begged me to help him hide it instead, so we could keep it. I wouldn't." He knew it had been the right thing to do. So why did it feel so bad?

Greta came closer and turned to face him. "You really liked Kit too, didn't you?"

How did she know that? "*Jah*."

Setting her pail down, she raised her arms as high as she could and placed a pudgy, little-girl hand on each side of his face. Then she met his gaze with her unexpectedly earnest one. "Your *bruder* is wrong to be mad at you. You did what your *daed* told you to, even though you knew it would make you and your *bruder* sad. I'm proud of you."

He blinked. The words were a soothing salve to a throbbing wound. But she was just a little girl who was probably parroting words. "You don't know what you're saying." He immediately felt guilty for his rough tone. But she seemed more insulted than frightened.

Her chin tilted up and her hands moved from his face

to her hips. "I do too know what 'proud of you' means." She retrieved her pail. "It's what *Mamm* says when I do something I don't want to but that's the right thing. Like helping my *shveshtra* finish their chores when I'd rather be outside playing." Her irritation was replaced with a dimpled, gap-toothed smile. "Like doing what your *daed* told you to, even though your *bruder* begged you not to."

"You really think so?" He couldn't help himself, he really needed some kindness today. Even if it was from an odd little girl.

Greta nodded, her expression solemn. "Obedience makes *Gotte* smile, ain't so? And that's a *gut* thing."

Something inside Noah eased and he was able to smile for the first time today.

"How did you do that with the rocks?" she asked, doing that twisting motion again.

"Do what?"

"Make it bounce on top of the water."

Noah hooked a thumb through his suspender. "It's a trick my *daed* taught me."

"Can you show me?"

He was surprised—it wasn't something little girls usually took an interest in learning. Then again, she wasn't like his sister or other girls he knew. "All right." He searched the ground for flat, smooth stones. "And then I'll show you the way home."

Chapter 1

Current Day (Seventeen Years Later)

Greta Eicher hopped out of bed and went to her window. She enjoyed watching the sun come up and she couldn't think of any better way to start off this New Year's Day.

Kneeling, she rested her forearms on the windowsill as she admired the view. It was beautiful, breathtaking. Those shifting shades of gold, orange and purple were a wonderful testament to *Gotte*'s creation, and the patterns they created on the snow this morning were particularly lovely. If only she could capture such beauty in her own quilt designs.

The morning light bathed the milking barn where the inside lighting proclaimed that *Daed* and Amos were already at work. Skip, their dog, raced out of the barn then back in, obviously full of energy. The fields beyond, blanketed with four or so inches of snow, looked pristine, as if providing a clean slate for the new day.

With a happy sigh, she thought again about what a wonderful *gut* year this would be. She'd waited long enough for Calvin Stoll to figure things out on his own, to see past their friendship to what was so obvious to her, that she and he would be *gut* together. This was the year it would happen, she could feel it.

Even if it meant she had to prod him a bit to help him see it.

"Greta!"

Martha's impatient call interrupted her pleasant thoughts. "I'm up!" she replied, quickly scrambling to her feet. The exasperated tone in her older *shveshtah*'s voice told her she'd been daydreaming at the window longer than she'd intended. She rubbed her arms against the chill, then glanced out the window once more. The shifting colors of dawn playing against the snowy fields suddenly sparked an idea for a new quilt pattern. She grabbed the sketchbook she kept close by for just that purpose and quickly drew a rough outline, capturing the vision before it got away.

Another, more insistent call from Martha forced her to set aside her pad. She dressed quickly, humming as she pinned her apron and cape in place. Then she put her hair up and donned her *kapp*, securing it with a single hairpin. Nothing could destroy her good mood today, not even Martha's responsible-to-the-point-of-asperity attitude.

The familiar aroma of coffee and breakfast that hit her when she opened her door set her stomach rumbling. It seemed Martha and Hannah were already at work in the kitchen.

She entered the kitchen just in time to see Hannah, her

younger *shveshtah*, pull a pan of sticky buns from the oven. Martha was frying eggs, with platters of cooked bacon and potatoes already resting on the counter beside her. As usual, they were getting in each other's way. How many times had she told them about ways to schedule their time at the stove so they could work more efficiently? But they never listened.

Martha, who took her role as lady of the house much too seriously, was the first to notice her. "*Ach*, you finally decided to join us. I thought I'd have to go knock on your door."

"Sorry. I got lost in the beautiful sunrise this morning and it inspired a new quilt pattern. What can I do to help?" The quicker they got everything ready, the sooner they could head to *Onkel* Simon's place. It was his and *Aenti* Ruthanne's turn to host the Eicher family New Year's Day gathering.

Hannah, who was arguably the best baker in Hope's Haven, gave her an understanding smile. "I could use some help with the sugar cookies. Just take the dough and form balls to place on the sheet pan."

"Of course."

"Be careful of the hampers," Martha warned, as Greta moved to the counter. "I've already packed up most of the food we're taking to *Onkel* Simon's today."

Greta looked at the array of hampers and rolled her eyes. She knew Martha and Hannah had cooked and baked all day yesterday—she'd contributed by doing the housework they hadn't had the time for. Still, this seemed excessive even for her two industrious *shveshtra*. "You do know we're just guests and aren't expected to feed the whole army of Eichers on our own, don't you?"

Martha wasn't amused. "It's impolite to show up without bringing a contribution for the meal."

"But this is so much more than just a contribution."

Martha shot her an exasperated look. "Really, Greta, must you comment on everything?"

Greta snapped her mouth closed and went to work on the sugar-cookie dough, focusing her thoughts on something more pleasant, like her idea for that new quilt pattern. She could already picture it in her mind—the colors of the new dawn radiating from the top of the quilt and seeping down into the solid white of the bottom half. The quilt stitches would outline the hills and furrows of the fields covered in snow. Something clean and crisp and filled with promise—much like this new year.

And like her feelings for Calvin.

There really was no other man in the district for her, literally. Twice before she'd thought a young man would ask for her hand. Once during the early days of her rumspringa, Henry Knepp had seemed interested, but he'd eventually turned his attentions to another. And three years ago Karl Schmucker had actually courted her for two months before deciding they were not suited.

But Calvin was different. Where others thought of her as too outspoken and forward, Calvin respected her spirit and encouraged her independent thinking. They'd make the perfect couple. Not that she was head over heels in love, but this was no fictional romance novel either. Instead, she and Calvin had a solid friendship and mutual affection. That made for a strong bond, love would grow between them over time.

Besides, not only were they well suited, but Calvin was a hard worker and progressive thinker like herself.

Though he'd only been eighteen when his *daed* died, he'd done a *gut* job of running the family farm ever since. Noah, the older brother, had already begun establishing himself in his woodworking business by then and hadn't wanted to return to full-time farm work. So Calvin had stepped up to shoulder most of the load. And the farm had flourished under his—

The door opened, interrupting her thoughts and letting in a blustery burst of cold air. *Daed* entered, stomping his work boots on the mat, and right behind him was Amos Kurtz, the neighbor who worked as their farmhand.

"It smells like breakfast is ready." *Daed*'s booming voice filled the room

Amos inhaled deeply as he unwound his neck scarf. "Your *dechder* are the best cooks in the county, Isaac, ain't so?"

"Martha and Hannah take after their *mamm* in that respect," *Daed* replied.

"Happy New Year, Amos," Hannah called out.

"*Danke*, Hannah." The lanky farmhand grinned at all three girls. "And Happy New Year to all you lovely ladies as well."

Amos had a contagiously jolly personality that never failed to draw a smile from those around him.

The two men shed their heavy coats and hats, then Greta's *daed* rubbed his hands together. "It's mighty *kalt* out there, but the sky is clear. I don't think we'll be getting any more snow today."

"*Wunderbaar*." Greta could hardly contain her good mood. "Everyone should be able to make it to *Onkel* Simon's."

Everything was going her way today. *Aenti* Ruthanne

and Calvin's *mamm* were sisters, which meant the Stoll family would show up at the gathering sometime today. And when they did, she'd find an opportunity to talk to Calvin and perhaps give him that little nudge he so obviously needed. Others might consider that too forward, but Calvin would see it for the initiative it was.

Martha swiped the back of her wrist over her forehead, then waved toward the table. "*Daed*, you and Amos have a seat. I'll have breakfast served in a few minutes."

That was Martha, not only was she *gut* at all things domestic, but she took her responsibilities to keep the house running smoothly very seriously.

As the men settled into their seats, Greta navigated her way around her *shveshtra* and grabbed the coffee pot from the back of the stove. She quickly poured up two cups of the hot brew, adding two teaspoons of sugar for Amos and a generous dollop of cream for *Daed*.

"To warm you while you wait," she said, as she set the cups in front of them. "You finished the milking in record time today."

"*Jah*." *Daed* pointed his coffee spoon at Amos. "Amos was already at work when I got up this morning."

Amos nodded. "I promised *Mamm* I'd be quick about helping you with the milking. I need to head back to help with the chores at home so everything would be taken care of before our guests arrive."

Within minutes, the table was set and the food laid out. After silent prayers of thanks were offered, the platters were passed around.

"So Amos, is your *mamm* preparing a big meal today?" Hannah asked.

"For sure and for certain. She was already up and

cooking when I rose this morning. We're expecting *Onkel* Philip's family and *Onkel* Michael's family to eat lunch with us. There'll be at least twenty of us."

Greta hid a smile. There would be more than double that many at *Onkel* Simon's today. *Daed* had five siblings, and all of them, along with many members of their families, would be there. And of course some of *Aenti* Ruthanne's family would be there as well.

"I have an extra strawberry pie you must take to her." Hannah, as usual, was willing to share the fruits of her labor. Greta also spied her slipping some cheese in her napkin. No doubt it would make its way to Skip on their way out.

Greta lost track of the conversation after that. It was all she could do not to bolt her food down. She just wanted the morning to rush by. The new year wouldn't really kick off properly for her until she was able to talk to Calvin.

* * *

"Here, let me help you with that." Greta grabbed one of the urns of coffee while Esther Mast grabbed the other.

"*Danke*." Esther hefted the urn to get a better grip. "They're so awkward to carry."

Greta nodded, then shifted her hold as she opened the door. They stepped outside, headed for the barn using the path that had been cleared of snow. A number of the men had gathered out there this afternoon, and *Aenti* Ruthanne wanted to make sure they had access to the hot brew.

"You know," Greta mused, "someone should build a

cart with special holders to keep these containers from tipping over. It would make transporting them so much easier." She waited for Esther to follow her through and then shut the door.

Esther laughed. "How do you come up with these ideas?" She gave Greta an arch look. "Me, I'd settle for a couple of strapping young men to carry them for us."

Greta grunted. "I'd rather count on a cart." Then she cut her friend a sideways look. "Maybe I'll share my idea with Noah. He could build them to sell."

"Noah is always open to moneymaking ideas, though he has to be convinced that's what they are before he acts."

"Calvin's *bruder* is a good businessman, for sure and for certain." It was Noah Stoll who'd had the foresight to expand his woodworking shop and display floor to include three shops in addition to his own, creating the Hope's Haven Amish Craft Mall.

And she not only admired him for that, she was also grateful he'd done so. She and Esther were partners in one of those shops, The Stitched Heart Quilt Shop, which not only sold their own work, but accepted work from other area quilters on consignment too.

Noah wasn't just an astute businessman, he was also a fair landlord to the shopkeeper tenants and, from all accounts, a talented craftsman.

Feeling slightly disloyal, Greta spoke up on Calvin's behalf. "Calvin is a *gut* businessman as well. He's always open to trying new things on the farm. He's made lots of improvements, both in machinery and practices, and they're paying benefits now." And best of all, he'd let her have a small hand in that. He'd not only discussed his plans with her to get her opinion, but he'd truly listened to the suggestions she'd had to offer.

Esther cut her a knowing look. "And has Calvin offered you a ride in his buggy yet?"

Greta felt her cheeks heat. A young man offered a girl a ride home in his buggy when he was ready to court her. "Not yet. But I'm thinking I might give him a little nudge today."

Esther's eyes widened, but she didn't respond right away. They'd arrived at the barn now, and it was full to almost bursting with men in black hats and dark coats. The bearded faces outnumbered the clean-shaven ones, indicating many of the single men had congregated elsewhere.

Noah, along with Esther's younger *bruder* Daniel, stepped up to take the urns from them.

When they headed back to the house, Esther's startled look had been replaced by a considering one. "Well, that's one way to find out where you stand."

Greta didn't let her friend's skepticism throw her. "That's the idea." Then she changed the topic. "I was thinking we could keep the shop closed tomorrow. I don't think there'll be many folks out shopping for quilts so soon after Christmas."

Esther nodded. "I suppose it wouldn't hurt. We need time to replenish our stock after the Christmas rush anyway."

"We did have a good season, didn't we?" It had been the best sales month they'd had since they opened the shop three years ago.

"So why do you want the day off tomorrow? Do you have special plans?"

What she hoped to be doing was making plans with Calvin for their new life together.

But before she could say anything, Esther looked past her and frowned. "*Ach*, there goes David, running around without his mittens. That boy goes through mittens like *Daed* goes through horse feed." She started toward him. "I'm sure Noah brought an extra pair." David was Noah's four-year-old son. Anna, David's little *shveshtah*, was somewhere around as well.

"Let me get him while you fetch the mittens," Greta offered. Truth be told, she loved Noah's *kinner*. Esther was Noah's cousin, and he occasionally brought his little ones to the quilt shop for her to watch when Maisie, his younger *shveshtah*, was unable to care for them. Greta had happily helped and had grown to love the motherless pair. It would be so nice when she married Calvin and the little ones could call her *Aenti* Greta.

Once David's hands were again swaddled and he'd been admonished to keep the mittens on, Greta and Esther headed back to the house.

"Speaking of courting"—Esther cut her an arch look—"I hear your latest pairing went well."

Greta nodded, feeling a glow of satisfaction. "Carl and Malinda are courting now and from all accounts are both very happy." Over the past couple of years she'd found herself taking on the role of a sort of matchmaker. It had started out almost by accident. Her cousin Philip, the painfully shy youngest son of her *mamm*'s sister, had asked her to speak to Esther on his behalf. Unfortunately, Esther wasn't interested in him in that way. Not wanting to see her cousin retreat even further into his shell, Greta had offered to help him find a woman who was interested. She'd matched him with Elsie Wengerd, and the two had been happily married for over a year now.

While she'd intended for this to be a onetime thing, Philip had sung her praises to a couple of his friends. Those two others had come to her at different times, and she'd been able to help them as well, though it had taken more than one attempt to pair them up. And while she never actively sought out these opportunities, the idea that she'd played a part in helping friends find happiness brought her much joy.

Of course she wasn't a matchmaker in the literal sense. Her approach was more to figure out the kind of person who'd complement them, help them see the possibilities, perhaps initiate a meeting, then leave the rest up to them.

And now it was her turn to find that happy ending for herself, and the anticipation was like a song bubbling up inside her.

Once back inside, Greta went about visiting with her cousins and helping where she was needed. All the while she waited for an opportunity to speak to Calvin privately. But whenever he seemed unoccupied she was busy helping her *aenti* or watching someone's *boppli*. Several times when she had free time she lost sight of where Calvin was.

At one point she saw Calvin's *mamm* sitting alone in a corner of the living room. Debra Stoll had the repu-tation of being a difficult woman—a woman who was demanding and set in her ways and who always thought she knew best. But Greta figured if she was going to become a member of the Stoll household as Calvin's *fraa*, then she should learn to get along with the family matriarch. After all, a little tact and kindness could go a long way.

Pasting on a smile, she approached the woman. "Hello, would you like me to get you something to drink or some of my *shveshtah*'s snickerdoodles? They're quite *gut*."

Debra looked down her nose at her, a surprising feat given she was seated. "Do you think I'm too infirm to get it for myself?"

Greta blinked. "Not at all, I just thought I'd save you the trouble—"

"It would be no trouble at all for me to fetch them myself. I'm not helpless."

"Of course you're not." She'd obviously stepped on a sensitive area of Debra's life. Time to try a different approach. "*Aenti* Ruthanne told me you made that rhubarb pie with the cherry topping. I don't think even my *shveshtah* Hannah has ever made one as tasty."

The older woman settled back down. "It's a recipe I got from my *grossmammi*. My own family claims it's their favorite, especially Calvin."

Greta filed that information away. She'd want to learn how to make it once she and Calvin were wed.

She settled in a nearby chair and spent the next twenty minutes with Debra, mostly listening to unasked-for advice and reminiscences about how things were done much better in the older woman's day. But Greta didn't mind, she considered herself to be laying groundwork for the future relationship she hoped to have with this important member of Calvin's family.

When Greta finally stood and excused herself, she saw Calvin head toward the back door, and for once he was alone. At last—this was her chance. She quickly donned her wool coat and slipped out the door behind him. She was in luck. Calvin stood alone, stroking the nose of one of the buggy horses.

She studied him as she approached through the ankle-deep snow. He wasn't as tall as his older *bruder*, but he had fine, broad shoulders and muscular arms, attributes that must serve him well in his work around the farm. His dark hair curled under the brim of his hat, and his profile was striking. He was already handsome, but with the beard he'd grow as a married man he'd gain a mature appearance that would only improve his presence.

She stopped a few paces short of him, waiting for the moment when he'd look up and notice her. When it came, his expression brightened in the smile he'd always reserved just for her. That smile was one she always looked forward to, one that could warm her on the coldest of days. It was what assured her he had to feel for her what she felt for him.

"Happy New Year, Calvin," she greeted, speaking first.

"And to you as well. You're looking nice today."

"*Danke.*" Surely his words were confirmation that she was doing the right thing by approaching him. "Why are you out here with the horses?"

"I love *Aenti* Ruthanne's family." He smiled at her as if sharing a secret. "Some more than others. But it's nice to have a few moments away from everyone, ain't so?"

Some more than others—could he mean what she hoped? "You seem particularly happy today."

He tilted his head with a sheepish expression. "So it shows."

"To someone who knows you well, *jah*."

A gust of wind ruffled her *kapp* strings and she crossed her arms against the chill.

Calvin frowned. "You're cold. Perhaps we should go back inside."

"Not just yet." What excuse could she use to keep him here a little longer? "My friend Grace said again yesterday that I'm too outspoken, that it's unseemly and prideful for me to draw attention to myself. Sometimes I think you're the only person who truly understands me." Would he take the hint?

His expression turned earnest and he touched her sleeve briefly. "I've told you before, don't let what others say bother you. You're a *gut* person, not at all prideful." His serious demeanor gave way to another smile. "And I should know, you and I have been best friends since our schooldays."

The conversation was going just as she'd hoped. "We have. But we aren't scholars any longer."

He nodded. "True. We're adults and have adult responsibilities now. But we'll always be friends."

Time to be more direct. "Do you think we can ever be more than just friends?" There, she'd said it. She couldn't be much clearer than that.

"We *are* more than just friends. You are my closest friend."

Okay, perhaps she did need to be clearer. This shouldn't be so hard for someone folks accused of being too forward, but today she felt tongue-tied.

However, before she could say more, Calvin spoke up again.

"And, as my best friend, there's something I want to share with you. I know it's not normally spoken of so soon, but I could never keep secrets from you."

Confidant wasn't the role she was looking for, but she could hardly say so. "Of course."

"I just have to tell someone." His voice vibrated with an intense emotion and his face practically glowed. "Wanda has agreed to let me court her."

Chapter 2

Greta stilled as her whole world shifted around her and began to fray at the edges. Her chest tightened and she had to force herself to breathe, as if her body had forgotten how to do so on its own. "Wanda? You mean Wanda Beachy?" Her own cousin.

If any of her distress showed, Calvin didn't appear to notice. "*Jah*. Isn't it *wunderbaar* that a girl as pretty and sweet as Wanda agreed to date me?"

Greta tried to wrap her mind around what he was saying. "But, I mean, I didn't realize you were looking for someone." Someone that wasn't her.

He grinned. "Doesn't everyone want to find a person to spend their life with?" His expression had a faraway look. "I finally have the farm running smoothly again, the way it did before *Daed* died. It's time for me to find a *fraa* and start a family of my own."

Apparently the idea that she would be that someone had never crossed his mind.

He eyed her hopefully. "She's your cousin, ain't so? Don't you think she'll make a *gut fraa* for a farmer like me?"

Did he honestly not see what this conversation was doing to her? "For sure and for certain." She just barely managed to keep her voice steady.

His expression lost some of its dreamy quality and he focused on her, as if just realizing something was wrong. "Are you all right?"

Greta tried to pull herself together. She couldn't let him see how hard this had hit her. "*Jah*, of course. I'm so happy for you."

Calvin's expression changed as he looked past her, and it was as if he'd forgotten her presence altogether.

Greta turned, but she already knew who she'd see. She could see now that the warm smile Calvin had always reserved just for her hadn't meant what she thought it had. It was a pale shadow of the glowing, you-are-my-world smile that suddenly lit up his whole face, the smile he was focusing on the girl exiting the house. And Wanda's smile was every bit as luminous, even though her downcast eyes and pinkened cheeks made it difficult to see.

She had to get away from the two of them before she unraveled completely. "Excuse me. I promised to help *Aenti* Ruthanne in the kitchen." It was weak as excuses went, but it didn't matter.

Calvin was already moving toward Wanda.

* * *

Noah Stoll slowly crossed the yard, moving from the barn to *Aenti* Ruthanne's house. He knew David and

Anna were being looked after, but he liked to check up on them occasionally.

Across the yard a group of children were building a snowman, though it seemed a snowball fight was in progress as well. And David was right in the thick of things. But Maisie and Benjamin, Noah's two youngest siblings, were also there so he knew they'd allow David to have fun while also making sure the older *kinner* didn't inadvertently get too rough with him.

David spotted him just then and came running over as fast as his little legs could carry him.

"*Daed*," he greeted, raising his arms in an obvious request to be picked up.

Noah obliged, lifting his son up over his head, making the boy giggle in delight. It was a sound he dearly loved but didn't hear nearly often enough. Easing the boy down to his hip, he checked out the chapped red skin on his son's cheeks while he pulled out a handkerchief and wiped the equally red nose.

David squirmed, obviously not liking the assault on his nose. Then he pointed back in the direction he'd come from. "We're building a snowman," he said proudly. "Do you see it?"

"*Jah*, and a very fine snowman it is." He gave the boy a squeeze. "Would you like to come in the house with me to get a cup of hot cocoa or would you rather go back to your snowman?"

David thought about it a minute, obviously torn, but then a wave of laughter drifted over from the group playing in the snow and he squirmed to be set down. Without a backward glance he ran over to join the others.

Noah met and held fourteen-year-old Benjamin's gaze

for a moment. His little *bruder* nodded in understanding, then went back to the impromptu snowball fight, pulling David to his side.

After watching the mock battle a moment, Noah turned to resume his trek to the house. As he did so, he saw Calvin in conversation with Greta Eicher. Calvin and Greta had been friends since they were young scholars together. And in recent years Noah had sensed Greta wanted to be more. Unfortunately for her, he didn't think Calvin felt the same. Or rather that was unfortunate for his *bruder*, because he could certainly do a whole lot worse than having Greta for his *fraa*.

Shaking his head, Noah stepped inside and found his twenty-month-old daughter seated in his cousin Esther's lap.

"There you are, sunshine," he said, lifting Anna. "Do you know they're building a snowman outside? What do you say we take a look and let Esther visit with her friends?"

Esther stood and tapped Anna's nose. "This little lamb is the best company I could ask for. But I know I'm no competition for a snowman."

Anna giggled and snuggled deeper into Noah's arms as he gave her a squeeze.

Maisie approached just then, her face still red from the weather outside. "I just ran into Calvin," she said with an arch smile. "He wants us to squeeze Benjamin in with us when we leave."

Interesting. Noah thought over the implications as he bundled his daughter in her coat and mittens. It sounded like Calvin was planning to drive a young lady home tonight. The conversation he'd seen between Calvin and Greta earlier took on new significance.

It wasn't totally unexpected—Noah had been aware that Greta was interested in his *bruder* for some time, but apparently he'd misjudged Calvin's feelings.

Noah wasn't sure whether to be happy for the two of them or not. He'd been quietly protective of Greta ever since she'd shown such kindness to him all those years ago when he'd badly needed a friend. She'd been a child then, six years old to his twelve, but it had impacted him deeply nevertheless.

He only hoped Calvin was prepared to treat her as she deserved.

Then he mentally wished the two of them well and pushed those thoughts aside as he spotted David. He waved and carried Anna closer to the snowman so she could place the walnuts he'd given her as her contribution to the icy gentleman's decoration.

Anna wanted to get down to perform her task, and Noah complied, smiling at his daughter's independent spirit. Then he looked up and his smile slowly faded.

Calvin was walking side by side with a young woman who was most definitely not Greta.

What had happened? Could his *bruder* have ignored Greta's obvious affection to pursue another? Did Greta know?

He looked around, searching for some sign of Greta, but she must have gone inside. He had to fight the urge to check on her and make sure she was okay.

Not only wasn't that his right, but his attention would likely not be welcome.

*   *   *

Greta had headed straight to the washroom when she made it back to the house, not even bothering to remove her coat.

She'd closed and latched the door behind her and sat on the edge of the bathtub, numb. She wasn't sure how long she sat there, unable to even think beyond the fact that, in a matter of minutes, her dream of finding a man who would appreciate her enough to want to spend a lifetime with her had been ripped away, leaving nothing behind.

Calvin had been her last chance to find a husband, a man who would accept her as she was. With what her *daed* believed about a woman's place and how her two previous boyfriends had eventually moved on to girls who were more biddable than her, it had already become abundantly clear that few men in this community would see her as an acceptable *fraa*. She'd thought Calvin would see her differently, would consider her an, if not appealing, at least suitable helpmeet.

But obviously she'd been wrong.

Finally she straightened, gathering her thoughts, trying to figure out what she should do now. The one thing she wouldn't do was cry, not here, not now. Perhaps tonight, in the privacy of her room, but for now she had to hold herself together.

Calvin and Wanda weren't engaged yet, they were just entering the courtship stage. And she herself was proof that courting didn't necessarily lead to marriage.

Then she gave her head a mental shake. She wasn't one to throw herself at a man. If he didn't want her, then so be it. It was obvious to her now that they never had been, and never would be, more than *gut* friends.

But how could this have happened? Not that Wanda wouldn't make a *gut fraa*. She was a sweet girl, very shy and with a generous heart. She'd overcome a lot in her short life. As a child she'd had a severe stutter, one that caused her to withdraw into herself. It had mostly disappeared in her adolescence, but the shyness remained. Greta loved her dearly and couldn't begrudge her a chance at happiness, which made this doubly painful.

Was Calvin just like all the other young men, looking for someone biddable, someone who aspired merely to be a *fraa* and a *mamm* and nothing else? Not that those were bad things, but she'd thought Calvin was looking for a partner who could also help him in other ways.

All those hours they'd spent discussing his dreams for the farm operation, when he'd bounced ideas off of her, ideas for changes and improvements, times when he'd listened to her opinions and ideas, and even changed some of his plans based on her suggestions. She'd thought they were stitching together plans for their future. Apparently he'd only wanted the opinion of his *gut* friend.

She'd thought he appreciated her spirited nature, her imagination and creativity. But again, it seemed those were qualities he appreciated in a friend, not in a wife.

Was everyone right? Did she need to change her ways if she ever hoped to marry? And if so, was getting married worth changing who she was?

She knuckled her eyes, reminding herself she wouldn't cry.

The only bright spot in this whole situation was that Calvin had seemed unaware of her true feelings and had told her his news before she could make a fool of herself.

At least she wouldn't have to bear seeing him look at her with concern or pity in his eyes.

And since she hadn't confided her feelings to anyone else except Esther, she should be able to move forward with most of her dignity intact.

Better start looking for a future that didn't include marriage.

But what would that look like?

Chapter 3

When Noah finally managed to drag his *kinner* away from the snowman and back to the house, he looked around for Greta. After a few moments he spotted her in a corner of the room telling a story to a group of the younger *kinner* who seemed thoroughly spellbound by her words and lively expressions and movements. Anna immediately wanted him to let her down so she could join them. It was all he could do to get her squirming body out of her coat and mittens before she was off.

When Greta spotted Anna and David she gave both of them a welcoming smile and a quick hug. Then she made sure the others made room for them in their circle before returning to her story.

Studying her, he could tell she'd heard the news, probably from Calvin himself. Not that her distress would be obvious to someone who wasn't looking for it. But if one looked closely, there was something about her that seemed off. And it was more than the redness in her face, a redness that didn't seem related to the cold.

It took him a moment to put his finger on it, but then it hit him. Though she was smiling and had playfully tapped Anna's nose, below the surface there seemed to be a vulnerable, brittle air that hadn't been there earlier. The smile she was focusing on the *kinner* didn't quite reach her eyes.

Oh yes, she knew Calvin's affections were focused elsewhere, and it had hit her hard. But he admired her for the way she kept herself outwardly calm.

She made a grand gesture just then, no doubt reaching some dramatic high point of her story, and her gaze met his. Not just met but snagged and held for a heartbeat. Her eyes widened and there was a moment of connection that caught him off guard.

Then she turned back to the children and continued with her story.

Had he imagined it? Or had it been a holdover from her reaction to Calvin's courting intentions?

Again he had a strong urge to offer her comfort. But this crowded room wasn't the place, even if she would welcome such a gesture.

He spotted Wanda just then, joining a group of other girls near the kitchen.

Perhaps it was time he had a little chat with his *bruder*.

Entering the barn a few minutes later, Noah spotted Calvin talking with a couple of his friends. He approached the trio, and as soon as there was a break in the conversation, he turned to his *bruder*. "Would you mind walking over to my buggy with me to look at something?"

Calvin appeared surprised but, with a farewell nod to his friends, he swept a hand to indicate Noah should lead the way. "What is it you wanted me to look at?" he asked as they exited the barn.

"Actually, I just wanted to have a private word with you. Maisie tells me you want me to take Benjamin home in my buggy."

Calvin's face split in a wide, I've-got-a-big-secret grin. "That's right. I won't have room in my carriage because I'll be taking Wanda Beachy home this evening."

Noah frowned at his *bruder*'s self-congratulatory tone. "What about Greta?"

Calvin's brow drew down, as if confused. "What about her? I mean, Greta and I are friends and she said she was happy for me."

"So you did tell her." Thank goodness he'd had the good sense to take her feelings into consideration.

"*Jah*. Just a little while ago."

The offhand way he spoke raised Noah's suspicions again. "You do know she has some affection for you, don't you? I hope you let her down gently."

Calvin waved a hand dismissively. "I've never given Greta a reason to think we were anything but *gut* friends."

That wasn't an answer. "But you never did anything to discourage her either, did you?"

"You sound like you're *her* big *bruder* rather than mine. And I think you're reading more into Greta's feelings for me than is really there."

Was Calvin really that blind? "I don't think so. Surely you had at least an inkling of her feelings."

"You're making it sound like I did something wrong,

like I set out to hurt her. As I said, Greta's my friend. We were scholars together. She has a sharp mind and is a *gut* listener, but those aren't the qualities one looks for in a *fraa*. Friendship is all I've ever felt for her, and friends are all we could ever be. I'm much more suited to marry a girl like Wanda than one like Greta."

Noah's jaw worked as he strove to hold his temper. "And knowing how she felt, did it occur to you to let her down easy before now? To let her know how you felt so she could move on?"

They had stopped walking by this time, and Calvin breathed into his cupped hands to warm them. "Not that I have any reason to explain myself to you, but I figured she'd eventually grow tired of waiting." He lifted his chin. "And what did it hurt? After all, there weren't any other men vying for her affection." He shrugged. "At any rate, she knows now."

Noah's hands clenched at his side. "I thought better of you."

"You're blowing this out of all proportion. Greta is made of tougher stuff than your average Amish girl— she'll get over any bruised feelings quickly enough."

Before Noah could respond to that ridiculous statement, Calvin continued. "I assume there really isn't anything you need me to see in your buggy."

Noah shook his head.

"Then if you'll excuse me, I'll return to my friends." And with that he spun on his heels and headed back to the barn.

Noah couldn't believe how offhand Calvin's attitude had been when discussing Greta's feelings. Had his *bruder* been that unfeeling when he'd broken the news to her? No wonder she'd looked so bruised when he'd last seen her.

As soon as Noah entered the house, Maisie was at his elbow. She nodded toward their mother. "*Mamm* is ready to go home."

Noah followed her gaze and noted the tired lines in their mother's face. He nodded, then looked around for his *kinner*.

Greta was still entertaining a dozen or so little ones with her storytelling. He smothered a sigh, thinking about pulling Anna and David away from the story they seemed so thoroughly engrossed in and having to wrestle them back into their winter gear.

But Maisie gave him a little nudge. "You let Benjamin know and get the buggy ready while I bundle up the little ones."

Giving his nearly sixteen-year-old sister a grateful smile, Noah nodded and headed back outside.

Fifteen minutes later, when he pulled the buggy up near the front entrance, Maisie ushered his *kinner* out— Anna on her hip and David preceding her. Benjamin was right behind them but waited near the door.

"Where's *Mamm*?" he asked as Maisie climbed in the back seat with his kinner.

"She said she forgot to tell *Aenti* Ruthanne something," Maisie answered. "She should be out in a moment."

Mamm stepped from the house just then, calling something over her shoulder before heading for the buggy. Noah noted how slow her movements were as Benjamin hurried to assist her, and how stooped she appeared as she leaned heavily on her cane. She was having more problems with her health lately. Not that she'd admit to it. And woe to anyone who dared mention she should take it easy. He made a mental note to try to coax her to visit the clinic in the coming weeks.

She made one protest as Benjamin took her arm, but he ignored it and she let him assist her without further comment. His *bruder* was showing a lot of maturity these days for his fourteen years.

As they settled into the front seat, Noah's thoughts turned once again to Greta and the lost look he'd seen in her eyes.

*   *   *

As eager as Greta had been to arrive at *Onkel* Simon's this morning, she was that much more eager for the visit to end. So she wasn't disappointed when her *daed* decided to leave in the late afternoon rather than stay for the evening meal.

She helped Martha and Hannah gather up all the dishes they'd brought and get them loaded in the buggy, hurrying things along as best she could. Once they were ready to go, she took a seat in the back of the buggy, settling in the far corner. Hannah joined her in the back, and Martha sat up front with *Daed*.

"Did you enjoy the start of your new year, *Daed*?" Martha asked as he picked up the reins.

He shrugged. "I suppose. Your *aenti* sets a good table." He set the buggy in motion. "There's a lot you girls could learn from her."

"*Jah*," Martha agreed, though her cheeks had reddened. "*Aenti* Ruthanne is always so organized and efficient, and yet so gracious to her guests."

Hannah leaned forward. "Well I certainly enjoyed my day. Visiting with everyone and catching up on their news is always fun."

"That's nice." Martha turned to her. "And you, Greta? You seemed eager to get to *Onkel* Simon's this morning. Did the day live up to your expectations?"

Greta had known the question was coming, so she was ready to give an honest but not-very-revealing answer. "Telling stories to the little ones always does my heart good. They're so bright and curious that spending time with them is a delight." It had also given her an excuse to avoid conversation with Esther. They'd exchanged one glance across the room and she could tell Esther realized things had not gone well.

Unaccountably, her mind went back to that moment during story time when her gaze had latched on to Noah's across the room. She'd had the oddest sensation he wanted to say something to her.

"*Ach*, that reminds me," Hannah said, interrupting her thoughts. "Did you see Cousin Paula's new baby? He's the sweetest little thing."

Greta was pleased to have Hannah take the spotlight off her, right up until their *daed* picked up the conversational thread.

"Speaking of *bopplin*, when do you girls plan to give me a few grandbabies of my own?" *Daed*'s question had a sly edge to it. "Paula is the same age as Greta, and already she's starting a family." He'd cut a look at Martha as he said this.

Greta winced at her *daed*'s thoughtless comment. Martha, at twenty-five, was well aware that most women her age were already married and raising *kinner* of their own.

But their *daed* wasn't finished. "I even heard a rumor that your cousin Wanda has a new boyfriend. She's a year or two younger than Hannah, ain't so?"

Hannah's gaze swung to Greta, her gentle gaze probing, as if looking for a reaction.

Did she know? Greta forced her expression into something she hoped reflected only a casual interest. "Remember what you always tell us when we get impatient, *Daed*," Greta said in as calm a voice as she could muster. "Everything happens in *Gotte*'s timing."

But it was very difficult for her to see where *Gotte*'s providence would lead her from here.

Chapter 4

Noah guided the buggy down the lane in the faded evening light. Knowing Calvin would likely be late returning home, he'd stayed a couple of hours at the farm so he could help Benjamin with the evening chores.

But he was headed home at last. Anna lay snuggled on Maisie's lap, wrapped in a blanket and half-asleep. David sat next to him, his head and shoulder leaning heavily against Noah, a precious burden. Even Maisie, who sat on the other side of David, looked drowsy.

He appreciated his little *shveshtah* more than he could say. Not so little, he supposed, she would turn sixteen in a couple of weeks. She'd been fourteen, just out of school, when Patsy died. Their *shveshtah* Faith had stepped in to help him care for his two very young children in those early months. After Faith got married he'd tried nannies for a while, but that hadn't worked out very well. Finally

Maisie had stepped up a little over a year ago and she'd been caring for them ever since.

But with her upcoming birthday, Noah had some choices to make. Many of Maisie's friends were already experiencing the freedom of rumspringa, and it wasn't fair to hold her back any longer. At Christmas he'd promised her that he would have arrangements in place to free her up no later than Valentine's Day. That gave him a little less than a month and a half.

Another nanny was an option, but he'd rather not put his *kinner* through that again. Anna and David deserved something more permanent in their lives. With a tightening in his gut, he accepted that it was time he started his search for a new *fraa*. With Maisie on rumspringa and *Mamm*'s health getting worse, he was running out of alternatives. Besides, these were his *kinner*, his responsibility. The best solution for everyone was for him to find a *fraa*.

Who should he approach? He hadn't even thought about dating since he'd lost Patsy. Patsy herself had been very young and naïve when they married. Even though she hadn't complained, he'd realized early on that she missed life on a farm.

Then there was her relationship with his *mamm*. She was his *shteef-mamm* really, but Debra had married his *daed* when he was only five and raised him as her own. Though he dearly loved her, and knew her to be a good-hearted person, he also knew she could be difficult at times.

He'd told Patsy to stand up for herself, knowing his *mamm* would respect her all the more for it. But that hadn't been Patsy's way.

He'd accepted her meekness as just a part of her gentle personality. It was only in the last six months of their marriage that he'd come to view things differently.

Giving his head a mental shake to brush away those sour memories, Noah focused on the future rather than the past.

He had several requirements for his next *fraa*. For one, he'd prefer not to have to deal with the almost martyr-like resignation that Patsy had sometimes displayed. He'd also be looking for someone a bit more mature and someone who didn't prefer farm life over the one a craftsman could offer. Of course, it went without saying that she'd need to love his *kinner*.

And right near the top of his list, the woman he married would need to be someone who'd put away romantic notions of what a marriage entailed. Someone who would be satisfied with a marriage based on friendship and mutual respect.

Because after Patsy's betrayal that was all he had to offer.

He had absolute confidence such a woman existed. Trouble was, how would he find her quickly? Should he ask Esther for help? Surely she'd know some women, perhaps even among her friends, who'd be of the right age and who would love little ones.

For a moment Greta's face came to mind. He thought his *bruder* had shown poor judgment in choosing Wanda over Greta. But then again, he hadn't chosen his first *fraa* particularly wisely himself.

Calvin's choice did have an unexpected benefit—it meant he was now free to pursue Greta himself. And David and Anna were already fond of her.

The idea was surprisingly tempting...

Then he dismissed it. Greta deserved someone who could provide her with a bit of romance in her life, who could love her fully. That hadn't been Calvin.

And given his record, that certainly wasn't him either.

Maisie spoke up, rescuing him from his thoughts. "What's on your mind, Noah? You haven't said a word the whole drive, and we're almost at your place."

Noah shrugged, unwilling to broach the subject with his children beside him. "Just wondering what this new year will bring."

"It does no *gut* to worry about such things," Maisie said in a fair imitation of their *mamm*'s voice. "Only *Gotte* knows what the future will bring."

"Yes, of course," Noah answered with a smile.

But hopefully, with Esther's— and *Gotte*'s—help, this year would bring him a new *fraa*.

So why didn't that excite him?

* * *

After getting her morning chores taken care of, Greta spent the next day in her quilting room. It was her favorite place, her retreat and sanctuary. No one else came in here as a rule, not even to clean. It was also where she felt closest to her *mamm*.

Mamm had had the same passion for quilting, and the two of them had spent many an hour over a quilt frame talking about anything and everything. *Mamm*, more than anyone else, had encouraged her to be herself. Oh, how she wished she were still here so she could pour her heart out to her now.

She tried to bury her wounded feelings in her work, but it was no use. She kept picturing Calvin's and Wanda's faces as their gazes met across *Onkel* Simon's backyard. Would someone ever look at her like that?

Somewhere along the way she'd convinced herself that being loved like that wasn't for her, that a strong friendship was a good enough basis for a marriage. But now she wondered if she was setting the bar too low. She deserved more than good enough. Truth was, Calvin's actions hadn't so much broken her heart as stung her pride.

But if all the men in her community wanted to wed meek and even-tempered women, then she was doomed to spinsterhood.

Perhaps she should embrace the life of a spinster. After all, when had she ever worried about living a traditional life? And there was a certain freedom a woman enjoyed when she had no husband to care for. And once Hannah and Martha married, she'd have many nieces and nephews to help love and spoil.

She could also focus more attention on her quilting, something that brought her joy. Designing new patterns, having the pieces fit together in new ways to form a pleasing whole, embroidering intricate designs on the pieced fabrics—these were things that brightened her days.

But apparently not today.

Greta jabbed her needle in the star quilt she'd been working on and pushed back from the quilt frame in frustration. This was the third time in less than an hour she'd had to pick out misplaced stitches. She stood, stretching and twisting her neck, trying to ease some of the tension from her muscles.

Looking for a measure of peace, she gazed at the three quilt stands on the other side of the room. Her *daed* had made those stands for her the Christmas after her *mamm* passed. Two of them bore precious burdens— quilts folded and displayed to their best advantage. Both quilts had belonged to her *mamm* and held very special places in her heart.

The third quilt stand was empty. When *Daed* had gifted them to her, he'd said the extra one was to give her a place to display her own wedding quilt someday. Today that empty stand seemed to be mocking her.

Refusing to wallow, Greta resolutely turned her focus to the two quilts, seeking the peace and clarity they always brought her.

The one closest to her was in excellent shape despite its age. It was a classic double wedding ring with the curved patches forming large, nearly perfect circles in vibrant shades of blues and yellows. The stitches were tiny and perfectly even. It was a quilt any woman would be proud to have in her home.

The second quilt was an intricately fashioned star pattern made with hundreds of tiny diamond-shaped patches. And while still lovely, it showed signs of use and wear. The colors had muted with age, and a few of the patches had begun to fray and needed to be restitched.

With a soft smile, she remembered her *mamm* telling her the story of these two very different quilts when she was just ten years old.

"This is my wedding quilt," Mamm had said, brushing a hand softly over the wedding ring quilt. "It was lovingly made for me by my sister and friends when your *daed* and I announced our engagement." *Mamm*'s face softened as she spoke. "Whenever I look at it, it reminds me of each of them and the time and love they put into making it. It's beautiful, ain't so?"

When Greta nodded agreement, *Mamm* continued. "It's very well preserved because I cherish it so much and only use it for special occasions such as when we have guests staying with us."

Then she'd set it aside and placed her hand on the star quilt, which was draped over her bed. "This one isn't nearly as well kept or as beautiful as my wedding quilt, but in a way I consider it my wedding quilt as well."

"How so? Did another group of friends make this one for you?"

Mamm smiled down at her. "No, I made it myself as a *youngie* specifically to put in my hope chest. And because it was for my hope chest, I fashioned it exactly as I wanted it, without worrying about others' opinions. I used the starburst pattern because it's my favorite design. I put houses in two of the corners to represent the future home I hoped to have. And I put hearts in the other two corners to represent the love that I hoped would fill that home. I selected colors that make me happy, colors of the sky and the primroses that grew in *Grossmammi*'s garden and the wild violets down by the stream."

She rested her hand lovingly on the quilt. "After your *daed* and I married, this became our everyday quilt, the one that brightened our room and kept the two of us warm on many a freezing winter night." She sighed. "There was a lot of love that went into the making of this quilt and even more into the use of it."

Greta could still see the soft glow of remembrance that infused her mother's smile as she spoke.

She straightened. Perhaps that's what her new quilt design could be—something she made for the pure joy of it, something that would reflect who she was and what she wanted out of life.

A quilt that she could someday share with someone she could love and be loved by.

Then she grimaced. It seemed she wasn't ready to accept the role of spinster just yet.

Speaking of which...

Greta moved to her worktable and reached for her sketchbook. She quickly turned to the rough drawing she'd made the morning before. Studying the design she'd considered so symbolic of promise, she tried to recapture that happy glow she'd felt when she first conceived it.

She pulled out her set of colored pencils and slowly began sketching a more polished version, tweaking the design in places, adding the colors of dawn washing over the pristine landscape. And gradually, as she worked, she lost herself in the joy of creating something beautiful, in seeing how the separate pieces of the puzzle, from the tiniest scrap to the largest block, would all fit together to form a harmonious whole.

She referred back to her stores of fabric at certain points, letting the materials themselves inform her design. At other times, Greta simply let the design go where it would. She lost herself in what was evolving on her sketch pad, letting everything else slip away but the joy of creating.

A knock at the door interrupted her work. At her "Come in," Hannah opened the door and stepped inside. "It's lunchtime. Aren't you going to join us?"

Greta set her pencils down. "I'm sorry, I lost track of time."

Hannah stepped closer and studied the sketch. "*Ach* Greta, that's beautiful. Is it for a quilt you plan to sell in your shop?"

Greta studied her sketch. "I haven't decided yet. This one may go in my hope chest."

"I wouldn't blame you." Then Hannah gave her a thoughtful look. "Are you all right?"

"Of course." Greta stood and smoothed her skirt, not meeting her younger *shveshtah*'s gaze. "Why wouldn't I be?" All the heartsick feelings she'd pushed aside while she was sketching came flooding back.

"I don't know. You've just seemed quieter than usual since we left *Onkel* Simon's yesterday. Made me wonder if something happened there, especially since you seemed so happy earlier."

How did she answer that without sounding pitiful?

Before she could say anything, Hannah spoke again. "Would this have something to do with Calvin?" she asked gently.

It seemed Hannah saw more than Greta gave her credit for. "So you know about that." And she thought she'd hidden her feelings so well.

"All I know is that you care for him a great deal. Perhaps a little more than you ought."

"More, apparently, than he cares for me. He confided in me that he intends to court someone else." She was pleased that she could say that without her voice breaking.

Before she could so much as blink, Hannah pulled her into an embrace. "Calvin is a *gut* man, but I always thought he wasn't very perceptive. You deserve a man who really sees and appreciates you for the wonderful person you are."

Greta gave a hiccuping laugh but she had the panicked feeling she wasn't far from tears. Apparently it wasn't as easy to just move on as she'd hoped. If Hannah didn't let her go—

Hannah stepped back. "Now you know Calvin Stoll isn't the one for you. That just means that it's time to open yourself up to new possibilities."

Greta very much doubted there was anyone out there more suited for her than Calvin but kept that thought to herself.

"Come have lunch. You'll feel better with some of Martha's cooking inside you."

Greta nodded. "Give me just a minute."

"Of course. Take your time. I'll make your excuses."

Before following Hannah from the room, Greta's gaze fell on her drawing and she took a moment to really study it. It wasn't exactly what she'd imagined yesterday morning. Yesterday's events had no doubt colored her outlook. But studying it, she could see it was something richer, deeper and totally unlike anything she'd ever done before. She could see the bright promise there, the promise of hope and new beginnings.

Was there a message for her in there?

Chapter 5

Greta entered the craft mall the next day, a new quilt top in hand. They kept a small stock of tops at the shop for the customers who wanted to try their hands at quilting but were intimidated by the piecing process.

She glanced in the Sweet Kneads Bakery window as she passed by. Hannah, who ran the shop, always arrived several hours earlier than Greta to get her ovens going and to prepare for her early morning customers. The wonderful aroma of cinnamon sticky buns and coffee wafted out into the mall lobby, and Greta counted a half-dozen customers standing in line for her *shveshtah*'s delicious pastries. Several of her prior customers were seated on the wooden benches that dotted the lobby, obviously enjoying their purchases.

Across the lobby, the sales floor for Noah's woodworking creations was also open. She could see young Reuben Zimmerman dusting some of the display pieces.

Noah was undoubtedly back in the workshop along with Andrew Wagler and Paul Habegger, his two woodworking employees. Reuben looked up just then and gave her a wave. She waved back and then bustled over to the quilt shop, nestled between Hannah's bakery and Charity Umble's candle and gift shop.

The door was still locked. Seemed she'd arrived before Esther for a change. Once she set her bag and quilt top on the counter and shed her coat and scarf, Greta took a look around. The shop wouldn't open for another thirty minutes or so, and preferring to keep busy rather than dwell on her thoughts, she decided to rearrange a few of the displays. In addition to quilt tops, they also stocked quilted throw pillows, potholders, place mats, baby quilts, table runners and some wall hangings. They also had bolts of fabric, some suitable for their Amish customers to use in making clothing and some to add punches of color for quilts.

As she worked, however, thoughts of yesterday flitted through her mind unbidden. She'd spent the rest of yesterday piecing the top together, using the need to finish it as an excuse to keep to herself as much as possible. But she'd taken herself to task last night, deciding she'd done enough moping and that it was time to get on with her life. If she was destined to remain single, then she'd better start looking for another worthwhile way to spend her time.

There had to be some kind of project she could focus her energies on. She moved to their shop's workspace. She and Esther each had individual one-person quilt frames where they worked on custom orders when they weren't attending to in-store customers. There was also a treadle sewing machine between them that they shared.

Working on the custom orders in the shop wasn't only an efficient use of their downtime, but walk-in customers seemed to enjoy seeing them at work. Greta was always happy to pause to answer questions and often made additional sales as the result of those discussions.

She studied the project she was currently working on, a log cabin quilt an English customer had ordered as a wedding gift for her niece. It was about two-thirds complete and she really ought to sit down and get to work finishing it.

The sound of knuckles rapping on the shop door caught her attention and saved her from making a choice. Turning, she spotted Noah with Anna on his hip and David at his side. Hurrying to the door, she unlocked it and waved him in.

"Sorry to intrude before you're open." Noah stayed on the threshold. "But I was hoping to speak to Esther."

"She's not in yet, but if you're looking for someone to keep an eye on these two cutie pies, I'll be glad to step in."

Noah smiled, the expression restrained. "*Danke*. I'll take you up on your kind offer."

He set Anna down, then stooped so he was eye level with the pair. "You two listen to what Greta tells you. And I'll be back to get you for lunch."

"I hope this doesn't mean something's happened to Maisie." Greta liked Calvin and Noah's younger *shveshtah*. She was a sweet girl with a quiet intelligence and strong sense of duty to her family.

After giving his *kinner* each a quick kiss on the

forehead, Noah stood and met Greta's gaze again. "Maisie wasn't feeling well this morning. I dropped her off at *Mamm*'s on my way here."

"I'm sorry. I hope she feels better soon." Then she turned to the children. "In the meantime, I'll enjoy having these two sweetie pies for company."

Noah nodded. "*Danke* again. But I do need to speak to Esther about something if you would let her know when she comes in."

Greta noted an unusual tension in him, which immediately drove her curiosity up, but she refrained from commenting, focusing instead on what he'd asked. "Of course. I'll let her know as soon as I see her." Then she turned to her two temporary charges. "Who wants to hear a story?"

Amid choruses of "I do!" Noah left the shop with a wave.

Greta had barely settled the children down and started her story when Esther walked in.

"What have we here?" she asked as she took off her coat and scarf. "Has our shop been invaded by a couple of monkeys?"

The kids immediately popped up to greet her, then grabbed her hands and tugged her toward Greta.

"Greta is telling us a story," David said.

"About a dancing pig," Anna added with a giggle.

Esther nodded with a grin. "Greta tells very *gut* stories."

Then her gaze met Greta's with a silent question.

"Maisie is a little under the weather this morning, so we get to spend time with these two. Oh, and Noah said he'd like to speak to you when you have a few minutes."

"Did he say what about?"

"*Nee*. But we don't open for another ten minutes. I'll be fine if you want to go ahead and take care of it now." She smiled at Anna and David. "The three of us have a story to finish."

Esther nodded, then gave Greta a meaningful look. "But then we need to talk."

"Talk?"

"About what happened New Year's Day."

Greta swallowed a groan. That was the last thing she needed right now. But before she could say so, Esther headed back out the door.

When she returned fifteen minutes later, it was all Greta could do not to ask what was going on. Luckily her friend was more than willing to be forthcoming. Esther glanced over to where Anna and David were playing with a set of wooden blocks they kept at the shop for just such times, and motioned for Greta to join her on the other side of the room. After checking to make certain the pair were still engrossed in their play, she turned to Greta. "It seems Noah is looking for a new *fraa*."

It wasn't what Greta had expected. It seemed both Stoll *brieder* were looking for *fraa*s. Shaking off that thought, she nodded. "He's been widowed nearly two years now and he has two little ones to care for. I suppose it's time." Patsy had died from complications only one day after Anna was born. The poor *boppli* had never known her *mamm*.

Esther studied her with a worried frown. "I'm sorry. I know this is probably not something you want to talk about after what happened with Calvin."

Greta brushed her friend's words aside. "I'm okay."

She returned to the original topic before Esther could say more. "Is there a particular reason he wanted to let you know?"

Esther's look said she knew Greta was deliberately avoiding talking about Calvin, but she gave in. "He asked me to help him."

"Help him? You mean he asked you to play matchmaker?"

Esther nodded. "I know matchmaking is something you're more experienced with than I am. I even hinted that he might want to ask you instead of me."

And he'd apparently brushed the hint aside. But there was no need for Esther to feel bad about it. "I'm sure he's more comfortable keeping this in the family. After all, selecting a helpmeet is a very personal thing."

Esther grimaced. "Not the way he wants to go about it."

"What do you mean?"

"In his words, he wants to be very businesslike in his choice this time around."

Greta frowned at that. "What exactly did he say?"

Esther wrinkled her nose. "He gave me a whole list of really practical requirements the candidates should meet."

"Such as?"

Esther repeated the list Noah had given her. Then she crossed her arms. "To be honest, I wouldn't even know where to start. Does that sound like anyone you know?"

Greta brushed the question aside. "Actually, I'm not sure what he described is what's really best for him."

The space between Esther's brows crinkled. "What do you mean?"

"I usually try to ask enough questions to get a real sense for what kind of partner the person needs, not what he or she thinks they need. Noah probably came up with this list by approaching the issue logically. But it's not logic he needs if he wants to have a happy marriage. Instead he should be paying more attention to his heart."

Esther didn't look convinced. "I know you mean well, but Noah isn't like the other men you've helped, he's not a passionate man with big romantic notions. I know my cousin. He's sensible and logical and content with an orderly life. Besides, I think Noah knows what he wants in a *fraa* better than you or I."

Greta had a moment of self-doubt. After all, if she'd been so wrong about Calvin and what he wanted, perhaps she wasn't as good at matching couples as she thought.

Then she rallied. "Perhaps Noah isn't looking for real romance because he's never experienced it before."

She held a hand up, forestalling whatever Esther seemed poised to say. "Or perhaps it's just the opposite—he had it once and doesn't think he can have that again." She straightened. "In either case, he's wrong. He should at least leave himself open to that sort of relationship in his marriage. Not only is that good for him and his future *fraa*, but it makes for a happy and secure home for his *kinner*."

"I wish I had your confidence in these matters," Esther said. "What sort of woman would you look for?"

Greta considered that. "Noah is a *gut* man and obviously a *gut* provider, but he's always so serious. He needs someone with spirit and tenacity, someone who can challenge him and make him laugh occasionally."

Esther gave her an arch look. "Sounds to me like you're describing yourself."

Greta laughed outright at that. "Even I know I'm much too far on the other side of meek for Noah. No, we need to find someone with more spirit than Patsy had but who won't send him running for the hills like I likely would."

"And do you know of such a woman?"

"Not right off the top of my head. I'd need to speak to Noah to get a better sense for what kind of woman would complement him."

"Compliment?"

"Not in the sense of flattery, in the sense of completing."

"Oh." Esther straightened. "Then that's what you should do."

"What?"

"Speak to Noah."

Greta frowned. "You said he brushed that idea aside."

"True. But you said he doesn't really know what he needs." She shrugged. "And you and I both know you'll do a better job for him than I ever would. You already seem to think you have some insight into what will make him happy."

"Actually, I've given up my matchmaking efforts. I realized if I can't figure out what sort of man would be a match for me, I have no business doing it for someone else." She understood now that she'd only looked at one side of the equation—what made sense for her—and failed to think about what her potential groom would be looking for.

"Surely you can make just one more exception. This

is Noah after all, and he's looking for a *mamm* for those two little lambs."

Greta looked back toward the counter, picturing the sweet *kinner* there. Helping Noah find a *mamm* for them was a different way to look at it. Perhaps this was the answer she'd been looking for. This was just the sort of project she needed to take her mind off of the disaster with Calvin.

Still she hesitated.

Then she remembered that little boy at the pond, how sad and yet how kind he'd been to her that long-ago day. The grown-up version deserved so much more than what he'd told Esther he was looking for.

"I'll do it," she said impulsively. Then she took a half step back. "Assuming he's willing, of course."

Greta's mind was already spinning with possibilities. "It'll be a bit of a challenge given that he seems to have his mind made up, but I think I really can find the right person to make this family complete."

"You sound eager." Esther grinned as if saying *I told you so*. "Since we don't have any customers at the moment, why don't you go talk to him right now?" She waved toward Anna and David. "I can watch those two."

Greta nodded. "You're right. Might as well find out if he'll even agree to this."

As Greta stepped out into the mall lobby, she spotted Noah leaving his workshop. She waited until he neared, then met his gaze and smiled.

"What is it?" he asked as he approached. "Is there something wrong with Anna or David?"

"*Nee*, they're both fine."

He relaxed at that, then grimaced. "I'm sorry I keep

imposing on you and Esther to watch them. I know you have a shop to run."

She waved a hand dismissively. "It's not imposing—I love having these sweet *bopplin* to watch over."

He gave her a short bow. "For which I'm grateful. *Danke*."

"You're quite welcome. Your little ones are a delight."

Noah gave her a polite smile tinged with curiosity. "So, is there something else I can do for you?"

Might as well dive right in. "Esther told me you asked her to help you find a new *fraa*."

Something akin to irritation flashed across Noah's face before his guard went up. "And why did she feel the need to speak of it to you?"

"She and I are *gut* friends and she knew I would help in any way I can."

"Help?"

"Help you find a new *fraa*, of course." She smiled. "And a *mamm* for your *kinner*."

His guard eased a bit, but now he seemed ready to dismiss the subject, and her. "I appreciate your desire to help me, but I think this is something best left to Esther. She knows me and she knows my preferences."

Greta wasn't going to let him dismiss her that easily. "I realize Esther is your cousin and you might be more comfortable dealing with her. But perhaps you don't know that I have experience helping other young men find a helpmeet."

"*Jah*, I'm aware that you've played matchmaker in the past."

The way he said "played" got her back up, but Greta decided to ignore his tone and keep her focus on convincing him he needed her help. "Then perhaps you'll understand why Esther thought I'd be able to help in your search as well. If you give me a chance, I know I can find a woman who'll make you happy."

"What do you know about what will make me happy?"

Good question, especially after her spectacular failure on her own behalf. And for a moment her certainty wavered.

But then she rallied. This was different. "I believe I understand people well enough to know who'll get along well together and who won't." At least when it came to others.

He raised a brow at that. "Do you now?"

She refused to let his skepticism affect her again. "It probably sounds like pride and boastfulness to you, but it isn't. I believe this is a gift from *Gotte*, just as your skill with woodwork is, and that it would be wasteful not to use it."

She saw him sober at that and study her thoughtfully.

Trying to press her advantage, she quickly added, "But of course you'll need to help me figure out some of your own specific likes and dislikes." Would he agree? She realized she wanted to help him, that she needed to find some purpose to fill the emptiness that was stretching out in front of her.

But rather than respond directly, he asked a question of his own. "Why do you want to do this?"

"Because I love your *kinner* and want to help see they are well cared for. And also because I think it's something I can do well."

"And for no other reason?"

She squirmed a bit under his steady, much-too-perceptive scrutiny. Surely he didn't know about her feelings for Calvin and what had happened New Year's Day.

She tilted her chin up. "What other reason would there be?"

* * *

Noah saw the slight reddening of Greta's cheeks that belied the confident expression on her face. Was she thinking of Calvin? If she'd been so wrong about his *bruder*'s feelings, how could she possibly know what he needed? But somehow it seemed cruel to point that out to her. And what could it hurt to let her try, if even Esther thought she would do a better job for him? "I suppose we could give it a try."

Her face blossomed in a smile that made him blink— it had been a while since he'd seen those impish dimples of hers.

Her hands clasped tightly together as if trying to hold in some big emotion. "*Gut.*" Her tone was charmingly businesslike. Apparently she'd wanted to do this more than he'd realized.

"Now, there are a few things we need to discuss, and it would probably be best done away from where passersby might overhear. Since your little ones are in the quilt shop, would you like to go back into your workshop?"

Noah hesitated a moment. He'd prefer his employees not overhear any of this either. "My office would be better."

She nodded and fell into step beside him. His office was in the second-floor loft, accessible by a set of stairs tucked away in the back corner of the building. When they reached the narrow stairs, she went first while he followed her up. When she reached the loft, she paused at the window that overlooked the open fields, and her face took on an appreciative, faraway look. "I've never been up here before. The view is lovely."

She stood in the direct path of a sunbeam. The light streaming in through the window spotlighted her in a way that made her face literally glow.

A lovely view indeed.

Greta wasn't pretty in the usual way of things—the gap between her teeth and her blunt nose saw to that. But even so, in the light from the window, there was an arresting quality to her that made words like *pretty* and *attractive* seem inadequate.

Noah blinked, not sure where those thoughts had come from. He cleared his throat and swept an arm to his left. "My office is this way."

She looked around as she followed him. "There's a lot of unused space up here."

He shrugged. "I'd rather not have customers going up and down those narrow stairs on a regular basis, so there's no point in trying to put shops or other offices up here."

"Still, there has to be some good use you can put all this space to. I'll give it some thought."

Rather than responding to that bit of presumption, he led the way into his office and gestured toward a chair in front of his desk. "Please, have a seat." Once they were both sitting, he leaned forward, resting his elbows on his desk. "Now, what did we need to discuss?"

"First, Esther told me your requirements, but I'd like

to hear it from you, along with any personal likes and dislikes you might have."

Noah leaned back. "It's quite simple. The woman I marry must love and care for my *kinner*, of course. She should understand and accept the life of a craftsman's *fraa* rather than a farmer's, and she should be happy with a businesslike arrangement rather than a love match."

"And that's it?"

He spread his hands. "I told you my requirements were simple."

"What about cooking or housekeeping skills? Do you care if she's from this district or not? Are you okay if she's a widow? If she has other children?"

All fair questions, he supposed. "Cooking and housekeeping skills should be at least adequate. It isn't required that she be from this district, but I would want to meet her face-to-face before making a decision, so keep that in mind. A widow, with or without children, would be acceptable if she meets the other requirements." Then he rethought that point. "However, not so many children that Anna and David get lost in the mix." He crossed his arms. "Anything else?"

The smile she gave him was almost condescending. "Those were just questions to cover the basics. There are all sorts of little things that go into helping us find the right match. Think for a minute what you'd like to see when you return home in the evenings? Is there something Patsy did that you particularly liked or didn't like?"

At the reference to Patsy he stiffened momentarily. Then he forced himself to relax. "What I would like to see when I return home is an orderly house, *kinner* who are well cared for, and a good meal on the stove." He waved a hand. "As for what I like and don't like, other than what we've already discussed, the rest is inconsequential."

"And what are you willing to provide for your *fraa* in exchange for this?"

"Exchange?"

"*Jah.* A marriage, even a businesslike one, is a partnership, ain't so?"

"Yes, of course."

"So, in exchange for providing you and your *kinner* with a well-kept, pleasant home, what can she expect from you?"

"I'll provide her with a safe and secure home and with whatever else she feels she needs from a marriage, within reason."

She smiled as if he'd passed some sort of test. "*Gut.*" Then she gave him a probing look. "Are you absolutely sure there's nothing else you want to add?"

Noah hesitated a moment, then added, "Only that even though I'm most definitely not looking for a love match, I do want the woman I marry to be someone I can like and respect and who will like and respect me as well."

"Very well. Now, how would you like to approach this? I can come up with the names of some women I think would be a good match in just a day or two. Once that's done, would you like me to give it to you to look at before I interview them in case there are names you want to eliminate from consideration? Or would you rather I talk to them first so I can come to you with more information?"

It seemed to him that she'd gotten ahead of herself here. "Talk to them about what?"

"Well, I can be direct and let them know you're looking for a *fraa* and see if they're interested. Or I can be indirect and just find out more about them and what they want out of life and marriage in general."

The idea of her speaking to women on his behalf was more than a little alarming. "I prefer the indirect approach," he said quickly. "And yes, I'd like to see the list first." There was no telling who would end up on her list, and he definitely wanted to have a look at it before she approached any candidate with such a sensitive matter.

"Very well. The only reason I asked is because Esther said you were in a hurry."

"I am. I promised Maisie I'd free her up to enjoy her *rumspringa* by Valentine's Day."

"That's good to know. Now we have a timeline."

"But just because I'm in a hurry doesn't mean we can't be deliberate in how we approach this matter."

"Of course."

Did she just roll her eyes?

But she was already moving the conversation along. "There's something else we need to talk about."

"And that would be?"

"Your *mamm*."

"*Mamm*?" She was the last person he wanted to get involved in this. It would just make her feel more guilty than she already did for not being able to help with the *kinner*.

"*Jah*. Even though I know she's a *Gotte*-fearing woman with a *gut* heart, she does have a very strong personality."

Noah just barely managed to keep from laughing. That seemed a bit of the pot calling the kettle black.

But Greta wasn't finished. "Some young women find her a bit off-putting. So they may need some reassurances that you would stand up for them with her."

"I'm not sure a woman who would need me to do that is one I would want to marry." He waved a hand. "But of course I'll stand up for my *fraa* if she needs me to." He straightened. "At the heart of the matter, I need a woman with at least a scrap of self-confidence."

She gave him an understanding smile. "Noted. And the heart of it is definitely what we want to get to."

Was she trying to twist his words into something more than he'd intended?

But before he could comment she changed the subject. "Now, is there anything else you think I should know before I get started?"

"*Jah*. Although I want this all to go as quickly and smoothly as possible, we're talking about finding a woman who'll be a part of my and my *kinner*'s world for many years to come. So the matter should be handled prayerfully and with a proper seriousness."

She nodded. "I understand and I assure you I wouldn't approach this any other way." Then she folded her hands in her lap. "One last question—may I ask if you've thought about what happens if you don't find your match by the deadline you set?"

Noah stiffened. "Are you saying you don't think you can do it?" Had he made a mistake agreeing to let her do this?

She didn't seem at all intimidated by his tone. "Not at all. But there aren't any guarantees in this. One can't rush *Gotte*'s timing."

He could hardly argue with that. "Of course. But

doesn't the fact that I'm not looking for a love match simplify things?"

"It does and it doesn't."

His exasperation ratcheted up a notch. "That's not an answer."

"Let me explain." Her tone was that of a teacher talking to a young scholar. "What you're looking for is only half of the equation. The fact that you don't want a love match removes a restriction and makes it easier for me to find a woman you'll approve of. On the other hand, finding a woman who wants to enter into a marriage that's more of a business partnership than a true love match adds something to the woman's side of the equation, which will likely make it more difficult to find one who'll find you compatible."

That aspect hadn't occurred to him before she brought it up. "I see."

"Now, back to my question. I take it from your response that you haven't given the matter of missing your deadline any thought. It's about five weeks until Valentine's Day, so you have a little time. But I do suggest you give it some thought."

She stood. "Unless you have anything else to add, I really should head down to help Esther. And don't worry, I have every confidence that I can find the right woman to fit your needs."

He stood as well, feeling unaccountably irritated at the way she'd taken control of the conversation. And what made her so confident she could handle this? Sure, she'd had a few successes, but who's to say those couples wouldn't have found each other on their own, especially if she didn't hold to a deadline?

As far as her understanding people and what they needed, with her outspoken manner she was more likely to upset people than otherwise. In fact, if she didn't approach this project with delicacy, she could do more harm than good to his objectives.

A moment later he took himself to task. Greta was a well-meaning person with *gut* intentions. If she'd directed the conversation, it was because she knew what information she needed in order to perform the task he'd set her. As for her headstrong personality, that was the way *Gotte* had made her.

She deserved a chance to see what she could do.

Chapter 6

Greta slowly descended the stairs, trying to process what she'd learned during that discussion with Noah—not the verbal part but the nonverbal, which was always more telling.

His reaction when she'd mentioned Patsy had surprised her. It hadn't been the grief she'd expected, or even a bittersweet nostalgia. She couldn't quite decipher exactly what emotion it had been, but her instinct was telling her that whatever it was, it was the reason behind his insistence that he wasn't looking for a love match.

What had happened to him?

She shook off that question and decided to take a quick detour into Hannah's bakery. She exchanged quick greetings with her younger *shveshtah* and ordered a half-dozen sugar cookies. Then, with the bag of treats in hand, she headed back to the quilt shop.

She found Esther dealing with a customer who wanted

to commission a piece and who seemed to have some very specific ideas of colors and materials. Greta handed a cookie to David and Anna and then settled them down for a nap.

Now the customer had departed, leaving only the two of them and Noah's *kinner* in the shop.

"So what did he say?" Esther moved to her quilt frame, giving Greta an arch look.

"He was perfectly fine with me taking on the match-making for him," Greta said confidently.

"Perfectly fine?"

She grinned at her friend's perceptive comment. "Well, it did take him a moment to adjust to the idea, but in the end he agreed to let me help, so that's what counts." She lifted her chin. "And I plan to do a fabulous job for him."

"I'm sure you'll do your best, just as you always do."

Greta eyed her friend closely. "Is that a hint of doubt in your tone?"

Esther glanced at the counter as if trying to make sure Anna and David were truly napping, then she turned back to Greta. "It's just that Noah is sometimes difficult to please."

Greta had suspected as much. "Tell me a bit about your cousin, other than the fact that he's sometimes difficult to please." She held up a hand. "Not gossip, just information to help me understand him better."

Esther studied the quilt she was currently working on. "I know he seems overly serious, but things have been difficult for him since Patsy died. Not only did he lose his *fraa*, but I don't think he was prepared to be a single *daed*, though I guess no man ever is. He loves David and Anna fiercely, and they're his main concern now."

As they should be. "Is there anything he likes to do when he wants to relax and have fun?" Had she ever seen Noah relaxed? Then she smiled as she remembered the little boy who taught her to skip a stone that day she'd encountered him by the pond.

Esther didn't answer right away, taking a moment instead to tie off her thread and roll the completed portion of the quilt to reveal the next section. "Noah relaxing..." she finally said absently. "Well, he likes to read."

That caught Greta off guard. "Read? You mean like the Bible or *The Budget*?"

Esther shrugged. "*Jah*, of course. But he also likes fiction, Western stories mostly."

Westerns? So he had an adventurous side. Greta filed that bit of information away for another time. "What else does he like, or not like, to do?"

"Other than playing with his *kinner* and caring for his horses I'm not sure. Even when we were *youngie* I remember Noah as someone who kept to himself a lot."

It seemed Noah was even more walled off from people than she'd thought.

"Will any of this information help you find Noah a *fraa*?"

"It gives me a clearer picture of the kind of lady who'll best complement him." Noah definitely needed someone who'd help draw him out.

"I hope so." Esther sighed. "Noah deserves to be happy."

Before Greta could agree, there was movement from behind the counter. "I want a drink of water." David's drowsily worded request put an end to their discussion. But Greta's mind was already processing the information Esther had given her, adjusting the earlier picture she'd had of Noah and mentally sorting through the names of the single ladies she knew who were of the appropriate age.

As chance would have it, two Amish women walked in just then. Exchanging only a glance, Greta moved to the children while Esther bustled forward to assist their customers.

The two customers were followed by three English women, and for the next hour, both Esther and Greta were kept very busy. Once things quieted again, Greta headed behind the counter and pulled some catalogs from a cabinet there.

Esther peered at the books across the counter. "Looking for some new fabrics? I thought our inventory was in good shape considering fabric isn't our biggest seller."

"I'm looking at what's available for a personal project I'm working on. I need some special pieces."

"Another one of your original designs?"

Greta nodded and pulled out her sketchbook. She opened it to the page with the sketch of the new design she'd been working on, what she'd come to think of as her Promise Quilt. "What do you think?"

Esther studied the sketch, her expression changing to one of delight. "Greta, it's beautiful. I think it's your best design yet."

"*Danke*. I'm looking for some special fabric to depict the sunrise colors—I have something very specific in mind."

Another customer entered the shop just then, and

while Esther bustled over to take care of her, Greta checked on their two charges.

But her mind was still on her self-assigned match-making task. She wanted to find the perfect woman for Noah, someone who would appreciate what a *gut* man he was. Even though he hid it well, she was convinced Noah did have a sensitive side.

Because she'd seen it that long-ago day. He might have buried it as he grew up, but it was still there. It would be obvious to anyone who'd ever seen him with his family.

*　*　*

Noah leaned over his current project, rubbing a custom stain over the surface of the rich rosewood chest with special care, taking his time to apply the coat smoothly and evenly. As he studied the way the wood took the pigment, he pictured the finished product, a hope chest for Maisie for her birthday. She'd been storing her keepsakes and other items collected for her future home on a shelf in her closet. It was time she had a proper receptacle.

As he worked, his thoughts turned to his earlier meeting with Greta. Had he made the right choice by agreeing to let her play matchmaker for him? It was ridiculous to leave such an important selection to someone who insisted on inserting notions of romance into the selection process. He'd come very close to finding a polite way to refuse her offer and send her on her way.

But there'd been something about her when she spoke to him about this, an enthusiasm that was underlined with just a hint of vulnerability. The enthusiasm was something he could have ignored—Greta seemed to tackle everything she got involved in with a great deal of enthusiasm and fearlessness. No, it was the vulnerability that had given him pause. In the past, Greta had always struck him as a totally confident young woman who went her own way regardless of the opinions of others. Yet twice in the past few days he'd seen this fragility about her, and he felt his *bruder* was very much to blame. As head of the family it made him feel oddly responsible, regardless of how illogical that feeling was.

Besides, she was very good to his *kinner*, and he could overlook a lot for that.

He finished applying the second coat and stepped back to review his work, arching his back to ease the stiffness in his muscles. After a moment he nodded, satisfied with how the chest was turning out.

He checked the clock on the wall, noting it was nearly noon. Time for him to have lunch with Anna and David. He scrubbed up and then rolled down his sleeves and headed to the quilt shop. When he arrived he saw Greta was dealing with two English customers while Esther was fussing with the arrangement of some quilting supplies on the wall behind the counter.

His *kinner* weren't immediately visible but he wasn't particularly worried—both Esther and Greta were very responsible when it came to his little ones.

He took a moment to study Greta as she spoke animatedly to her customers, answering their questions about the origins of some of the pieces and the possibility of ordering a custom quilt. It was reflective of his earlier thoughts about her being enthusiastic in whatever she tackled.

A moment later the customers nodded and moved away, obviously prepared to browse. Noah stepped forward before he could be caught staring and moved toward Esther. "And where are you hiding Anna and David?"

"*Daed!*" David came rushing out from behind the counter with Anna close behind him.

"Are you two ready for your lunch?"

"*Jah!*"

Greta came up just then. "Let's put away the toys before you join your *daed.*"

Firm without being authoritarian, he liked that.

Then she turned to him. "I already have a few ideas for you. But I want to give it some more thought. I should be ready to talk to you in the morning."

Apparently she'd taken what he'd said about his timeline to heart. "I look forward to hearing what you come up with."

And, a bit to his surprise, he actually *was* looking forward to it.

* * *

That evening after the chores and dinner had been taken care of, Greta slipped inside her quilt room. She brushed her hands across her *mamm*'s wedding quilt, smiling at the memories that evoked.

She remembered the hours her *mamm* had patiently schooled her on how to quilt. *Mamm* had been a very talented quilter in her own right—her stitches tiny and perfectly placed. She could bring any pattern to life with her artistry. But when it came to cutting and piecing, she always followed existing patterns, saying that she had no talent for pattern making. Later, when Greta first started designing her own patterns, *Mamm* was delighted and she actively encouraged Greta to explore her talent.

Her support, however, had gone beyond quilting. *Mamm* had been one of the few people to both understand her spirited outlook toward life and also actually encourage her in all that she attempted, not just quilting. Above all, she'd always encouraged Greta to be true to herself.

Greta had been thirteen when *Mamm* died, and she'd felt that she'd lost not only her mother but the only person who really understood her.

What would *Mamm* think of her now? Would she encourage Greta in this matchmaking endeavor or tell her it was something best left to Noah and his family?

She missed being able to discuss such things with her, missed being able to show her the new designs she'd sketched, missed being able to just feel her comforting presence as they sat stitching together.

Resisting the urge to wrap herself up in that quilt again, Greta gave it another pat and then carried the lamp to her worktable. She had two names for Noah but she'd like to have at least three before she presented the list to him tomorrow.

Greta pulled out her sketchbook, ruler and tissue paper. Focusing on something else, like transferring her sketch into actual pattern pieces, was the kind of work that freed her mind to think.

An hour later she had pattern pieces for about a third of the quilt cut and meticulously labeled so that they cross-referenced to her sketch.

Not only that, but she'd also come up with the third name for her list. A list that, if all worked out, contained the name of Noah's next *fraa*.

Why did the thought of that not fill her with the same kind of excitement it had on her previous matchmaking attempts?

* * *

"I have three names for your consideration."

It was the next morning and Greta again sat across from Noah in his office, feeling just the tiniest bit smug.

"Three? You work fast."

"You did say you were in a hurry." Greta noted the look of surprise and something akin to panic on Noah's face. It seemed he'd had his doubts about her. And perhaps about himself?

Noah cleared his throat, reclaiming her attention as he leaned back in his chair. "Well, let's hear them then."

She nodded and sat up straighter, confident his next *fraa* was indeed on this list. "First there's Lizzie Yoder." She watched him closely to gauge his reaction.

His forehead furrowed. "You mean Joseph Yoder's widow?"

"*Jah.* She has a two-year-old son, but that just means she knows how to take care of little ones and that there'll be a new playmate for your *kinner*. And Joseph was a farrier rather than a farmer, so she shouldn't be averse to marrying a craftsman. Also, as a widow who's living with her husband's parents, I would think she'd be amenable to setting a wedding date in the near future." She also had a great sense of humor, was funny without being unkind, which was something Greta thought would add a needed bit of levity to their future life together.

Noah nodded slowly, a promising sign. "She does sound like a *gut* candidate. But tell me about the other two names on your list."

More confident now, Greta leaned back in her chair. "The next person I think would be a good match for you is Sara Kauffmann."

"The schoolteacher?"

"*Jah*. She's a couple of years younger than me," Greta continued, "but mature for her age. I know she's on the quiet side, but as a schoolteacher she also knows how to stand up for herself." Which would come in handy when dealing with Noah's *mamm*.

"And her scholars like her very much, so you know she'll be good for your *kinner*." Unfortunately, Sara didn't have a noticeable sense of humor, but perhaps she had enough spirit to make up for that.

"That's *gut* to know." Noah was more noncommittal with Sara than he'd been with Lizzie. "And the third name?"

"That would be Rachel Lapp. You probably aren't familiar with her—she lives over in Heartwood Crossing, in Bishop John Basinger's district. I met her during my rumspringa—Calvin knows her as well if you want to check with him."

Noah waved a hand. "Not necessary."

Greta felt bolstered by this show of confidence. "She's my age or perhaps just a little older, is sweet natured, and quite graceful in her movements and actions. One additional point in her favor is that her father is a furniture maker, so she should already be familiar with the kind of work you do."

Rachel also had a touch of the mischief-maker in her, something Greta believed would be a good foil to Noah's much-too-serious disposition.

Noah stroked his beard. "Is she by chance Asa Lapp's daughter?"

"I believe so. Why, do you know him?"

"Not personally. I know his work, though. His craftsmanship is excellent."

Another positive note that should predispose him to like Rachel. "It's been a while since I've spoken to her, but if you'd like, I can contact her again to gauge her interest."

Having exhausted her list, Greta folded her hands in her lap. "What do you think? Do any of these women interest you?"

He took his time responding, and when he finally did speak, he didn't answer her question directly. "It appears you've really put a lot of thought into this."

She would have been flattered by his words if he hadn't sounded so surprised. "Of course. I told you, if for no other reason than that your new *fraa* will be caretaker to your sweet *kinner*, I'm committed to finding the best possible match for you."

He nodded, waving a hand as if asking her to continue.

"So, do I need to keep looking for other candidates or do you want to pursue one of the women on this list?"

"They all have their good points." Noah's voice and expression were businesslike, as if he were merely discussing plans for a new table he planned to build. "I'm acquainted with Sara and Lizzie, and they seem to be fine young women. But, as you suspected, I've never met Rachel Lapp. Perhaps we can find a way for that to happen so I can have all the information at hand before I decide which one to focus on."

There was that logical, analytical mind of his at work. "Of course. Let me think on how I can arrange that. I'll try to come up with something quickly so it doesn't delay you too much."

Greta left his office with mixed feelings. There was a sense of accomplishment—she could tell he was pleased that she'd found promising candidates so quickly. But she was also a bit sad for him that he wasn't able to just go with his first instinct. Surely one of those women had appealed to him more than the others. Since he had a deadline for completing his search, he should have been willing to do whatever he could to move forward.

Was it just his deliberate nature, or was something else at work here holding him back?

* * *

When lunchtime rolled around, Noah was still trying to decide how he felt about his morning meeting with Greta. At least two of the women whose names she'd brought to him were surprisingly good choices. Of course, Lizzie wasn't quite as serious minded as he would have liked, and he had the impression Sara could be stubborn at times, but neither of those traits was serious enough to rule them out if the women were otherwise suitable. He was realistic enough to know there wouldn't be any one woman out there who could perfectly check all the boxes on his wish list.

Then there was Greta herself. He didn't know why

her apparent competence at this matchmaking business surprised him so much. After all, just because she was opinionated and forward didn't mean she was also inept.

He glanced down at David and Anna, playing on the floor of his office. Maisie was still under the weather, so Esther had watched them for him this morning, but he kept them with him when he was in his office rather than the workshop.

David had the two wooden horses Noah had carved for him, and he was putting on a show of sorts for his little sister, who was clapping her hands in appreciation. Noah's heart hitched at the sight of the two of them playing together. They deserved so much more than he alone could give them. Whatever other faults Patsy had had, she'd been a *gut mamm*. He needed to give them that again.

But after the way Patsy had pushed him out of her life those last few months, he didn't want another love match for himself.

A knock interrupted his thoughts. Who could that be? Folks seldom came up here unless there was something that needed his immediate attention. He rose quickly, then realized it was Greta standing there, one hand behind her back. Before he could say anything, however, David jumped up, abandoning his toys and his sister, and ran to her.

"Greta!" His voice rang with delight as he hugged her legs.

She ruffled his straw-colored hair affectionately.

Then David stepped back and leaned to his left as if trying to see around her. "What do you have behind your back?"

Greta pulled her hand around, looking at what she held as if just remembering she had it. "You mean this? Why it's just a few cookies I got from my *shveshtah*'s bakery. I was wondering if there was anyone up here who would be willing to help me eat them."

David nodded vigorously. "I will."

"Cookie!" Anna pushed up from her seat on the floor and came toddling over.

Greta glanced at Noah for belated permission, which he gave in the form of a nod. She handed Anna and David each a large sugar cookie, then turned back to him. "Can we talk for a minute?"

Noah turned to his *kinner*. "David, Anna, you sit and eat your cookies while I talk to Greta."

The children nodded and happily obliged.

Noah gestured for her to step into the area outside his office and followed close on her heels, leaving the door open so he could keep an eye on the *kinner*. "What is it? Did you think of something else?"

"Actually, I have an idea on how you can meet my friend Rachel."

He almost smiled when he heard the excitement in her voice. "I'm listening."

"Rachel works at a fabric store in Heartwood Crossing. I believe there's also a lumber supply store there, ain't so?"

"*Jah*. I occasionally do business there."

"Tomorrow's Sunday, but could you find a reason to go there on Monday?"

He rubbed his jaw, understanding what she was leading up to. "I suppose I could."

"*Gut*. Then I can tag along while you run your errand

so that I can visit with Rachel. And you can come into the fabric store with me and meet her. It's not ideal but it'll be quick, and if you don't feel a connection with her, she need never know why we were there."

He couldn't find any fault with her plan, and it did accomplish the goal of allowing him to meet Rachel quickly. "Very well. What time would you like to leave Monday morning?"

"I'm at your disposal. The quilt shop is closed on Mondays, so whatever time works best for you is all right by me."

"It's a little over an hour by buggy each way, so we should get an early start. Give me time to open the shop for Andrew and Paul—say, seven thirty?"

"I'll be ready."

The question was, was he ready?

*   *   *

When Greta returned to the quilt shop she found Esther assisting a customer, so she went directly to her quilt frame. Taking a moment to reorient herself with where she'd left off, she went to work. It would be *gut* to see Rachel again. It had been, what, six months since they'd last exchanged letters? She wasn't even sure who'd failed to answer who, but it was high time they reconnected.

If things worked out and Noah and Rachel ended up together, her friend would move to Hope's Haven and they'd be able to see each other more often. It was an outcome she hadn't considered until now.

The arrival of two customers brought Greta's wandering thoughts back to the present. She quickly jabbed her needle into the quilt and stood to greet the two women. "Is there something I can help you ladies with?"

The older of the two, a silver-haired woman with a wrist full of slender silver bracelets, waved a hand with a smile. "No thank you, dear, I think we're just going to look around for a bit."

"Of course." Greta waved toward her quilt frame. "I'll be just over there. If you have any questions or decide you need some help, please don't hesitate to let me know." And with that she returned to her quilting.

Once Esther's previous customer paid for her purchase and left, her friend approached one of the new arrivals, who was examining the throw pillows. The other woman, the one with the bracelets, drifted closer to where Greta was working.

"Oh, how lovely. Is it for sale?"

Greta looked up and shook her head with a smile. "I'm sorry but this is a special order for another customer."

"She's lucky. It truly is beautiful."

"*Danke.*"

"Do you think I could commission you to make something similar for me? My daughter is getting married this summer and I know she'd love this."

She seemed to be surrounded by people involved in weddings. "Of course. But only if you understand it won't be exactly the same. I rarely use the same fabrics in the same way twice."

The woman's smile brightened at that. "Even better, that means the quilt will be unique. In fact I'd like a different color palette if that's okay, one with more lilacs and blues, her favorite colors."

Greta nodded, sheathing her needle in the quilt once

more. "That sounds lovely. Would you like to pick out the fabrics or would you prefer to leave it to me?"

"Perhaps we can do it together?"

"Of course." Greta stood. "Let's take a look at the fabrics we have in stock. We can also special order other pieces if you like." As they walked to the other side of the shop, where the bolts of fabric were shelved, Greta stopped at the counter and picked up one of the order forms. "I'll also need to get information on what size bed this is for and how soon you'll need it, along with a few other things. Then we can discuss cost."

But as she worked with her newest customer, Greta's thoughts kept drifting back to the upcoming trip to Heartwood Crossing with Noah. The forced closeness and relative privacy would give her a chance to get to know him better. If she could get him to open up.

If not, it was going to be a very long, uncomfortable ride.

* * *

"How is Greta doing with the matchmaking?" Esther settled into the buggy with Anna on her lap and David squeezed in the middle. Noah had given her a ride this morning and was returning her home for the evening.

He paused with the reins in his hands as he shot her a surprised look. "Didn't she talk to you about it?"

"*Nee.* Greta says the details are yours to share or not. All I know is that she's spent a lot of time in your office today."

That surprised him. But there were a lot of things about Greta Eicher that had surprised him lately.

"Does your silence mean you're not going to share?"

The question made Noah realize he'd been quiet too long. "Not at all. Greta has given me the names of three women who she thinks meet my requirements."

"Already?" Esther shifted Anna into a more comfortable position. "And what did you think of her choices?"

"They seem surprisingly well thought out."

"And?"

"And one of the women is someone I don't know, so Greta is arranging for us to meet on Monday."

"And so it begins."

The hint of amusement in Esther's tone wasn't lost on him.

"*Daed*, what's matchmaking?" his son asked.

Noah had forgotten David and Anna were listening. He cut a quick glance Esther's way, but she gave a shrug as if to say he was on his own.

How did he explain the concept of matchmaking to a four-year-old? Especially if he wasn't ready to talk to him about bringing a new person into their lives just yet.

Then again, perhaps it was best to start laying a little groundwork. "A matchmaker is someone who tries to help a person find someone he or she might want to marry."

He left it at that and waited to see how David reacted.

The boy's nose wrinkled in thought for a few minutes, then he met Noah's gaze. "Does that mean you're going to marry Greta?"

"*Nee*," Noah said quickly, ignoring Esther's stifled laugh. "What it means is Greta is helping me find someone else to marry."

"Oh."

Was that a note of disappointment in his son's voice?

Then David brightened. "Well, I hope she finds you someone just like her."

Deciding there was no good way to answer that, Noah focused on the road, refusing to meet Esther's mirth-filled gaze.

Despite his son's wishes, a woman like Greta Eicher was the very last thing he was looking for. Because with Greta, keeping things businesslike would be nearly impossible.

* * *

"Greta?"

Greta paused with her hand on the knob to her quilt room. "Yes *Daed*?"

"You're not going to disappear in there again this evening, are you?"

Greta released the doorknob and turned to face him fully. "Is there something you needed from me?"

Her *daed* spread his hands. "Only to spend a little time with my middle *dochder*."

With a smile Greta moved toward her *daed*. "Of course. Sorry I've been so focused on my quilting lately."

He sighed. "You are so like your *mamm*."

"*Danke*." She walked beside him to the living room. "That's the sweetest thing you could say to me."

"I hear you've been playing matchmaker again." His tone held a note of displeasure.

Startled that word had spread of her work with Noah, Greta merely nodded.

"Carl seems quite happy with the young lady you matched him with."

So not Noah. "Malinda is a practical woman who'll be a good match for his touch of absentmindedness."

"This little hobby you have is all well and good, but do you think it might be keeping you from finding a husband of your own?"

So that's where the displeasure came from. "It doesn't work like that. Helping others find the right person to spend their lives with doesn't keep me from being open to finding the same for myself." Not that she'd be doing much more. Once she found a good match for Noah she was done.

"But the men who've come to you for help, you could have matched one of them with yourself, ain't so?"

"Again, it doesn't work that way. None of those men I found matches for were looking for someone like me." And they weren't what she'd been looking for either.

"Then perhaps that's a sign you should change your ways to become the kind of woman a fine young man would want to marry."

Greta loved her *daed* and didn't doubt that he loved her, in his own gruff way. But, unlike *Mamm*, he'd never understood her. And since *Mamm*'s death he'd closed off quite a bit, and lost some of his warmth in the process.

"I am as *Gotte* made me."

He frowned, his displeasure with her response obvious. "*Gotte* also gave you a free will and His word to guide you."

Greta held her peace, not wanting to make him angry.

"Think on that, *dochder*. Unless you're happy with the role of spinster." Then he pointed a finger at her. "And if you're determined not to change your ways, then think of your *shveshtra* next time you're making a match." And with that he turned and walked away.

Greta slowly made her way back to the quilt room. Did he have a point? She'd never once considered Hannah or Martha when she looked at matches for the men who'd come to her.

But thinking back over the three matches she'd made, she couldn't picture either Hannah or Martha being a good fit.

And as for Noah...

No, she couldn't see either of them as a match for him either. Hannah was too young and starry-eyed, she'd never settle for a businesslike marriage. And Martha was too pragmatic and serious, matching her and Noah would ensure neither ever learned to let down their guard.

As for *Daed*'s suggestion that she should find a match for herself, she was still trying to deal with the fact that she'd been so wrong about Calvin's feelings. She wasn't ready to open herself up to that kind of rejection again so soon. Even for a man as intriguing as Noah Stoll. A man who had two youngsters that she'd grown to love. A man she could bring light and laughter to.

Then Greta took herself to task. It was too soon for her to go down that road again.

Besides, if Noah had had any interest in her he would have said so when they discussed potential candidates.

Wouldn't he?

Chapter 7

Perhaps it would be better if I go into the fabric store alone."

They had reached the outskirts of Heartwood Crossing, and Greta was surprised by how quickly time had passed on the ride over. She'd worried when they first set out this morning that they wouldn't have anything to talk about. But she'd mentioned her idea about a special cart to transport coffee carafes, and they spent most of the hour-long drive discussing various ways to make such an item serve more than one purpose for a household. She was surprised at how easy Noah was to talk to. Even more surprising was that he'd actually been willing to listen to her ideas and even debate them with her.

Now Noah cast her a sideways look. "I thought the whole reason we took this trip was so I could meet your friend."

"It was, I mean it is. I just think it might be best if

I spend a little time with her first. You can come inside when you return to pick me up."

"You obviously know best how to handle this, so we'll do it your way. I won't be long."

She smiled at that, pleasantly surprised that he respected her judgment.

Heartwood Crossing was a much bigger town than their small community of Hope's Haven. There were a number of restaurants and fast-food places as well as a large hotel, several strip malls and two movie theaters.

Luckily the fabric store was on the main road into town, so it was easy to find.

Once Noah dropped her off, Greta walked inside and realized she didn't even know Rachel's work schedule. Would her friend be here today? Or had she talked Noah into traveling all this way for nothing?

Then she saw a figure wearing a *kapp* and Amish dress, standing on a step stool, sliding bolts of batting onto an upper shelf, and breathed a little sigh of relief.

She waited until Rachel saw her, then gave a little wave.

"Greta!" Rachel's eyes lit up with delighted recognition. She stepped down from the stool and bustled over to greet her. The two embraced, then Rachel stepped back. "It's wonderful *gut* to see you. But what are you doing in Heartwood Crossing?"

Greta unbuttoned her coat. "A friend was traveling here for business and I thought I'd tag along with him to pay you a visit."

"I'm so glad you did. It's early for me to be taking a break, but maybe we can chat while I unbox and shelve these notions, then we can get a quick cup of coffee together."

"Sounds *gut*. Besides, I want to pick up some fabric for a new quilt I'm planning to start soon."

Rachel grinned as she pulled out a box that had been sitting unobtrusively under a cutting table. "Don't you run a fabric shop of your own?"

Greta returned her grin. "It's a quilt shop that sells some fabrics as well. But we don't have anywhere near the selection this store has."

"Well, feel free to look around whenever you're ready." She tilted her head with an assessing look. "Still sketching out beautiful new quilt designs, I take it."

Greta shrugged. "I sketch whatever visions come to me."

Rachel set the box on the table. "So how long can you visit?"

"I imagine Noah will be back to get me in about twenty or thirty minutes."

Rachel opened the box and began to arrange carded buttons on a vertical rack. "Tell me about this Noah. Are you two courting?"

"*Nee*, it's nothing like that. Noah is just a friend."

"A friend you would ride all the way from Hope's Haven with just to spend thirty minutes with me? That sounds like a very *gut* friend."

Greta's cheeks grew warm for some unaccountable reason. Time to cut off that line of conversation. "Do you remember Calvin Stoll? Noah is his older *bruder*."

Rachel nodded. "If I remember correctly, you were sweet on Calvin. Did anything come of that?"

Greta waved a hand dismissively, hoping she appeared unaffected. "That was ages ago. We're just friends now."

Rachel gave her an arch look. "Are you just friends

with all the young men of your acquaintance? Or just the Stolls?"

"If you're asking me if I'm dating anyone, the answer is I'm not." She quickly took advantage of the opening. "And what about you? Is there a young man you're particularly sweet on?"

To her surprise, Rachel's cheeks pinkened.

"*Jah*. Just before Christmas, John Brandt, whose family has the next farm over from ours, asked to court me."

Greta struggled to keep her disappointment from showing. "From the expression on your face I take it you like this John Brandt very much."

Rachel nodded. "I've known him forever and we've always been friends. And then suddenly one day, we realized we were more than friends."

The way she'd expected it would happen with Calvin. Greta kept her smile firmly in place as she gave her friend a hug. "*Ach*, Rachel, I'm so happy for you." And she truly was. She just wished she hadn't gotten Noah's hopes up.

"*Danke*." Rachel stepped back and gave Greta's hand a squeeze. "I hope one day you can be this happy too."

Me too. Time to change the subject again. "Enough about men, tell me what else has been going on in your life since we last spoke."

And for the next fifteen minutes or so, they chatted about inconsequential things while Greta helped her unload the box of notions. When Greta finally stepped away to select some quilt fabrics, she tried to figure out just how she'd tell Noah that they'd made this trip for nothing.

* * *

Noah parked the buggy beside the fabric store, grateful many of the businesses here accommodated Amish vehicles. He didn't get out immediately. Instead he sat there for a moment, wondering if he would walk through the door and meet the woman he would marry one day soon. It was daunting, to say the least.

Finally he shook his head over his own foolishness and exited the buggy. He stepped inside the fabric store and paused, removing his hat. This was obviously a female domain and, unlike in Greta and Esther's smaller quilt shop, he felt completely out of place. It took him a few minutes to locate Greta, but he finally spotted her with another lady in Amish dress. Neither of them noticed him right away, so he took a moment to study Greta's companion. She was petite and appeared to smile easily. The hair peeking out from under her *kapp* was blonde, and she had a pleasant appearance.

Then Greta looked up as if she'd felt his gaze, and something flickered in her expression, there and gone in a heartbeat, before he could react.

She straightened immediately and began gathering her things. "Noah, there you are. I take it your business is completed."

He nodded. "It is." Why did Greta seem so flustered? Surely she wasn't nervous about introducing him to her friend all of a sudden.

She turned to her companion, who was smiling his way. "Rachel, this is Noah, the friend I told you about. Noah, this is Rachel Lapp."

Before they could do more than exchange greetings,

Greta spoke up again as she slipped an arm into her coat. "It was so nice visiting with you again, Rachel. But I've kept you from your work long enough, and I'm sure Noah is eager to return to his place of business as well."

He wasn't sure what was going on, but he followed her lead. "*Jah*, if you're through with your visit it's best we be on our way." He helped Greta with the other sleeve. "It was nice meeting you, Rachel."

"And you as well. Please tell your *bruder* Calvin hello for me."

Was that it? Had talk of Calvin upset Greta?

Then he discarded that thought. Greta might still be smarting over Calvin's lack of interest, but she wouldn't let that deter her from her goal.

As soon as they were outside, Noah stopped and turned to her. "I assume there was some reason you hurried me out of there before your friend and I could become acquainted."

Greta gave him an apologetic nod. "I found out Rachel already has a boyfriend."

"I see." Noah resumed walking toward the buggy, trying to decide if he was sorry or pleased by the turn of events. Perhaps a bit of both? What did that say about him? He absolutely understood on a logical level that he needed to find a *fraa* so Anna and David could have a *mamm*, but perhaps there was a small, illogical part of himself that wasn't quite ready to accept that yet.

It was only when he reached the buggy that he realized Greta was breathless from trying to keep up with him.

* * *

Greta tried not to fidget as Noah negotiated the buggy through town in complete silence. He hadn't said anything other than to ask her if she was comfortable when he spread the buggy blanket over them.

Was he angry that she'd wasted his time with this trip? Would he decide not to let her continue as his matchmaker?

Finally, when they reached the open road, she couldn't stand the silence any longer and spoke up. "I'm truly sorry."

Noah turned to look at her, his eyes squinted slightly in a puzzled expression. "Sorry for what?"

Had she misread him? "For making you come all this way for nothing."

He shrugged and turned back to the road. "I asked to meet your friend and you saw to it that I did. Now we know one name we can cross off that list of yours. I call that progress."

"So you're not angry?"

"Of course not. Why would you think that?" He seemed genuinely puzzled.

"It's just"—she waved a hand—"you were so quiet."

His lips curved in a wry smile. "In case you haven't noticed, I'm not the chatty type."

She smiled, surprised by the bit of teasing. "No, I suppose you're not." Since he was taking this setback so well, she decided to return to the business of matchmaking. "So, of the two names left on the list, who would you like to approach first, Lizzie or Sara?"

"I've been giving that quite a bit of thought since Saturday."

Of course he had. Probably analyzed it a hundred different ways.

"Both seem like *gut* candidates, but I think, since Lizzie has been married before, she's the one more likely to be content with what I'm offering."

Not the best reason to select a potential bride, but if that was the way he wanted to approach it, she'd go along. "*Gut*. I'll see Lizzie this afternoon with our quilting group and can speak to her there. Would you like me to just find out how open she would be to remarrying, or given the rush you're in, would you prefer I be more specific?"

He didn't answer right away, his expression pensive. Then he gave her a sideways look. "I suppose it's best to get on with it."

His uncertainty caught her off guard. Was he having second thoughts? "We can slow things down if you're not sure. I just thought—"

"No, ignore what I just said—it was a momentary lapse of focus. I promised Maisie she'd be free of me by Valentine's Day, and with *Mamm*'s health getting worse I don't have any alternatives. After all, I can't keep asking you and Esther to watch my *kinner* when you have your own shop to run." He shook his head. "No, the sooner I find a *fraa*, the better for everyone."

She could sense his hesitation and frustration, but it wasn't for her to second-guess him. "Very well then, again to my question, how would you like me to approach Lizzie this afternoon?"

His sigh was one of resignation. "I suppose you should just find out if she's interested in another marriage. If so, then I can approach her myself after services on Sunday."

He was still approaching this methodically. "All right. I'll let you know in the morning what I learn."

"*Danke*."

The silence stretched out for several moments before Greta decided to broach a different topic, just to keep the conversation going. "Do you mind if I ask you something?"

He cut her a wary look, then nodded. "Ask away."

"How did you get started in woodworking? I mean, your family has always farmed in one way or another, ain't so?"

He nodded. "They have. But from the time I helped *Daed* build a birdhouse when I was just a *kinner* myself, I've been fascinated by the craftsmanship involved in a well-made piece of furniture or cabinetry. After I asked *Daed* enough questions about it"—he cut a rueful glance her way—"in other words pestered him mercilessly, he took me to see Gideon Chupp, one of the best cabinetmakers in the county. I was about eight years old at the time and Gideon answered all of my questions. He even invited me to come visit him again if I had any other questions."

"I take it you went back."

"Many times. Before I knew it I was apprenticing with him. And eventually I was ready to go out on my own."

"So you never considered becoming a farmer like your *daed*?"

He shook his head. "That was always Calvin's interest. From the day I met Gideon I knew I wanted to work with wood. And *Daed* never tried to talk me out of it. He said if *Gotte* had put that desire on my heart and that skill in my hands, then who was he to hold me back."

"Your *daed* always struck me as a very sensible, caring man."

"For sure and for certain."

Intrigued by this side of him, a side that was neither practical nor analytical, Greta pressed for more info. "So what is it about woodworking that captures your interest?"

"You're the first person who's ever asked me that." He glanced her way as if judging how sincere her interest was. Then he nodded and turned his gaze back to the road. "There's just something about taking a raw piece of lumber and turning it into something functional and beautiful that I find so satisfying. I love the smell of sawdust, the feel of a smooth slab of wood, the beauty of a well-constructed dovetail joint."

The way he talked about his work seemed poetic, almost passionate, like a true artist who took joy in his work. In other words, completely at odds with the analytical persona he usually projected. She felt a little spurt of excitement—she was finally getting to the heart of him. "I'd like to see examples of your work sometime," she said impulsively. "If that's okay?"

He cut her a surprised look. "Why?"

She shifted in her seat, wondering if she'd been a little too forward. "The way you just described it, you made it seem so, I don't know, so artistic."

He chuckled at that and it transformed his whole face. "I'm no artist. But *jah*. Stop by the workshop whenever you have time and I'll give you a tour."

"I'd like that." Then, because she suddenly felt self-conscious, she reached beneath the seat and pulled out a small basket. "I think it's time to bring out the hot chocolate and peanut butter cookies I brought for us to share. Would you like some?"

He grinned and nodded. "I was wondering if you'd ever let me have a taste of those."

She removed her gloves and handed him a cookie. While he munched on that, she uncapped the thermos and poured up a cup of still-warm cocoa. As soon as he finished the cookie, she handed him the cup of cocoa.

His hand closed over hers for a moment as he took the cup, and Greta was surprised by the totally unexpected tingle of awareness she felt.

Flustered, she pulled her hand back a bit too quickly, and some of the cocoa spilled. "*Ach*, I'm so sorry." She could feel the heat rise in her cheeks as she fumbled for a napkin.

But he only laughed. "It was just a few drops. No harm done."

She clutched the napkin and reached over to blot at his sleeve. Then she stopped herself, her cheeks getting increasingly warmer. What in the world was she doing?

Apparently noting her distress, Noah handed the cup back over to her and took the napkin. After wiping at the barely noticeable spot on his jacket, he traded back. "There we go, good as new."

Without saying anything, Greta tucked the napkin back in the basket and took a cookie for herself. She nibbled on it, more as an excuse not to have to talk than because she had any kind of appetite. Had his hand closed over hers deliberately or had it been an accident? He *was* looking for a *fraa* after all.

Then she gave her head a mental shake. She was just being fanciful. Noah had never shown that kind of interest in her, and there was no reason to believe he ever would.

Noah sensed Greta's discomfort. Was it just the spill or had that momentary touch sparked something in her too? He pushed that thought away to process later. Right now he needed to put her back at ease. He took a big sip from his cup, then lifted it as if to toast her. "Mmmm, this is wonderful *gut*."

Some of her tension sccmcd to evaporate. "Hannah made the cookies but the hot cocoa is all me."

"There's a little something different about it, ain't so? It's very *gut*, but 1 can't quite figure out what it is." He didn't have to fake his appreciation.

"I like to add a little cinnamon to the mix," she admitted as she poured herself a cup. "It's the way my *mamm* used to make it."

He heard the wistful tone in her voice. If he remembered correctly, she'd been young when her *mamm* died, around thirteen or so. "She taught you well."

They were quiet for a while after that, both sipping on their cocoa. Noah decided that sensation he'd felt at her touch had been nothing more than static clectricity.

Then Greta cleared her throat. "I got the impression earlier that you're not completely comfortable with this search for a new *fraa*, ain't so?"

He glanced at her from the corner of his eye, trying to gauge her intent. He'd hoped she hadn't picked up on that, but he should have known better. "Not exactly."

"Is it because of my matchmaking? Is there something I should be handling different or better? I know you said you were all right that Rachel had a boyfriend, but if I did—"

He cut her ramblings short. "Not at all. You're doing just as I asked."

She relaxed against the seat back. "Then what?"

How much should he say? He supposed it was best to be open. "I do want to find another *fraa*, just as I said. Not only out of necessity, but because I know everyone is happier when they have someone to share the burdens of life with."

She made a noncommittal sound at that, and he suddenly realized she was probably still dealing with the hurt Calvin had dealt her. How long would she feel the sting of that rejection?

There was no taking the words back now, so he moved on quickly. "The hesitation you sensed comes from the fact that I'm uncomfortable making a big decision like this in such a short period of time. I'd prefer to have the opportunity to really get to know these women better before asking one of them to become my *fraa*." He grimaced in frustration. "It's my own fault—I should have taken care of this sooner."

She stiffened again. "This is not some chore to take care of," she said, her tone sharp. "This is finding a *fraa*, a *mamm* for your little ones."

He waved a hand in surrender. "*Jah*, of course. Which is why I'd like to take my time." He handed her back his empty cup and accepted another cookie. "My main concern is that the woman I select truly understands what she'll be agreeing to."

"Ever the practical thinker."

She said that as if it were a bad thing.

"That conversation might be difficult to have," she continued, "but it won't be time-consuming. I'll even step in and do it for you if you prefer. So what are you really worried about?"

He grimaced. "You don't pull your punches, do you?"

Greta didn't seem bothered by his accusation. "The more information I have, the better I'm able to match you with the right woman."

"Do you think there's only one right woman for every man?"

"I believe that *Gotte* has prepared a woman and a man to complement each other and it's when we find this match that we can be truly happy." She lifted her chin. "So, will you answer my question?"

Noah held his peace while he negotiated the turn off of the main highway onto the road that would ultimately take them back to Hope's Haven.

Had Patsy been the woman *Gotte* prepared for him? If so, had he failed her as a husband? Their first few years had been pleasant if not wildly happy. David had been born before the end of the first year and they'd both lavished their love on him, and that had seemed to be enough. And then a year and a half later she'd become pregnant again and they'd seemed on their way to building the family they both wanted.

Then her *daed*'s accident had happened and everything had changed. He'd stepped in as the senior man in the family, as her *mamm* had asked him to. He'd made the decisions that had to be made, and she'd turned her back on him for it.

He gave his head a mental shake, remembering Greta was waiting on his answer. "My hesitation comes from the fact that no matter how carefully I choose, adding a new member to our household will lead to changes for both myself and my *kinner*, and I'm not sure I'm ready for that." He glanced her way to gauge her reaction. "I guess that sounds grudging."

"A bit." Then she smiled, removing some of the sting from her words. "But change, even change for the better, can be unsettling."

"And does this information truly help you find me a match?"

"It tells me something about you, which will help me better understand what to look for."

"You really do take this seriously, don't you?"

"Of course. I've prayed for you, for guidance, and for the woman *Gotte* has selected for you, whoever she may be, every day since I agreed to be your matchmaker."

"*Gut* to know." Then he changed the subject. "I know it's only eleven, but what do you say we stop in at Eberly's for a burger and some fries?" Eberly's was a fast-food place in the center of Hope's Haven that catered mainly to the Amish, though it wasn't unusual to see English there as well.

She rewarded his suggestion with a dimpled smile. "I can never say no to Eberly's. They make the best burgers, ain't so?"

Noah returned her smile. "Eberly's it is."

Once they were seated in a booth with their burgers and fries in front of them, Greta decided it was time to take back control of the conversation. "Have you been thinking about what we discussed in your office?"

"You mean about what I'll do if you miss the deadline?"

That sounded a bit confrontational. "I'd have worded that differently, but *jah*."

"A nanny is always an option, though not one I care to use."

"Why not?" It was the backup plan she'd expected.

He munched on a fry for a moment. Then he shifted in his seat. "When Patsy died, Anna was just a few days old so she didn't feel the sting of that loss, but David was two and a half so he did. My *shveshtah* Faith came to help us. I don't know how I would've gotten through those early days without her. But she was engaged to a man in another district, and two months later she was setting up her own household."

Greta remembered Faith's wedding. She'd seen Noah there, looking stoic and somehow all alone in that crowd of over three hundred.

"Then I hired Ellen Kauffmann," he continued. "She was efficient and took good care of my *kinner*, but it was obvious her heart wasn't in it. When she told me she was going to step down after three months, I wasn't surprised. Next was Darla Miller. She agreed to help me until her *shveshtah*'s *boppli* arrived, which happened two months later. Maisie has been their caretaker ever since."

"Maisie's been watching over them for over a year now, ain't so?"

He nodded. "The point is, my *kinner*, especially David, would get attached to each woman as she came into our home, and then would be upset when she left." He dragged another fry through ketchup. "They'll miss Maisie when she moves on, but I'll make sure they spend time with her periodically so they don't feel abandoned again."

"That's a *gut* plan."

He nodded but he wasn't smiling. "I'd prefer the next woman who comes into their lives be someone who'll stay for the long term."

"I understand. And I promise I'll do everything I can to make that happen." She lifted a hand in a gesture of surrender. "But it's ultimately in *Gotte*'s hands."

"Of course. But let's pray you're the instrument He'll use to get it done."

Greta took a bite of her burger, feeling the weight of those words.

Gotte's instrument to help him find his future helpmeet.

Somehow, that made it more important than ever that she succeed.

Chapter 8

Greta smiled apologetically as she entered Dorothy Wagler's home. "Sorry I'm late." She'd gone straight home when she and Noah returned from Heartwood Crossing and had gone back to work on her Promise Quilt. Despite the fact that today's outing had resulted in scratching a name off the list, she felt it had been productive in other ways. She knew Noah much better now than she had before they set out.

He was a serious, thoughtful man who cared deeply for his *kinner* and considered what was best for them in a mindful manner. He was an artisan who loved his art and he was a man of reason and honor.

He deserved a special woman to share his life with. Had she truly found the best candidates for him?

Greta removed her coat and hung it on a peg by the door. "I suppose I'm the last one here."

"*Jah*, but you're not very late. We were just getting started."

Greta followed Dorothy to the large open room where the quilting frame was set up.

"Well, look who finally showed up." Esther smiled at her from where she sat next to Debra Stoll on the far side of the quilt.

Aenti Ruthanne, who, along with Lizzie's sister Marylou, sat with her back to the door, turned and gave her an arch look. "Verna Bixler mentioned she saw you riding out of town with Noah Stoll early this morning."

Greta smothered a groan. Of all people to spot them, it would be the biggest gossip in the county. Not that she and Noah had anything to hide.

Glad to see one of the remaining empty chairs was next to Lizzie, Greta nodded as she moved toward it. "We went to Heartwood Crossing this morning. Noah had an errand to run and he graciously allowed me to tag along. My friend Rachel Lapp lives there, and it's been nearly a year since I've had a chance to visit with her."

"And how was she doing?" The question came from Esther, who no doubt knew exactly why they'd gone to Heartwood Crossing.

"She's doing well. She has a boyfriend now and she was eager to tell me all about him."

Esther's disappointed nod said she understood the implications.

Aenti Ruthanne, however, gave her a sympathetic smile. "Don't you worry, Greta, the *gut* Lord has a young man in mind for you too, I'm sure of it."

Greta barely managed to avoid wincing. Her *aenti* had no idea her hopes had been dashed just a few days ago.

Taking a moment to gather herself, she bent over to fetch her needle and thimble from the sewing basket she'd brought with her. Rather than dwelling on her own feelings, she told herself to focus on finding a way to bring up the subject of a second marriage with Lizzie. It certainly wouldn't be easy to do it under everyone's noses here. But she was determined to find a way—after all, she'd given her word to Noah.

The women settled into their work. The quilt was a simple tumbling blocks pattern, one nineteen-year-old Marylou had pieced together. When the quilting was done it would go in the quilt shop for sale by Greta and Esther. The quilt shop wouldn't take any of the profits from this work. Instead, the profits, as with all the quilts they worked on as a group, would be split evenly between the primary creator, in this case Marylou, and the Christian Aid Ministries.

Thirty minutes later, Dorothy signaled it was time to take a break. "I have coffee and snickerdoodles in the kitchen," she said as she stood. "And Ruthanne brought a coffee cake as well."

Greta stood, arching her back to relieve the sitting-too-long-in-one-position kinks.

As the women filed out of the room, Lizzie paused to pick up something she'd dropped. This was her chance. But she couldn't just blurt out her question, she'd have to lead up to it. Perhaps a comment about her son. "How's Otto?" she asked.

Lizzie smiled with maternal fondness. "He's doing well, growing like a weed and more curious than a monkey."

Greta returned her friend's smile, then nudged the

conversation forward. "I imagine it must be difficult raising a son without a husband to help you."

Lizzie's smile faded. "Joseph would have been a *wunderbaar daed* and it's a tragedy that Otto will never know him. But I don't question *Gotte*'s will, and Joseph's *daed* provides a *gut* role model for our boy."

"That's *gut*. And perhaps someday you'll find another husband?"

Lizzie nodded. "If it's *Gotte*'s will, I wouldn't be averse to that."

So now Greta had her answer. Not that she was surprised. She'd figured the young widow would be open to the idea, if for no other reason than the same one Noah had, to have a helpmeet to partner with through all life had to offer. The tricky part was, would she settle for the kind of relationship Noah was offering, or would she only be willing to marry again if it were a love match?

She'd inform Noah in the morning that Lizzie wasn't opposed to a second marriage.

The rest was up to him.

* * *

Tuesday morning, after Noah opened the workshop and checked that Paul and Andrew were set with projects for the morning, he headed upstairs to his office. Paperwork was his least favorite part of owning his own business, but he was meticulous about keeping up with it.

When he reached the top of the stairs he was surprised to see Greta standing there studying the open area beyond his office. "*Gut matin*. Can I help you?"

She turned, and there wasn't a trace of guilt at being found up here on her own in her smile. "Hello. I was looking at all this open space and wondered if I could speak to you about a possible use."

She was still chasing that rabbit trail? "What might that be?"

She gave a sweep of her hand that took in a large area beside his office. "How difficult would it be for you to build another room up here?"

He joined her and studied the area she'd indicated. "There are already windows in place and it would be a simple matter to put up two walls to enclose it, so no, it wouldn't take much."

She nodded in satisfaction. "I thought not. So would you be willing to do it?"

He crossed his arms, not sure if he was amused or put out at her high-handedness. "That depends. Why would I need another room up here?"

"I was thinking about making it available for the shopkeepers to use as a break room or meeting room. You have to admit it's such a waste to have all this space up here lying idle."

Ignoring the last part of her statement, he rubbed the back of his neck. "Do you think there's really a need for something like that?"

"Absolutely." Then she turned her hands palms up. "I mean, I'm sure it wouldn't be used on a daily basis, but there are times when it would definitely come in handy."

"I'll think about it." Noah figured it was time to change the subject. "Was there a reason you came up here, other than to rescue this space from being wasted?"

"*Ach*, of course. I was waiting to speak to you."

He waved a hand toward his office door. "Then let's have a seat, shall we?"

"This won't take but a moment," Greta said as she followed him inside his office. "I wanted to let you know that I did speak to Lizzie yesterday."

Why had she decided to save this news for last? And why hadn't he bothered to ask? "What did she say?"

Greta settled into a chair. "She said if it be *Gotte*'s will to send her another man to marry, she would be happy."

He felt more resigned than pleased by that news. "And you didn't mention my name?"

"*Nee.*"

"*Gut.* I'll approach her on Sunday. The service is to be held at *Mamm*'s house, so that may make it easier." He tried for a smile and a lighter tone. "It'll give me the home field advantage, so to speak."

Her head tilted slightly to one side. "Are you nervous?"

He shrugged. "It's not every day a man makes the decision to go courting."

"I thought you made that decision several days ago?"

"That was more of an abstract I-need-to-do-this decision. This is something more concrete."

She nodded. "I understand. But smile—you're one step closer to finding the woman you want to share your life with, and that should make you happy."

He didn't respond to that. Instead he decided they both needed a distraction. "If I remember correctly, you asked for a tour of my workshop."

"So I did."

"If this is a good time, then..."

"We don't open the quilt shop for another twenty minutes, so yes, this is actually the perfect time."

Noah led the way out of his office, but allowed Greta to precede him down the stairs. As he followed, he wondered why he wasn't happier about the news she'd brought him. True, he was as determined as ever to marry again and give Anna and David some security in their home life. But when he closed his eyes and pictured his new *fraa*, it wasn't Lizzie's face he saw.

Once they reached the ground floor, Greta fell into step beside Noah. They walked half the length of the mall, entering the woodworking shop through a door marked Employees Only.

As soon as Greta stepped inside, she smelled the not unpleasant scent of fresh sawdust, wood stains and varnish. There was also the sound of hammering coming from somewhere to her left. She looked around, noting the stacks of lumber and cans of finishes along one wall, and there were at least four worktables set up in different areas of the large room. Hanging on the wall near the door were a fire extinguisher, fire alarm and first aid kit. It reminded Greta that Noah, along with several other men of the district, had taken first aid training when the local clinic had offered it six months ago. Another sign of what a responsible man he was.

Noah led her toward the sound of the hammering, where she saw Andrew Wagler hard at work. Andrew paused at their approach and looked up.

Noah swept a hand in his employee's general direction. "Greta, I believe you already know Andrew."

She gave the man a smile. "I do. His *fraa* Dorothy hosts our quilting circle."

"Andrew's working on a set of kitchen cabinets an English customer ordered from us. He's almost ready to take them to the customer's home where he'll do the installation."

Andrew nodded acknowledgment, then went back to work.

Noah escorted her a few feet farther along to another work area.

"Paul's building a worktable for Trudy Yutzy's greenhouse."

Greta nodded a hello, then admired the worktable. "I know Trudy is going to really like this."

Then she turned to Noah. "And what are you working on?"

"It's over here." He led her to another part of the workshop and pointed to a large hope chest.

"*Ach*, it's lovely." He truly was an artisan. "Are you making it for someone in particular or will it go on your sales floor?"

He opened the lid, revealing a large tray inside. "It's a birthday present for Maisie." He removed the tray, showing just how spacious the trunk was.

Greta studied the cloth lining on the bottom and sides, and the stain on the exposed wood. "Oh, Noah, she's going to really cherish this."

He replaced the tray and closed the lid. "I feel bad that she had to wait so long. *Daed* made Faith's hope chest, and I know he intended to make one for Maisie, but he passed before he could. I should have thought of doing it sooner."

"It'll be all the sweeter to her for the wait." Then she traced the edge of the lid with a finger. "The color is such a rich, lovely shade. What kind of wood is it made from?"

"The tray is made of cedar but the chest itself is made from rosewood." He studied it as if seeing it for the first time. "Some of the color comes from the wood itself, some from the stain I applied."

She could tell he was being critical of his work. "Is it finished?"

"I want to add some handles to make it easier to move, but other than that, yes, it's done."

"So do you already have your next project in mind?"

He straightened with a nod. "I have an order for two side tables that I've already gathered the materials for, and I want to add a few more pieces to the sales floor."

* * *

Noah watched as Greta walked around the workshop, her curiosity evident in her expression. This had always been a decidedly male domain, he couldn't remember the last time a woman had been in the workshop. Even Patsy had rarely visited him here.

"You seem to have lots of different kinds of wood here. How do you know which variety is best for which project?"

He was surprised by her question—it showed she had more than a casual interest. "The selection of the wood is partly dictated by the project itself and partly by aesthetics. For instance, I used cedar for the tray in Maisie's hope chest because it's good at keeping away moths. Which makes it a good material for things like closet shelves and wardrobes too. Oak, maple and birch are examples of hardwoods that can stand up to a lot of abuse. Cherry, rosewood, mahogany are all great for showpieces." His lips quirked up in a half smile. "And that's probably a lot more than you wanted to know."

"Not at all. So specific woods are better for specific types of projects?"

"For sure and for certain. Just as some fabrics probably work better for your quilts than others."

She nodded her understanding. "I suppose Calvin draws on your expertise when he has a project that involves wood. I know he was experimenting with different materials for some storage bins he wanted to construct in the barn."

She seemed mighty familiar with Calvin's projects. For some reason that irritated him. But he kept his voice carefully neutral. "No, my *bruder* rarely asks for my opinion."

She nodded. "Calvin is independent minded that way."

He could hear the admiration in her voice. He didn't like the thought that she might be comparing the two of them and finding him wanting.

"*Ach*, what do you have here?" She stooped down to peer at something under a worktable.

Chapter 9

Noah was glad of the change of subject. He stooped beside her, knowing he would see a wooden crate that currently provided a bed for a yellow tabby and five kittens. "That's Sawdust. She showed up here about five months ago and made herself at home. Then about seven weeks ago she surprised us by birthing this litter."

Greta was already rubbing the cat's head. "What sweet babies you have, Sawdust."

Sawdust responded with a contented purr.

"Well now, that's surprising. Sawdust rarely lets anyone touch her."

Greta grinned, obviously pleased. "She's probably just all tuckered out from caring for her babies." She rubbed the cat's ears one last time, then put her hands on her knees as if to stand.

Noah stood quickly and offered her his hand.

With a smile she accepted, and with a quick spring she was on her feet.

But something happened, some unevenness in the floor or just a wobble in Greta's balance, and she stumbled, falling against him. Almost too fast for him to form intent, Noah wrapped his arms around her to steady her.

Their gazes locked, and her wide-eyed stare shifted from that of a startled doe to something warmer, more aware.

His own breath caught in his throat and his pulse quickened. Noah wasn't sure how long they remained frozen like that, but this time there was no denying the awareness sparking between them.

A cough from Paul—or was it Andrew—brought him back to his senses. He quickly righted her and stepped back, though he kept a supportive hand on her elbow. "Are you all right?"

Greta nodded. "*Jah*." Then, as if hearing how breathy her voice had sounded, she cleared her throat. "I'm fine, *danke*." This time her voice was clearer, near normal.

He dropped his hand. What was he thinking? What were Paul and Andrew thinking?

Besides, Greta still had feelings for Calvin, that was clear from what she'd said a moment ago, and how she'd said it. It didn't matter that Calvin didn't return those feelings, Greta was still smitten.

She was focused solely on being his matchmaker. And no matter what his racing pulse might indicate to the contrary, he wasn't looking for emotional entanglements, in fact just the opposite. He'd learned his lesson on that front all too well.

Noah tried to read Greta's expression. But she was brushing at her skirt, her face downturned. "I should head back to the quilt shop," she said. "It'll be time for us to open soon."

Her voice was steady, if slightly lowered. She seemed to have pulled herself back together just fine. Had he imagined that moment of awareness? "Of course. Let me walk you out."

Trying to find a way to break the awkward silence, Noah reached for a safe topic.

"Yesterday I told you what woodworking means to me and how I got into it. What about you? With quilting I mean. Is it something you feel passionate about, a calling so to speak, or is it just a way to earn money for your family?"

Greta was taken aback. He wanted to talk about quilting after what had just happened? Had she misread his reaction? The way his eyes had darkened and his hand tightened on hers? Had she been wrong when she thought his breath hitched?

Had it all just been wishful thinking?

No, no, she hadn't meant that. Wishful thinking indeed. She was just confused was all.

Well, if he wanted to pretend nothing had happened, she could too.

Forcing her mind back to his question as they stepped through the doorway, she pasted on a smile. "I actually do love what I do. I guess you could say it's a calling."

"Esther said you're very creative."

"Esther is very kind." She waved a hand, trying to explain how she felt. "Like you, I enjoy the creative aspect of what I do. Taking small, sometimes raggedy scraps of fabric that on their own have very little value, pieces that would otherwise be thrown away, and using them in such a way that they become integral parts of a beautiful whole is very satisfying."

He nodded. "I can see that."

"The real joy for me," she continued, "comes in the design work, in finding new ways of arranging various shapes to make a pleasing image that brings happiness to those who see it. When I start a project, I try to visualize the emotion I want the future owner to feel, and then I look for the design and color palette that I think will best evoke that."

She cut him a sideways look, smiling sheepishly. "That probably sounded boastful and much too dramatic."

He blinked, caught off guard by her uncharacteristically shy smile. "Not at all. I think it's the way any artist feels about their work."

"Like yourself you mean."

He raised a brow, his expression skeptical. "You think of me as an artist?"

"Of course. Don't you?"

He nodded slowly. "I suppose. But not everyone does."

She wondered if he was thinking of anyone specific.

"But back to quilting," he said. "I don't think Esther feels quite the same way you do about it."

"True. We've had a number of discussions about that. She's really good at quilting, but she has other dreams."

"Such as?"

"That's Esther's story to tell."

And with that she took her leave of him and headed across the mall lobby to the quilt shop.

As soon as Noah was no longer at her side, Greta allowed herself to remember their near embrace. Not that he'd intended to embrace her, that was obvious from how quickly he'd focused on other things. Why was she even calling it an embrace? He'd apparently acted out of gentlemanly instinct and caught her before she could fall. It probably meant nothing more than that to him.

Not that it meant anything more to her either. It had just caught her off guard is all. And coming on top of her unexpected reaction to touching his hand in the carriage yesterday, her reactions were just confused.

There was nothing more to it than that.

Chapter 10

By the end of the workday, Noah had convinced himself the incident in the workshop had just been what it seemed on the surface—one friend helping another in a moment of need.

It was time for him to focus on this whole matchmaking process. Was it possible Lizzie Yoder was the woman *Gotte* had prepared for him and him for her? He pulled an image of her up in his mind. Blonde hair the shade of unvarnished oak, a nice, easy smile and a young son. Other than that, he couldn't remember much else about her. He couldn't recall the sound of her voice, wasn't even sure if he'd ever spoken to her. She'd told Greta she was open to marriage again, but what did that mean to her? Would she be willing to move as quickly as he needed her to? Would she be happy with a marriage of convenience as opposed to a love match? Was she looking for something completely different in a husband than what he had to offer?

Joseph, her late husband, had been burly and strong, with a booming laugh and a clap on the back for anyone he spoke to. Was that the kind of man Lizzie preferred? If so, they were wasting their time, because he was nothing like that.

Then again, Greta had thought they would be a good match, and he was coming to trust her instincts, so there had to be something to it. Still, his concerns refused to be quieted.

Perhaps it was better he not look too closely at the reasons why.

After supper that evening, Greta washed the dishes while Hannah dried. Martha was in the living room with *Daed*, taking care of some mending while he read from his Bible.

Greta handed her *shveshtah* a clean dish. "So, how was your day today?" she asked.

Hannah dried the plate and stacked it on the counter with the others. "A busy morning but slow afternoon. I'm confident it'll get busy again when we get closer to Valentine's Day, though." Then Hannah met and held her gaze. "Tell me the truth, is there something going on between you and Noah Stoll?"

Greta tried not to look guilty. "Why would you ask me that?"

"That's not an answer. But to answer your question, I have a pretty good view of the loft stairs from my shop, and I've seen you go up to his office several times in the past few days. Then you went to Heartwood Crossing with him yesterday, and I saw you coming out of the woodworking shop with him this morning."

How much should she tell Hannah? After all, it was Noah's business and she doubted he would want the whole district to know he'd asked her to play matchmaker for him.

She turned her gaze to the bowl she was washing and carefully chose her words. "I went there yesterday because I wanted to visit my friend Rachel Lapp. I was in the workshop this morning looking at a cat and some kittens who've taken up residence there. And as for the loft, I had some suggestions I wanted to make on how he might make better use of all the empty space he has upstairs." There, every bit of that was true and she hadn't betrayed Noah's trust.

Hannah giggled. "I can imagine how Noah reacted to you making suggestions on how he could use his own space."

Greta tilted up her chin in mock dignity. "He actually said he'd think about it."

"Now that's interesting." Hannah gave her an arch look. "Seems like you have an answer for everything."

"You sound like that's a bad thing."

Hannah accepted the bowl. "You know, I always thought Noah was much more self-assured than Calvin."

But it was Calvin who'd always championed her, made her feel she was special. "And why are you telling me this?"

"I just thought it was worth mentioning."

Deciding that didn't require a response, she changed the subject. "So exactly how is your business doing now that the holiday rush is behind you?"

Hannah's look said she knew Greta was deliberately changing the subject. But she let it go. "It's slower than it was in November and December, of course. But like I said, I expect it to pick up in February with Valentine's Day. Especially since I want to feature a small line of chocolate candies this year."

"You do? When did you decide that?"

"When Ada Mullet asked if she could have space in the shop to sell her candies during February." Hannah smiled serenely. "I'll get a small portion of her sales and I figure anything that brings customers into the shop is a *gut* thing."

"I agree. So you're only going to do that during February?"

"We said we'd see how it goes and then decide if it makes sense for her to continue. But she brought me some samples of her work to taste and I have a *gut* feeling about how she'll do."

"If it works out, perhaps she can eventually partner with you, the way Esther and I do."

Hannah nodded. "That thought had occurred to me."

It seemed her little *shveshtah* was more of a businesswoman than Greta had given her credit for. Perhaps if she'd misjudged her in that sense, she'd misjudged her in other areas as well.

Could it be that Hannah saw something in Noah that she herself had missed?

* * *

Wednesday morning, Noah had an appointment at the home of an English customer who wanted him to build a dining room table and eight chairs. The couple wanted him to see the room where the table would be placed so he could get a feel for the space and their style preferences.

Once Noah returned to the mall, he went up to his office to figure out materials and costs. This was the kind of project he'd like to work on himself. But he had to make sure that it made the most sense from a workload standpoint.

When he stepped out of his office he turned to the stairs, then paused. Greta's suggestion that he put a room up here for the mall shopkeepers' use actually had some merit. He stepped past his office to look at the available space. It really wouldn't take much.

Because the back wall was already in place and the new room would butt up against his office, he'd only need to erect two new walls. The most complicated part would be installing a door, and even that was a simple, straightforward task.

As for the materials, again it would be minimal. He had just about everything he'd need already in the workshop.

Fetching a notebook and tape measure from his office, he made quick work of sketching out the job and figuring out the materials.

It was only when he'd made the final set of notes and closed the notebook that he realized that, somewhere along the way, he'd decided to go ahead and build the room Greta had requested.

He supposed she'd want him to furnish it as well.

Might as well add that to his list of things to take care of.

Greta decided to go in early on Thursday so she could finish up the quilt project she was working on and get it out to her customer. She had a new project she was eager to get started on.

Amos hitched Velvet to the buggy for her while she bottle-fed an orphan calf and then fed Skip. Her buggy was a small open carriage, so she had her winter bonnet, gloves and wool coat on. She also spread a heavy buggy blanket over her lap.

During the cold but sunny drive, as she listened to the clip-clop of Velvet's shoes on the paved road, her mind was on the Promise Quilt. Last night she'd pulled out the box of fabric scraps she had left over from other projects along with the fabric she'd purchased at the store where Rachel worked and the yardage she had on hand.

Like an artist mixing colors on a palette, she'd combined different pieces, moving them around, creating different light and shadow effects, different gradients of color, until she was pleased with the results. It was only when she stepped back that she realized how late she'd stayed up working on her design.

Added to the fact she had gotten on the road extra early this morning, it was no wonder she found herself yawning as she plodded toward the quilt shop. Seeing the vision for her quilt start to come together, though, was worth a little bit of missed sleep.

But before she could unlock the door, she heard hammering coming from the loft. Could Noah have already begun work on the new room she'd suggested?

Quickly heading for the stairs, she couldn't help but smile. He had actually acted on her suggestion. Not even Calvin had moved so quickly and completely on one of her ideas.

Noah really was a thoughtful man with a *gut* heart, even if he didn't show that side of himself often.

She topped the stairs and moved past Noah's office until she spotted him kneeling and hammering a board onto the floor. He didn't notice her right away and she took a moment to study him. His hair was the color of walnuts but for the first time she noted some lighter strands shining through.

He'd removed his jacket and rolled up his sleeves, and his movements as he wielded the hammer were confident and powerful. As he pounded away, the downward motion stretched his shirt across his back, emphasizing the breadth of his shoulders and the muscled tone of his arms. Why hadn't she noticed before just how—

Before she could finish that thought, he looked up and spotted her. Embarrassed to have been caught staring, she pasted a bright smile on her face and stepped forward. "Sorry, I didn't mean to interrupt your work. I just heard the hammering and my curiosity got the better of me."

He had a couple of nails between his lips, which he quickly removed. "No need to apologize." He set down his tools. "This is as much your project as it is mine." Then he stood and brushed at the knees of his pants. "You're here mighty early this morning."

"I wanted to get an early start on my current quilt project this morning." She waved a hand at the work he'd been doing. "You decided to build the room." She couldn't hide the note of delight that crept into her voice.

Noah grinned, no doubt at her stating the obvious. "I did." He turned to study his work, hooking a thumb absently through his suspenders. "After thinking it over, I decided the idea had merit, especially since building it out was a small job I could do in my spare time."

Then he turned back to her. "I have the bottom plate down now, so you can see the outline of the room. What do you think?"

Greta studied the area he had marked off and nodded her approval. "I like it. You've been generous with the size. And including two of the windows will make the room feel light and open."

He nodded in satisfaction. "That was my plan."

"Is there anything I can do to help?"

"I'm actually done for now. I may do a little more on it this afternoon, but there's a project in the workshop I need to get back to."

"Of course, the work for your customers must come first. But if there's anything I can do to help..."

He looked at her as if to gauge her seriousness, then nodded. "When it comes time to paint, I wouldn't mind having a bit of help."

Pleased he'd taken her offer seriously, she nodded. "Absolutely."

"And speaking of painting, do you have any thoughts on color?"

She didn't hesitate. "A soft blue would look nice." It was her favorite color.

"Blue it is." Then he wrinkled his brow as if pondering something. "I was thinking, the only real furnishing it needs is a large table and some chairs. Do you agree?"

Pleased that he was actually asking her opinion, she looked around. "Perhaps a bookshelf or tall cabinet for storage if that's not too much trouble."

"I should be able to come up with something that'll serve the purpose."

"*Gut*. And I'll do what I can to help make it feel welcoming." She actually had an idea for something she wanted to add to the room, something to help it feel more warm and friendly. But rather than tell Noah about it, she decided to save it as a surprise. After all, it was beginning to look as if she wouldn't have any other use for the items in her hope chest.

Noah worked on the new room off and on for the next couple of days and by Saturday morning he had all the wall studs up and the door framed out. He'd brought some paint cards with various shades of blue for Greta to look at today so they could start painting next week.

He smiled as he climbed the stairs to his office, wondering if she'd be here early again this morning. When he reached the top of the stairs he glanced out the window, and sure enough he saw a carriage being pulled by Greta's horse, Velvet.

Would Greta have hot cocoa for him like she'd had yesterday?

Then he noticed another buggy, this one pulled by Calvin's horse. What was his *bruder* doing out so early? When the buggy turned in beside Greta's, Noah stiffened. Had Calvin come to fetch him? Was something wrong at home? But Calvin spoke to Greta for a few minutes, then as Charity Umble's buggy pulled up, he headed out again.

Noah turned and slowly headed to his office.

Fifteen minutes later he saw Greta walk past his door, headed for the new room.

When he joined her she smiled up at him and handed him the thermos. "You've gotten quite a bit done."

Noah accepted the thermos but didn't open it right away. "I have some paint chips in my office for you to look at if you have a moment."

"Of course."

He led the way back to his office and handed her the sample cards.

She set the bag she was carrying on a chair and took the cards from him. "I wish there was this wonderful range of shades for the quilt fabrics I purchase." A moment later she held a card out to him. "I like this one."

Their hands brushed together as he accepted the card, and he again had that pulse-spark reaction to her touch. Could he blame it on static electricity again?

She turned to reach for the bag she'd set on her chair, making it impossible to see if she'd had any kind of reaction to that touch.

Not that it should matter.

When she turned back to him, her expression was free of anything but a friendly smile.

He glanced at the bag she was currently digging through. "What do you have there? Something to go with the cocoa?"

"*Nee*. It's something for your *kinner*." She held up a doll. "I made this a while back when I thought we might offer them for sale through the quilt shop. Last time I saw Anna I noticed that her doll was fraying a bit." She brushed at the doll's apron. "I understand hers may be special to her and she would want to keep it, but I thought it couldn't hurt for her to have another one."

"That's very thoughtful of you." Why hadn't he noticed his *dochder*'s toy was wearing out?

She set it on his desk and reached back in the bag. "And since it didn't seem right to give Anna something and not David, I made a little stuffed dog for him."

"Again, very thoughtful." Noah studied her. Should he press her for the answers he needed? "I have to say, you seem to be going out of your way to be kind to us."

She brushed at her skirt. "It's only a couple of toys. That doesn't require a lot of effort."

"You've also brought me hot cocoa for two mornings now. It all seems above and beyond."

She appeared confused. "It's just a little kindness to repay you for your work on the loft room. But if it makes you uncomfortable—"

He interrupted her. "Is it perhaps because of Calvin as well?" He mentally winced at his bluntness, but he always found it best to get right to the point when one wanted answers.

Greta stilled as his words sunk in, and she felt the blood drain from her face. "Calvin?"

"I'm sorry if I'm being rude, but I have a good idea of how you felt, perhaps still feel, toward my *bruder*. I'm curious as to whether you're helping me out of some misguided sense of loyalty to him. Or even because you think he might view you more kindly because of it."

He knew? Her cheeks heated as she realized she hadn't hid her feelings as well as she'd thought. How many others knew or guessed? "I wasn't aware my feelings were so obvious." Did Calvin himself know? The thought of that set her stomach churning.

"Not obvious. But yes, I picked up on some signs. And I did see you on New Year's Day, the day Calvin began his courtship of Wanda. Or at least made it public." He studied her a moment, then softened his tone. "You did a good job of hiding it, but subdued isn't your usual demeanor."

What did he mean by that? Did he see her as much too forward, just like everyone else?

He spread his hands. "I'm only bringing this up because if you think this will make me inclined to speak well of you to Calvin—"

She couldn't allow him to finish that statement. "My feelings for Calvin have nothing to do with my helping you." She was pleased to note her voice didn't crack or waver. "I thought you knew me better than that." So much for any thoughts she might have that Noah understood and appreciated her forthright attitude.

When would she ever learn?

She had to get away from Noah, away from everyone, and pull her swirling thoughts together. "Now, if you'll excuse me, I need to get back to the quilt shop." Hopefully Esther wouldn't have arrived yet and she could be alone for a few minutes.

She turned to leave and it took all of her self-control to simply walk rather than flee.

The ironic thing about this was she hadn't thought about Calvin in that way for a while, and even when she'd seen him a few moments ago, none of the angst or sting she'd felt on New Year's Day was present. Even the pining for things to be different had disappeared.

Did that mean she was fickle?

To be honest, she'd latched on to Calvin because of the way he'd seemed to accept her as she was. No young man had ever done that before. Even the two boys she'd dated had tried to change her in subtle and not so subtle ways. But she'd never been in love with Calvin in the romantic sense. Stepping back and viewing it with clearer eyes, she could see that unlike her own willingness to settle for friendship and respect, Calvin had rightly been looking for love.

Perhaps she was fickle after all.

Or perhaps there was something else at work here.

But now, knowing she hadn't been as discreet as she'd thought, how in the world would she face Calvin again?

Or Noah himself for that matter?

Noah absently picked up the cloth dog as he watched Greta walk away. She had her head up, displaying the regal lines of her neck. Despite her earlier reaction, she appeared more insulted than angry.

Hard to believe that just a moment ago her face had paled and then flushed. It was obvious she'd been surprised and embarrassed that he'd guessed how she felt about Calvin.

But his real question was whether or not she still had romantic feelings for his *bruder*. It would be better if she just moved on. For her own sake, of course.

In fact, the more time he spent with Greta, the more convinced he became that a marriage between her and Calvin would never have worked out even if his *bruder* hadn't turned his sights on Wanda. Greta was too spirited, too strong-willed for a young man like Calvin.

She needed to find someone with the sense and maturity to appreciate her.

Someone more like him?

Chapter 11

Greta was nervous as she got dressed Sunday morning. After her disastrous conversation with Noah yesterday, she wasn't sure how to react when she came face-to-face with Calvin today. She was cowardly enough to hope to avoid that altogether. To think that Calvin had even suspected what she felt for him was unsettling, to say the least.

As for Noah, the only communication she'd had with him since yesterday morning was a brief conversation just before she'd left the mall, asking if he needed anything from her before he talked to Lizzie. He'd told her he was fine.

His assurance that he was prepared for that important conversation had left her feeling restless. And if she didn't examine the reasons for that too closely, it was nothing more than concern for the outcome of her matchmaking efforts.

Trying to put those uncomfortable thoughts out of her mind, Greta pinned her Sunday white apron and cape to her dress and headed downstairs.

As soon as the service ended, Greta scurried to the kitchen, and almost beat the Stoll women there. While the men set up the tables and benches for the meal, she helped load platters with sandwich meat, cheese and bread. Other women gathered jars and small bowls of chow-chow, boiled eggs, pickled vegetables, jams, spreads and various sandwich fixings. While the food, along with pitchers of tea, lemonade and water, was carried out to the dining area, Greta managed to find things to do in the kitchen.

She wasn't exactly hiding, just making herself useful elsewhere. And all the time she worked, she couldn't help but wonder how much Calvin really knew about her feelings for him. She couldn't bear the idea that he might actually pity her.

After the entire congregation had been fed and the kitchen and tables cleaned up, Greta donned her coat and slipped outside for a breath of fresh air. She lifted her face, enjoying the sting of the wind after the heat of the crowded kitchen.

She was just congratulating herself on having avoided any direct interaction with Calvin, when to her surprise, he sought her out.

"Greta, could I speak to you privately for a few minutes?" He blew into his hands, warming them with his breath.

Not long ago those words from him would have thrilled her. Now she found herself studying him for signs of pity or awkwardness. But all she saw was the same old Calvin, though perhaps a little more distracted than normal. If he knew about the plans she'd had for him, he was kind enough not to let it affect their friendship.

Greta's apprehension eased and gave way to curiosity. Why had he sought her out? Surely he hadn't suddenly realized he'd made a mistake with Wanda. If so, she wasn't sure how she felt about that. But she was curious enough to want to find out what was on his mind. "All right."

He waved toward the left side of the barn. "Why don't I show you the new fence I built around the paddock?"

"Of course." She moved in the direction he'd indicated, and he fell into step beside her without speaking.

When they reached the paddock, Calvin stopped and rested his arms on the fence. There were other people milling around outside in the cold, but no one approached. Folks were used to seeing the two of them deep in conversation. Although one would expect that to change now.

Not ready to meet his gaze directly, Greta studied the fence Calvin had erected, remembering the debate the two of them had had over an article he'd read about more efficient methods of fencing. It looked as if he'd gone a different direction than the one she thought they'd finally decided was best. Had he agreed with her to end their debate? Or had he merely changed his mind later?

She finally grew impatient with the silence—it was time to get this over with. Whatever *this* was. "What did you want to speak to me about, Calvin?"

He met her gaze, his expression gloomy. "It turns out

Wanda is uncomfortable around *Mamm*. I think she's actually afraid of her."

Was that all? Greta tried to keep the exasperation from her tone. "Wanda is very shy, you know that. And you must know that your *mamm* can be intimidating. I'm sure once they get to know each other better that discomfort will ease." She turned to face him fully. "But why are you telling me this?"

He waved a hand in frustration. "I can't have the girl I love not want to be close to my *mamm*."

So he was already prepared to declare his love. That thought barely stung at all. Perhaps her activities on Noah's behalf these past few days had served their purpose, had given her something new to focus on.

"As I said, give it time," Greta counseled. "If Wanda loves you, that love will eventually extend to your family." If she were in Wanda's place, she'd never let someone get in the way of her and the man she loved. Not even his *mamm*.

Then she softened her tone, trying to reassure him. "If you make it clear to Wanda that she'll always come first to you, it'll go a long way to reassure her."

Calvin rubbed his jaw, giving her a pleading look, as if he hadn't heard a word she'd said. "Surely there's something we can do now to hurry the process."

We? With that one word, Greta suddenly realized that, to Calvin, nothing had changed between them. To his way of thinking, they were still the *gut* friends they'd always been.

For a moment she was tempted to shrug off his request and rejoin her friends. Whether he realized it or not, things *had* changed. And so had she. She loved Wanda and knew how fragile the girl was. There was no way she would come between her and Calvin.

But Calvin was her friend and she couldn't abandon him when he needed her. "I'm not sure what good it would do, but I suppose I could talk to her."

"I've tried that," Calvin said, glumly planting a foot on the fence wire. "I was hoping you might have a better idea." He looked at her with an expectant expression.

Why was he expecting her to solve his problems? Calvin had selected a girl who was meek and timid, he had to learn how to live with that.

Then she took herself to task for that very uncharitable thought. He'd come to her for help after all.

Suddenly she had an idea. "Perhaps there is a way to get your *mamm* and Wanda together in a comfortable social setting."

Calvin perked up at that, his expression suddenly hopeful. "How?"

"I can invite Wanda to join our quilting circle."

His eyes lit up. "That's right, *Mamm* is a member." He gave her a happy, relieved grin. "If they interact in a group like that, surely they'll grow to like each other."

Greta wasn't prepared to guarantee that. "It will certainly give them the chance to get to know each other better. The rest will be up to them."

Calvin placed his hand over hers and gave it a squeeze. "I knew I could count on you."

"For sure and for certain. I'm your best friend after all." If he only knew how much it cost her to keep her tone light after the way he'd dashed, not her heart, but definitely her hopes. "I'll speak to the others in the group today before folks start leaving."

"*Danke*."

She thought he would leave her then, but instead he leaned against the fence again. "I understand you've been spending time with Noah."

Greta wondered at the tone he'd used, almost as if he didn't approve. "*Jah*. I'm helping him with a project." She very nearly added that it had nothing to do with him, but restrained herself.

Calvin paused a moment, then seemed to come to a decision. "Just a word of caution, don't let my *bruder* take advantage of you."

Where in the world was that coming from? "He isn't taking advantage of me," she assured him. "He's merely looking for options on how best to care for Anna and David while letting Maisie enjoy the freedoms of her rumspringa."

But Calvin didn't let it drop. "He has money enough to hire someone to take care of his *kinner*. Don't let him play on your sympathies." Before she could respond, he continued, "Maisie offered to help Noah when the nannies he hired didn't work out, and he's still taking advantage of that offer over a year later. Our little *shveshtah* is spending her youth taking care of his family and home."

Greta met his gaze and said evenly, "That's between Maisie and Noah. Just as the work I'm doing is between Noah and me and is none of your concern."

Calvin stiffened at that. "Sorry. I was just looking out for you. I know my older *bruder* can be single-minded and doesn't always see what he's doing to those around him."

Realizing she'd hurt his feelings and that his intentions, while misguided, were honorable, she softened her tone. "I really do appreciate your concern, Calvin, but after all this time you of all people should know I'm capable of looking out for myself." She pushed away from the fence. "Now, if I want to talk to the other ladies in my quilting circle before they get away, I'd better get on with it. With any luck I can invite Wanda to join us before she leaves today."

"*Danke*." Calvin straightened as well. "I'll let you get to it. Just remember what I said about Noah."

Choosing not to respond to that absurd warning, Greta moved toward the house, trying to process the previous conversation.

Was Calvin's request that she help Wanda a sign he hadn't suspected her feelings for him? And had she imagined the undercurrent in Calvin's warnings, or was there really some bone of contention between him and Noah?

She gave her head a mental shake, trying to clear it of all but the one thing she could actually control right now. Time to find the members of her quilting circle and pave the way for Wanda to join them. Her gaze landed on Noah, who stood near the side stoop, deep in discussion with Lizzie Yoder. The young widow was smiling and nodding at something he'd said.

It appeared he'd begun his pursuit of Lizzie. Were the two getting along? Had he broached the idea of marriage with her yet in his reasoned, unemotional way? After all, his time was short if he was to meet the deadline he'd given Maisie.

Both of them seemed at ease and comfortable with each other. Was his search for a *fraa* over?

That thought gave her an oddly anticlimactic feeling.

And an emptiness as well that she couldn't quite account for.

A moment later, Noah looked up and his gaze met hers. The heat climbed in her cheeks as she realized she'd been caught staring, but somehow she couldn't look away from his gaze.

Then something in his expression shifted, his smile warmed. A heartbeat later, his gaze shuttered and the connection was gone. He turned back to Lizzie as her little boy rushed up to join them.

Trying to make sense of what had just happened, Greta slowly trudged back to the house in search of members of the quilting circle.

Noah listened to the story Lizzie was recounting about her son with just half an ear.

He'd noticed Greta and Calvin chatting alone a few minutes ago and had been curious about what was going on. At first he'd wondered if his *bruder* had changed his mind and decided Greta was the woman for him after all. Not that who Calvin courted was any of his concern. Except Greta was helping him out and he didn't like to think of her being caught in the middle of his *bruder*'s emotional seesawing.

Whatever they'd been discussing, however, Greta's expression when they parted ways had been anything but loverlike. In fact he'd describe it as more like irritation. Which he found rather interesting.

What was even more interesting was catching her staring at him. Except he'd quickly realized she was no doubt wondering how his interaction with Lizzie was going.

On that thought, Lizzie reclaimed his attention, pulling him back to the present as Otto came toddling up to them, bundled up so thickly he looked like a roly-poly toy.

"*Ach*, there you are, my little man," she said, her voice almost a coo. "Running away from your cousin Fredrick again, I see."

A teenager, who Noah assumed was the aforementioned cousin Fredrick, came panting up to them. "Sorry Lizzie, as soon as he saw you he took off."

"That's all right." She picked up the toddler and settled him on her hip. "I've got him now."

With a nod, Fredrick hurried off to join a group of other teens.

Lizzie gave her son an affectionate squeeze. "I don't suppose I have to tell you what a joy children are," she said. "Otto here is my whole world, especially now that his *daed* is gone." The look she gave Noah was one of shared experience. "Which I don't have to explain to you either."

Noah nodded, not quite sure how to respond to that. "Anna is inside napping and David is playing with the other *kinner*."

"It's good your *shveshtah* is able to help you care for them."

Deciding to test the waters just a bit, he cleared his throat. "I'm not sure how much longer I'll be able to count on Maisie. She turns sixteen on Sunday."

"*Ach*, it's time for her rumspringa then. But surely she'd continue to help you if you need her to."

"I don't want to ask that of her."

"You are a good *bruder*. But the good of your little ones comes first." She gave Otto a squeeze. "Just like this little *boppli* will always come first for me."

Then she smiled. "I'm sure *Gotte* will provide a way for you to get through this. Perhaps even a new *fraa* to be your helpmeet."

Did he detect a note of interest in her voice? The logical, practical part of him urged him to push forward, to see if they could form a mutually beneficial partnership. But something held him back.

So instead he nodded. "Perhaps."

She gave him a soft smile. "I know you still miss Patsy, just as I miss Joseph. But you must keep up the hope that *Gotte* will send you another woman you can love nearly as well, if not more so."

Is that what she was hoping for herself? He straightened. "I'll continue to pray for *Gotte*'s will to be done." Then he nodded. "If you'll excuse me, I should go inside and check on Anna." And with a tap to Otto's very red nose, he turned and headed back toward the house.

Would he find Greta telling stories to the little ones again? He was sorry for the wedge that had been driven between them over their discussion about her feelings for Calvin. He missed that easy camaraderie they'd shared.

He wanted to repair the rift between them, but he wasn't sure quite how to go about it.

Unless...

Chapter 12

It didn't take Greta long to track down all the ladies of the quilting circle and ask them about inviting Wanda to join the group. They each gave her the go-ahead, just as she'd expected. She did get a probing look from Esther, though, but thankfully her friend kept her thoughts to herself.

To Greta's surprise it was a little more difficult to convince Wanda herself.

"It's very kind of you to invite me," she responded, "but I'm not sure I want to intrude in your group. And I'm not sure I can spare the time."

Wanda was the only daughter in a family of seven children, so Greta understood that she had very little free time after helping her *mamm* with the housework. Still, she wanted to make sure her cousin understood the opportunity she was being offered. "Actually, I thought you might have a particular interest in joining us since Debra Stoll is a member."

"Oh." Wanda shifted uncomfortably. "Did Calvin ask you to invite me?"

Smart girl. "We did discuss how eager you are to get to know his *mamm* better. And it's just for a few hours once a week on Monday afternoons, so perhaps you can spare that much time."

" 'Eager' may be overstating the case."

Greta was surprised by Wanda's dry tone. Maybe the girl had a bit of spirit in her after all. "I understand Debra can be intimidating at first, but once you get to know her—"

"Intimidating! She terrifies me." Wanda looked around as if afraid she'd been overheard. "She snaps at people for no reason at all, and she glares if you try to help her. I'm doing my best to stay out of her way."

Greta resisted the urge to roll her eyes. "You're wrong about her being mean. She has a strong personality, I'll grant you that, and she's often convinced her way is the best and only way to get things done, but she's not truly mean. She's a *Gotte*-fearing woman with a *gut* heart."

Wanda didn't look convinced so Greta tried again, working hard to allay Wanda's fears. "If you feel you're right about something, all you have to do is stand your ground in a respectful manner. She'll actually think the better of you for it."

"I'm not sure I can do that." Wanda looked away, chewing on her lip. "I'm not as brave as you."

Trying to put her cousin at ease, Greta schooled her tone into something gentler. "At least you can take this first step of being in her company more." She held the girl's gaze. "Which will let Debra get to know you better. We're a group of seven women—with you it would be eight. You'd just be one of the group, so it wouldn't be as if you need to interact with her one-on-one. This way she can observe and get to know you in a small group setting."

Wanda seemed to think that over for several moments. Her expression was easy to read and Greta saw the internal struggle play out, waffling between timid uncertainty and yearning, until she finally nodded. "I suppose I could join your circle for a few sessions, just to see how it works out," she said reluctantly.

Greta patted the girl's hand in approval, reminding herself of all the times Calvin had stood up to support her. "We meet at Dorothy Wagler's home. If you like, I can pick you up tomorrow on my way there."

Wanda nodded in obvious relief. "Yes, please."

"Then I'll see you tomorrow at around one forty-five." And with a nod she turned to move away.

A moment later she caught sight of Noah. Though he was speaking to Esther, she had the distinct impression he'd been watching her a split second before she turned around.

Dismissing that fanciful notion, she went in search of Calvin to tell him the plans were set.

Noah had seen Greta in deep discussion with Wanda and wondered if it had something to do with the talk she'd had with Calvin earlier. From the demeanor of the two ladies, it appeared Greta was trying to convince Wanda of something.

When Esther mentioned Greta had talked to her about including Wanda in their quilting circle, part of the picture became clearer.

Calvin, of course, was behind Greta's issuing the invitation. Why had he turned to Greta rather than one of the other members of the group, like their cousin Esther? Surely his *bruder* knew this wasn't something Greta would want to get involved in, especially given the way he'd ignored her feelings for him.

And why had Greta agreed? Was it strictly out of kindness or was it because she still carried a torch for Calvin and wanted to please him? He simultaneously wanted to call his *bruder* out on his selfish actions and go to Greta to make sure she was all right.

Of course, he couldn't do either.

But he could let Greta know that he was still her friend, despite the wall that he'd inadvertently erected between them.

Looking around, he caught a glimpse of her slipping away toward the area where the buggies were parked. He followed and then paused when she stopped to rub her horse's nose.

"Hello," he greeted while he was still a little distance away. He didn't want Greta to feel he was sneaking up on her.

She looked up and her hand paused for a moment. Then she fixed her gaze back on the horse as she continued stroking the animal's nose.

"I have a confession to make," she said as she reached into her coat. "I confiscated this apple from your *mamm*'s kitchen to feed Velvet."

He leaned against the nearby fence and frowned in mock accusation. "So you're a self-confessed thief. I'll have to make sure to keep an eye on you."

That earned him a smile and she finally met his

gaze. "You can try, but I'm also quite elusive," she said dryly.

With a chuckle he moved to the other side of Velvet. After a moment he sobered. "It appears I owe you an apology."

She cut him a sideways, guarded look. "Oh?"

"I obviously upset you when I mentioned your feelings for Calvin. And for that I'm very sorry."

She'd stiffened at the beginning of his apology, keeping her guard up for a heartbeat after he'd finished.

Then, exhaling a soft sigh, the tension seemed to peel away from her. "Apology accepted." Then she grimaced. "I suppose I overreacted. I was just caught off guard."

And that too was his fault. "So, can we go back to you being my matchmaker?"

This time her smile was more relaxed. "*Jah*. Though I never really stopped. And speaking of that, I saw you talking to Lizzie earlier. How did it go?"

Noah rubbed the back of his neck. "She seemed like a very nice woman."

"But?"

Had his doubts been so obvious? "But I'm not sure we'd make a good match."

"May I ask why you think that?"

"A few reasons, but the main one is she seems to want a love match."

Her gaze searched his face. "And that's still something that absolutely will not work for you, even if freely offered?"

Did she still not understand? "No, romantic feelings just complicate things. And the inevitable expectation is that those feelings will be returned, and I can't promise that." Love was just not for him. He'd allowed himself to think it was, once upon a time with Patsy.

And that had eventually turned to ashes.

Greta's heart broke a little at those words. Had he loved Patsy so much he didn't think he could ever love someone else? If only she could convince him it didn't work that way.

And just a moment ago she'd felt so happy. His teasing, followed by that apology, had caught her by surprise, but pleasantly so. She hadn't liked the stiff awkwardness that had crept into their interactions yesterday.

But for now it was best to keep everything between them businesslike. "I'm sorry. The choice is yours. If you feel that Lizzie isn't the right match, then of course we'll scratch her from the list and move on."

He nodded. "*Danke*."

"I saw Sara earlier. I'll see if she's still here and try to speak to her today."

He looked around. "People are already beginning to leave. It can wait until later in the week."

For someone who claimed to want to move quickly on this he sure seemed okay with stretching things out. "Of course. In the meantime, I'll work on finding a few more names to add to the list, just in case."

He nodded. Then his expression changed, shifted into something unreadable. "Esther tells me you've invited Wanda Beachy to be part of your sewing circle."

What else had Esther told him? "I did. She wants to get to know your *mamm* better, now that she and Calvin are dating. This seemed a *gut* way to help that along."

"And Calvin asked you to smooth the way for her."

His words had been a statement, not a question. And there'd been something in his voice she couldn't quite identify. "He did ask me to help find a way. Inviting her to our quilting circle was my idea, though."

"Of course it was."

There it was again, that hint of something not quite right between the *brieder*, this time from Noah. What was going on between the two of them?

Chapter 13

As soon as Noah stepped inside the house, *Mamm* called him over to the rocking chair where she was enthroned.

As he crossed the room, his mind was still focused on Greta. It seemed, after everything that had happened, she still had strong feelings for Calvin.

Why else would she agree to help him this way?

Mamm thumped her cane on the floor, regaining his attention. "Help me up, I want to go for a walk outside."

Noah lowered his arm and let her grab on. As she released her cane and levered herself up with his help, he cautioned her. "There's still snow on the ground and it's mighty *kalt* out there. Are you sure you want to go outside?"

She stiffened and frowned up at him. "I'm not afraid of a bit of weather. Just fetch me my coat and scarf."

"As you wish." He handed her cane back to her and went off to do as she'd requested.

A few minutes later they were stepping from the house. "Walk with me," she all but commanded.

With a deferential nod, Noah took hold of her elbow and slowed his steps to match hers.

"I suppose you know your *bruder* Calvin is courting Wanda Beachy."

Did she have concerns about the matter? "I do," he answered noncommittally.

"She'll be a good match for him, no doubt."

"And she'll be a help to you if they marry."

Mamm lifted her cane and waved it dismissively. "I'm not ready to move into the *dawdi* house just yet—it'll still be my kitchen."

"Of course. I merely said Calvin's future *fraa* will be a help to you, not that she would take your place."

Mamm settled down a bit at that, then she cut Noah a sideways glance. "Perhaps it's time you find a nice young lady to court as well. Your *kinner*, my *kins-kinnah*, need a *mamm*, and you've grieved over Patsy long enough."

Noah felt a momentary flash of exasperation. How could she possibly know how long was long enough?

But apparently she took his silence as permission to continue. "I heard you and Greta Eicher rode over to Heartwood Crossing together last Monday." There was an inquisitive archness to her tone. "She's always struck me as a sensible, intelligent girl."

Uh-oh. He didn't like where this was going. "She is that. But that trip had nothing to do with me courting her."

"*Ach*, that's too bad—perhaps you should reconsider."

Then she lifted her cane again. "But far be it from me to try to manage your love life. If you're not interested in her, then you should find someone else. *Gotte* Himself says in the Bible that it isn't *gut* for a man to be alone."

"As it so happens, I am looking." As soon as the words left his mouth, he wished he could call them back. But it was too late and *Mamm* was already jumping on them.

"*Gut*! There are any number of eligible young ladies in our district and in the next one over. I can give you several names to choose from. And your *aenti* Reba from Berlin can provide candidates for you as well. And there's no reason for you to drag this out. Your *kinner* need a *mamm* now."

It was Noah's turn to hold up a hand. "Slow down. I appreciate your offer, but there's no need for you to provide a list or recruit *Aenti* Reba to help. As I said, I'm already looking." He was strangely reluctant to let her know Greta was helping him.

She gave him a considering look and then sighed. "I know I'm not your birth mother, but I've helped raise you since you were five years old and I love you as if you were my own. I want only what's best for you and would not knowingly lead you amiss."

He gave her hand a squeeze. "And I love you like my own *mamm*." He actually didn't remember much about his *mamm*, just vague recollections of a sweet voice humming to him and warm, comforting hugs. Debra had never made him feel he was anything less to her than her own *kinner*. The fact that she didn't always seem to understand him wasn't her fault. "And I truly meant no disrespect. It's only that when it comes to the selection of a *fraa*, I want to do things in my own way."

She shook her head. "*Ach*, headstrong, just like your *daed*." Her tone was affectionate rather than scolding. "Still, I hope you won't delay, if not for your *kinner*'s sake then for Maisie's. It's time she came home."

That last part stabbed at his conscience. "I'll do my best, but you must know these things can't be rushed."

She gave him that look that had always made him feel like a young scholar caught getting into mischief. "Nonsense. Many a match has been decided on a single conversation."

Noah refrained from comment, but that didn't stop her from pressing on.

"And there's no need for you to wait until the fall to marry. You're a widower with two young *kinner*. I'm sure the bishop will give you permission to marry as soon as possible."

Noah turned them back toward the house. "I think it best to save the discussion of wedding dates until after I find a bride," he said firmly. "Now, perhaps it's best we head back inside."

This time she let the conversation drop. But Noah wasn't fooled. Once *Mamm* got an idea in her head she was like a bulldog with a bone. He pictured her throwing an endless parade of single women in his path until he picked a new *fraa*.

If they hadn't been before, his days as a single man were most definitely numbered now.

Chapter 14

Greta smiled as Wanda climbed into her buggy and set her sewing basket on the seat between them. She was pleased her cousin had followed through—she'd halfway expected the girl to make an excuse to back out.

Sure enough, Wanda's first words were "I have to admit, I'm still not sure about this."

"There's no need to be worried." Greta set the buggy in motion. "You're at least acquainted with everyone who'll be there, and the more time you spend with us, the better friends you'll become. And that includes Debra Stoll."

"I hope you're right." She cut Greta a sideways glance while she nervously fingered her *kapp* string. "I'm not particularly good at quilting—I'm much better at knitting or sewing. I hope my inexperience doesn't make her think less of me."

Greta chose her words carefully. She had to put

Wanda more at ease before she interacted with Debra. "Don't worry, you'll be fine. It's not much different than sewing clothing." She quickly changed the subject. "As nervous as you are, you must really care for Calvin to do this for him."

Wanda's whole demeanor brightened. "Calvin is a very kind and handsome man, ain't so? And he's quite clever and charming as well."

"He's definitely that."

Wanda picked at her skirt, avoiding meeting her gaze. "It just seems too early to me. We only just started dating."

Was her cousin so unsure of her feelings? "Calvin appears to think your relationship is serious," Greta said carefully.

This time Wanda met her gaze. "Calvin seems to confide in you quite a bit."

That touch of jealousy in her tone was unexpected. It wasn't completely without basis, of course. But only on her side. "We're just really *gut* friends. We've known each other since our schooldays."

"He's known a lot of people since his schooldays. Yet you're the one he confides in."

Greta shifted uncomfortably. There wasn't accusation in her cousin's tone, just curiosity. Rather than responding, she tried to turn the conversation back to the earlier point. "Does this mean you're not as certain about your feelings as Calvin is of his?"

"It's flattering that such a wonderful *gut* man as Calvin is so attentive. It makes a girl feel special. But isn't the point of courting so a couple can get to know each other better before they decide if they truly belong together?"

"Of course." Greta wasn't sure why that mature attitude surprised her.

"I do like him, of course," Wanda continued with a soft smile. "And I'm ready to start my own family. But I want to make sure he's the right man for me." She brushed at her skirt. "And one doesn't marry just the man, his family is part of the mix as well."

Was she concerned about the entire family or just Debra? "Well, you're making a *gut* start. You'll get to know Debra better this afternoon."

"Esther Mast is one of the quilters in your group, ain't so?"

"She is."

"And she's your *gut* friend?"

Greta nodded, wondering why the change of subject. "*Jah*. Not only my friend but my partner in the quilt shop. She's also Calvin's cousin."

Wanda glanced at her with a touch of sympathy. "It must be difficult to deal with the English all day at your shop."

Greta kept her tone deliberately light. "Actually, it can be quite rewarding. Many of our customers admire and appreciate the workmanship that goes into our quilts. And it can be fun to answer their questions."

Wanda didn't appear convinced. "Still, I would think the most rewarding occupation for a woman is raising *kinner* and running a household of her own."

Greta's hands tightened on the reins and she did her best not to take offense. With six older *brieder*, Wanda probably didn't realize that having an outside job wasn't optional for some women in the community.

"About Calvin's *mamm*," she said, deliberately turning

the subject back once more, "your best approach would be to find some common ground and engage with her that way."

Wanda gave her a helpless look. "I'm not sure we have any common ground."

Greta's heart softened as she realized Wanda was truly nervous. "There's Calvin," she said gently. "You both care for him."

"True. But that doesn't seem to be a topic to start with."

"Well then, there's the fact that Debra is a *gut* cook. Did you try some of the rhubarb pie she made yesterday?"

"*Jah.* It was wonderful *gut.* But again that's hardly something to build a conversation around."

"Oh, I don't know. You could compliment her on it, ask if she'd share the recipe, discuss the finer points of her technique, ask about her own favorite dishes. That sort of thing."

"I could do that." Wanda sounded perkier, a bit more confident.

"Of course you can. And once the conversation gets going, you'll find other things to branch off on and can approach new topics the same way. Ask questions and listen to her answers so she can see you value her opinion. And her answers will also give you clues as to what subjects to broach next."

Wanda gave her an approving smile. "You really are as clever as everyone says you are."

Was that meant as a compliment?

They arrived at the Wagler home just then, effectively ending their discussion. Wanda didn't step out of the buggy, but sat there a moment chewing on her lip nervously.

Was she second-guessing this approach again? "I promise it won't be as bad as you think it will," Greta said gently. "And if things do get too uncomfortable for you, give me a signal and I'll make an excuse to leave early."

Wanda seemed to draw courage from Greta's backup plan. She nodded, straightened and stepped down from the buggy. A few minutes later they were entering Dorothy's enticingly warm kitchen.

Dorothy greeted them with a smile. "*Wilkom*, ladies. Today seems to be the day everyone arrives early."

"I hope you don't mind," Greta said quickly. "Since this is Wanda's first day, I wanted to give her a chance to settle in before everyone arrived." She'd deliberately arrived early and had nudged Esther to do the same, hoping that when she and Wanda walked into the quilt room there would be a number of open chairs to choose from.

"Of course I don't mind." Then Dorothy turned to Wanda. "*Wilkom* to my home. You're Ira and Susan Beachy's daughter, ain't so?"

"I am."

"Your *mamm* does beautiful crochet work."

Wanda brightened. "*Jah*. I hope to be as good as she is someday."

Apparently crochet was a subject that Wanda could discuss with enthusiasm. Good to know.

Greta turned to their hostess. "Is there something we can do to help?"

"*Nee*, I've got everything under control." Dorothy waved her hand toward the hallway. "Esther is already in the quilt room, why don't you two join her? I'll be there as soon as the others arrive."

Greta nodded. "Come on, Wanda, I'll show you the way."

Twenty minutes later everyone had settled in and started stitching. Greta had hoped Wanda would say something to Debra before now, but it seemed her cousin was too tongue-tied to speak up. It was up to her to smooth the way.

"Debra, Wanda was telling me on the way over here that she really enjoyed that rhubarb pie you served yesterday."

Debra nodded, a smile erasing her sour expression. "The secret is to add the juice of some blueberries to the mix when you're cooking the filling."

"Really?" Wanda leaned forward, finally finding her voice. "My *mamm* uses strawberries or cherries. I would never have thought to use blueberries. What made you try it?"

Obviously pleased to have someone ask about her methods, Debra launched into a story of how she had experimented with various recipes in her youth.

Before long the two women were deep in conversation, with Debra sharing stories of food and family.

Wanda encouraged Debra to elaborate every time the conversation seemed to wind down, and was particularly attentive when it came to stories that included Calvin.

Soon, Greta was free to relax and speak to others in the room.

By the time they were ready to put away their sewing supplies and make their exit, Wanda seemed much more at ease than she had earlier.

"You were right," she said as she settled into the

buggy, "Debra is still intimidating but she's really quite nice once you get to know and understand her."

Greta relaxed, happy Wanda was finally able to see past Debra's rough exterior. "So does this mean you'll join us again next week?"

"*Jah.*" Wanda shifted in her seat with a happy sigh. "I think Calvin's *mamm* is really starting to like me."

It appeared Wanda would fit into their quilt circle just fine. Calvin should be pleased.

And she found she was truly happy for the two of them.

* * *

Greta decided to go into the mall early on Tuesday morning. She was eager to see what Noah had done to the loft room yesterday, if anything.

She quickly climbed the stairs and was disappointed to discover Noah wasn't around.

But he'd definitely accomplished quite a bit yesterday. Except for the open doorway, the new room was completely enclosed. She stepped inside, looking around with a smile. It appeared everything was ready for the first coat of paint. Which meant she could finally pitch in and help.

"What do you think?"

She spun around to see Noah leaning against the doorjamb, watching her. "It appears you've made quite a bit of progress since I left here on Saturday."

He straightened and joined her inside the room. "*Jah.* The baseboards and crown molding have been stained and are in the workroom. I figured I'd wait until the walls were painted to attach them and mount the door."

"So when do I start painting?"

He raised a brow. "You were serious about helping with that?"

"Of course."

"Have you ever painted before?"

"I helped *Daed* when the kitchen needed repainting." Did he doubt her ability to do a good job?

But he nodded. "All right. Can you come in early again tomorrow? There's just one or two more things I want to do before we paint."

"I can probably manage."

"*Gut*. And make sure you wear an apron and a head covering you don't mind getting paint spatters on."

"I will."

A few minutes later, Greta headed back downstairs, pleased that Noah was allowing her to help. While Calvin had asked her advice at times, he'd never actually let her contribute in a physical way to any of his projects.

Thinking of Calvin brought back everything he'd said to her on Sunday. What kind of issue had come between him and Noah? And did they both feel the tension?

If only she could ask. But they would quite rightly tell her it was none of her business. Still, if she understood, maybe there was something she could do to heal the breach. Assuming there was one and she hadn't just imagined it.

When she stepped inside the quilt shop she found Esther already there. "Is there something going on between Noah and Calvin?" she asked impulsively.

Esther drew her brow down as she met her gaze. "That's not for me to say. If Calvin or Noah wish to make their feelings public, then they'll be the ones to speak of it."

Greta felt her cheeks warm at the gentle rebuke in Esther's voice. "I'm sorry. Of course I shouldn't have attempted to gossip about your cousins."

Esther waved a hand dismissively. "Curiosity is a powerful force." Then she smiled. "By the way, I need to leave early today. I promised *Mamm* I'd run an errand for her."

"Of course. I'll be fine closing up." She'd actually planned to leave early herself, hoping to talk to Sara before the teacher left the schoolhouse. But Esther had been covering for her quite a bit lately, so it was time she returned the favor.

Tomorrow should be soon enough to speak to the third candidate on her list.

* * *

Noah stepped back and studied his painting partner. She had a large triangle of cloth covering her *kapp* and an old shirt that probably belonged to her *daed* over her bodice. Both coverings were currently dotted with paint drips. But that didn't overshadow the broad smile of accomplishment on her face.

"That went quicker than I thought it would," she said, her voice reflecting a sense of accomplishment. "What's next?"

"Now we need to let this dry before we put on the second coat, so we'll call it a day and pick back up tomorrow."

Greta nodded. "I'm actually looking forward to it."

Noah started putting away the supplies, surprised she wasn't ready to give up.

"Are you busy this afternoon?" he asked impulsively.

"I'd planned to leave a little early so I could stop by the schoolhouse and speak to Sara. Why?"

"That can wait until tomorrow, can't it?"

"That's up to you since we're on your timetable."

He figured one more day wouldn't hurt anything. "I want to get Maisie something nice to put in that hope chest before I give it to her for her birthday on Sunday. Sort of a thank-you for all she's done for me and Anna and David this past year." He smiled self-consciously. "I'd appreciate a woman's perspective to help pick it out."

"I'd be delighted to help." She smiled, apparently not finding his request strange.

"Would three o'clock work for you?"

She nodded. "Just stop by the quilt shop when you're ready to go."

* * *

Promptly at three o'clock, Noah stopped by the quilt shop to let her know he was ready. A few minutes later Greta climbed into his buggy, a feeling of anticipation bringing a smile to her lips. She not only loved shopping for gifts, but she was pleased he'd invited her to help in such a personal task.

"Do you have any idea what you want to get her?" she asked as he set Jericho in motion.

He cut her a sideways glance. "If I knew, I wouldn't have needed to ask for help."

"Fair enough. So do you have a feeling for what

kind of item you want—linens, dishes, cookware, lamps, something else?"

"Again, I'm counting on you for direction." He glanced her way with a raised brow. "Pretend you're buying something for your own hope chest."

She nodded. "I can do that."

"The only parameter is cost." And he named a figure Greta felt was more than generous.

"Since I can't get you to narrow our search I think the best place to shop will be Spellman's Home Goods. They have a wide enough selection that we're bound to find the perfect gift." She grinned. "And when I take you up and down every aisle of that store, just remember it was you who said you were leaving it all up to me."

Noah heard the playful tone in her voice, saw the mischievous dimple make an appearance and found himself smiling in return. The store she mentioned was a large department store located on the main highway at the edge of town. Viewing items on every aisle would take quite a bit of time. "Spellman's it is."

When they walked in the store, Greta grabbed a shopping cart and headed for the far end of the store where towels and linens were located.

"Oh, look at these," she said, reaching for some blue towels with an embossed border of roses. She stroked them almost reverently. "They're not only pretty, but they're so thick and soft." She held them out toward him. "Feel."

He obediently ran his hand over the surface of the towel and nodded. "It *is* soft."

She set them back on the shelf. "I can see you're not impressed, so let's move on."

And before he could say anything, she'd moved on to bed linens. After pulling several from the shelves and then returning them, she again moved on. "*Ach*, look at the clocks."

Like a little girl she went straight for the most ornate wall clock on the shelf. "What do you think?" she asked. "Isn't it pretty?"

Noah looked at the brass-and-enamel creation. It was festooned with swirls of brass and had a bright blue and silver face. She thought this was pretty?

Then Greta laughed. "You should see your face."

Her teasing surprised a grin from him. "Thank goodness. I was beginning to wonder if I'd selected the wrong shopping partner."

"I just wanted to see if I'd get an honest response from you." She put the clock back and selected a simpler, more elegant clock. "Now this one might work."

"*Jah*, I like it much better. But I'm not sure if I want to give her a clock."

"Then let's move on."

As she'd warned earlier, Greta went through the store aisle by aisle. She offered suggestions based on the budget he'd given her and the kind of items she'd like to have for her own hope chest. It was interesting watching her browse, stopping to admire everything from the practical to the whimsical, from vases to serving platters. It gave him insight into another, more lighthearted side of his matchmaker.

Finally, when they were in the cooking section, she gave a little crow of delight. "This is it." She bent over and pulled a stockpot from the shelf. "It's large, sturdy and built to last a lifetime. Maisie will get a lot of use from this when she sets up her own household." She looked at the price tag. "And it just fits within your budget."

Noah took the heavy pot from her. "And this is something you'd be pleased to own yourself?"

"Absolutely. Trust me, this'll make her very happy."

He set the pot in the shopping cart. "Then the stockpot it is."

They headed for the checkout stand and were soon settled back in Noah's buggy. As Noah picked up the reins, he impulsively turned to Greta. "You were a big help to me this afternoon. Why don't you let me repay you by buying a burger and a shake at Eberly's?"

Greta gave him a surprised look. Then she glanced down. "There's no need to thank me, I had fun."

"But I want to."

She stared at him without answering right away, and he thought for a moment she'd refuse. And for some reason, it was important to him that she said yes.

She finally nodded. "I'd like that. *Danke.*"

Noah gave her a wide grin and set Jericho in motion.

* * *

Noah smiled to himself as he brushed down Jericho that evening. The shopping trip with Greta had gone well. Better than well. He'd already stowed the gift safely in the trunk, which was hidden away in the barn, waiting for his *shveshtah*'s birthday.

And at Eberly's they'd kept the conversation light. He'd gently nudged the discussion in the direction of her quilt designs, and she'd happily talked about the inspirations she drew from and some childhood memories of quilting with her *mamm*. Spending the afternoon with Greta had been...fun. It had been some time since he'd allowed himself to let his worries go for a few hours and just enjoy himself.

Twenty minutes later, as he walked into his home, David ran up to greet him.

"*Aenti* Maisie and I saw a red bird today. She said it was called a cardinal."

"Did you now?" Noah pulled up a chair and settled his son on his lap.

"*Jah*. I even found one of his feathers. See."

Noah dutifully admired the wispy feather his son held out. Then David added, almost as an afterthought, "And *Onkel* Calvin came by and brought me and Anna some of *grossmammi*'s cherry pie."

Calvin had been here? His *bruder* never visited. What was going on? But Noah kept his smile in place for his son's sake. "I hope you saved me some."

"Anna and David have already eaten," Maisie said. "I'll warm up the stew and have a bowl on the table for you in just a few minutes." Then she gave him a troubled look. "Once the *kinner* are in bed, we should have a talk."

"Of course." Whatever she had to say, he had no doubt it was related to Calvin's visit today. And from Maisie's demeanor, it wasn't happy news.

An hour later, when the kitchen had been cleaned and David and Anna had been tucked in, he sat across the kitchen table from Maisie. "So what do we need to discuss?"

She clasped her hands tightly in her lap. "I may not

be able to stay here and help care for your *kinner* much longer."

A not unexpected topic. "I know you'll be sixteen on Sunday, and I've already promised to have other arrangements in place by Valentine's Day—"

"That may not be soon enough." She waved a hand as if trying to wave away something unpleasant. "This isn't about my rumspringa. The reason Calvin came by was to talk to me about *Mamm*."

Noah sat up straighter. "What about *Mamm*? Did something happen to her?"

"Not exactly. But her health is getting worse, and the cold weather isn't helping matters. Calvin says she could barely stand at the stove to cook breakfast this morning for all the wheezing and her aches. It was one thing before Faith got married—she took a lot of the burden off of her. But now that Faith and Donald are married and have moved to Berlin, *Mamm* is trying to do everything herself again. You know how stubborn she can be. She won't let either of the boys help with women's work."

"Why didn't Calvin come to me with this?" He hated that his *bruder* had put their little *shveshtah* in the middle of this.

Maisie shrugged. "I think he wanted to know if I was ready to come home."

She probably wasn't even aware that she was wringing her hands. "It's okay, Maisie," he said gently. "If you feel you need to move back home to help *Mamm*, I can figure something out. You've done more than expected for me and my *kinner*." It seemed he was out of time. "Just give me this week to make other arrangements."

He was rewarded with a relieved smile. Some of her

tension melted away like snow in the spring. Then she turned serious again. "I don't want to leave you and your *kinner* stranded."

"Don't worry. I've already put some plans in motion so I could free you up by Valentine's Day. This news just means I need to speed things up."

He reached across the table and covered her hands with his. "I truly appreciate all the sacrifices you've made for us. And this may sound entirely self-serving, but don't get so caught up in helping *Mamm* that you miss the fun and excitement of your rumspringa. Promise me."

She nodded. Then she smiled hopefully. "I do have an idea that might help until you get whatever solution you're working on in place."

She almost sounded like Greta. "I'm listening."

"Why don't I take Anna and David with me and spend our days at *Mamm*'s house while you're at work. That way I can watch them and help *Mamm* at the same time. Once your workday is over, you can pick them up and return home. You could even share the evening meal with us before you leave."

Noah smiled fondly at his younger *shveshtah*, proud of the generous young woman she was becoming. "*Danke*, Maisie, but you've done plenty for us. It's up to me to find an answer." As tempting as her offer had been, it wasn't fair to expect her to run a large household with a working farm under *Mamm*'s exacting standards and take care of his *kinner* too.

"But—"

"I tell you what, we'll call that our backup plan. Now, you'll move back home by the end of the week, one way or another. I'll let Calvin and *Mamm* know." He wanted to have a word with Calvin anyway. "And I'll figure out a way to make sure Anna and David are well cared for." Even if it meant he had to hire a nanny after all.

She nodded but her expression was still troubled. Apparently she needed some tangible proof he and his *kinner* would be okay.

First thing tomorrow he'd have a talk with Greta and see if they could accelerate this hunt for a *fraa*.

Chapter 15

Noah pulled his buggy up to his *mamm*'s house the next morning, but before he could climb out, Calvin was there. Did he not want to have this conversation in front of their *mamm*?

"I suppose you're here to discuss my talk with Maisie yesterday."

"*Jah*. Don't you think you should have talked to me instead of putting her in the middle of this?"

"Maisie is old enough to make her own decision about where she needs to be."

Did his *bruder* really not understand? "Well, you'll be glad to hear that I've told her that after her birthday on Sunday she doesn't have to watch my *kinner* any longer."

"*Gut*." Calvin gave him a suspicious look. "I hope that doesn't mean you plan to replace Maisie with Greta."

Noah stiffened. "Why would you say such a thing?"

"You seem to be monopolizing a lot of her time lately."

If he didn't know better, he'd think Calvin was actually jealous. "She's helping me with some planning." He didn't feel any obligation to tell his *bruder* that she was playing matchmaker for him.

Then, before Calvin could dig deeper, he gave him his best get-out-of-my-way look. "Now if you'll excuse me, I need to get to work."

He held Calvin's gaze until his *bruder* moved away from the buggy, then set Jericho in motion again. It took him several minutes to cool down. When he finally did, though, he took himself to task for his reaction. Anger was a poison and he didn't want any part of it.

Funny thing was, he hadn't got his back up until Calvin asked about Greta.

Noah had just finished setting out the paint supplies when Greta breezed into the room.

"*Gut matin*," she said cheerily as she entered waving her thermos. "I brought the hot cocoa."

Noah, whose mood had lightened considerably, returned her smile. "Are you ready to wield a paint roller again?"

"Absolutely." She poured them each a cup from her thermos and handed him one.

He took a sip, then met her gaze. "*Danke*."

She rewarded him with a dimpled smile.

He took another sip, giving him time to pull his thoughts together. "Do you still intend to talk to Sara Kauffmann today?"

She nodded. "*Jah*. I plan to leave a little early and stop by the schoolhouse after the scholars go home for the day." She apparently picked up on something in his voice or expression, because her nose wrinkled in question. "Is everything okay?"

"I had a talk with Maisie last night. It seems I'm going to have to release her sooner than I'd expected."

She stilled. "How much sooner?"

"Sunday."

"Oh." Greta took a sip from her own cup.

He waited while she considered the implications of what he'd just said.

"May I ask why?" she finally asked.

"*Mamm*'s health has apparently gotten a lot worse. She needs Maisie's help sooner rather than later."

Greta's expression sobered. "I'm afraid even if Sara agrees to let you court her there's very little chance she can take on the care of your *kinner* so soon."

"I understand. But I just need to know if she's willing. If so, I can find a way to manage things temporarily while we get permission from the bishop to marry quickly."

"And if she's not?"

He didn't blame her for the hint of doubt in her voice. "I'll pray *Gotte* will provide another way."

She lightly touched his arm, then quickly withdrew. "As will I."

He appreciated her support. Because that was all that touch had been, he was certain of it.

Trying to lighten the mood, he turned the conversation as he set his cup down. "We should be able to finish up the painting today. Then it'll just be a matter of getting the trim and door installed and the room will be ready."

"Have you told any of the other shopkeepers about it yet?" she asked.

"Only in general terms. I didn't want to set any expectations in case I ran into delays." He cut a glance her way. "What about you, have you said anything to Hannah or Esther?"

She nodded. "Only that you're building a room up here, which everyone can see."

One thing he could count on with Greta was her discretion.

As they got to work, Noah tried to pull up an image of the schoolteacher in his mind. The woman who might soon be his *fraa*.

Sara Kauffmann was petite with light blonde, almost white hair. She was somewhat plump but it suited her.

That was all he could remember—not the sound of her voice, or her smile, or the color of her eyes.

On the other hand, he had no trouble picturing Greta without bothering to look her way. Her warm smile punctuated by a dimple, her delicately pointed chin, the gold flecks in her eyes that seemed more pronounced when she was excited or amused. The sound of her voice, its inflection when she was pondering something or happy or irritated. Or the way she used her hands when she spoke or wrinkled her nose when she was trying to puzzle things out.

He gave his head a mental shake, trying to clear it of all those inappropriate, totally unhelpful images. It was to be expected of course. He'd spent a lot of time in Greta's presence lately, so naturally she'd be on his mind.

It was nothing more than that.

Greta used the paint roller, enjoying the rhythmic up-and-down motions as she added a coat of that pretty shade of blue to the walls. But her mind was preoccupied with thoughts of what Noah had told her. She hadn't realized Debra's health had gotten so fragile—she should have paid better attention to her at quilting circle on Monday.

And she definitely should have talked to Sara before now. In fact, despite what Noah had told her, she should have tracked Sara down last Sunday and spoken to her then. It wasn't like her to put things off.

What was happening to her?

Noah was working on the wall adjacent to hers. There was a different feeling today. Rather than the easy back-and-forth of yesterday, Noah seemed lost in thought, rarely speaking except in response to something she said. And there was an undercurrent of tension in him that hadn't been there yesterday.

Was it because of his concern over the short time until Maisie moved on, or was something else on his mind?

Whatever the case, she needed to get some answers from Sara so that he could make plans, one way or the other.

Though Greta knew the wall of silence between them was more contemplative than troubled, she couldn't seem to break through. When they finally finished the painting, she quickly gathered her things and headed down to the quilt shop.

As soon as she and Esther exchanged greetings, she put in her request. "I hate to ask you to cover for me yet again, but I'd like to leave a little early today to run an errand."

Her friend gave her an arch look. "Would this errand have anything to do with your matchmaking efforts?"

Greta turned to wipe at the counter with a cloth. "Perhaps."

Esther raised her hands, palms outward. "Say no more. I'll be glad to do my part to support you and Noah."

Greta glanced up, trying to read Esther's expression. There was something about the way she'd said that last bit that seemed to carry a double meaning. But Esther had already moved to her quilt frame with a perfectly innocent expression. In fact she was humming softly to herself.

*   *   *

Greta pulled her buggy up to the white clapboard schoolhouse and saw three *kinner* heading down the lane in the opposite direction of her approach. The schoolhouse seemed isolated because of the woods on one side and open fields on the other, but it was actually in the heart of the Amish community.

The schoolhouse door was open, so Sara must still be inside. Hopefully she'd timed her arrival so all the *kinner* had headed home already.

As she climbed down from the buggy, she faced the coming interview with mixed feelings. Getting agreement from Sara was very important to Noah. So why was she feeling this strange reluctance to proceed?

Mentally shaking off her mood, she climbed the steps to the schoolhouse door. She walked inside to see Sara gathering up some papers. The petite schoolteacher looked up and her lips curved in a welcoming smile. "Greta. How good to see you. Please come in."

Greta moved past the rows of wooden desks to the front of the room. "I hope I'm not disturbing you."

"Not at all. In fact I just took care of the stove and was about to head home. What can I do for you?"

"Actually, there's a matter of some delicacy I'd like to discuss with you."

"Ah, let me guess. You're busy working one of your matchmaking cases, and you want to find out if I'd be interested in being courted?"

Greta always thought Sara was clever. "And how did you figure that out?"

Sara slid her papers into a large satchel. "Stephen Zimmerman is my cousin and he told me what you did for him."

Stephen was the second young man she'd helped find a match for.

"And since you don't have any *kinner* who go to school here," Sara continued, "I can't think of any other reason you'd make a special trip just to speak to me in private." She closed her satchel and moved to a coat hook where her coat and scarf hung. "And did I guess correctly?"

"You did, which allows me to be more direct than usual. The first question is, are you interested in marriage?"

The schoolteacher donned her coat. "I enjoy being a schoolteacher and I love all the young scholars I get to work with, but I do want to have a family of my own someday."

"So you *are* open to marriage."

She wrapped her scarf around her neck and reached in her satchel. "With the right man," she said, pulling out a pair of gloves.

At least it wasn't a no. "And what qualities would this right man have?"

"He'd need to be a man of faith and strong morals, someone I can respect, and someone who'll respect me."

So far, so good. "I notice you didn't mention love."

Sara waved a hand. "That's what the courting period is for, to see if love will develop. The other things I mentioned, those come first so I'll know whether to even begin a courtship."

Uh-oh. "So you consider love an essential part of a marriage."

"Of course." She eyed Greta, her brow drawn down in a puzzled expression. "Don't you?"

Greta worded her response carefully. "There have been certain instances where a couple enter into marriage for other reasons—companionship, mutual benefit, security."

"I suppose. But, much as I'd like to have a family of my own, I'm not willing to give up the life I have for a marriage without love." She straightened. "Why? Is the man you're working with looking for that kind of arrangement?"

Greta nodded. "From what you just said, I suppose there's no point in our taking this discussion any further."

Sara frowned. "I almost feel insulted that you'd think I'd agree to something like that."

"I'm sorry, Sara. But I don't presume to know how any woman will react to such a personal request as a courtship."

"Can I ask the identity of the man you're helping?"

Greta gave her a challenging look. "Would knowing change your mind?"

Sara grinned. "*Nee*. Besides, I think I already have a

gut idea. And I wish him well." She grabbed her satchel. "So, I take it we're done now?"

"*Jah.*" Greta followed her from the building. "Can I give you a ride home?"

"*Danke*, but I'm not going far and I find the cold bracing as long as the sky is clear. Besides, I like to walk."

A few minutes later Greta was back in her buggy, but she didn't set off right away. How was she going to tell Noah the news?

This was all her fault. He'd told her just what he wanted in a *fraa* but she'd thought she knew better. She'd wanted to give him her version of what would make him happy in the long run. If she'd searched instead for someone who met his stated requirements, someone who would likely be willing to engage in a marriage of convenience, he might already have his match and be able to move forward. How could she have betrayed his trust this way?

She bowed her head. Gotte, *I've been prideful, thinking I knew best, and because of that I've hurt a* gut *man. Please, help me to know how to fix this for him.*

Greta wasn't sure just how long she sat there, but the sound of an approaching buggy brought her back to her surroundings.

As the vehicle pulled up beside her, she recognized Calvin's horse. What was he doing here?

As soon as Calvin's buggy pulled to a stop, he stepped out and headed her way.

Curious as to what he wanted, Greta smiled and greeted him. "Hi, Calvin. Is everything all right?"

"*Jah.*" He leaned against her buggy. "I need to speak to you about something important."

Wanting to make sure she kept their relationship firmly in the just-friends category, Greta spoke first. "Did you hear how well Wanda did at our quilting circle on Monday? It was difficult for her but she was so brave." She gave him a bright smile. "It was worth it, though, because I think she and your *mamm* got along really well."

He waved her words aside. "That's *gut*. But that's not what I want to talk to you about."

"Oh?" What was he up to?

"I miss the way we used to talk about things. In fact I'm starting to think I might have made a mistake when I asked Wanda if I could court her."

She had to nip this in the bud. "Calvin, no."

Her protest only made him press harder. "Just listen. I know you feel affection for Wanda. And Wanda is a sweet girl, but I've begun to wonder if what I really need is a woman with a little more spirit, a little more confidence than she has." He gave her that smile that used to melt her insides. "A woman like you."

Greta drew back in dismay. "That's not fair to Wanda. Two weeks isn't enough time for you to see who she really is." She waved a hand. "Wanda has more spirit and courage than you give her credit for."

"Can you honestly say you no longer have feelings for me?"

How dare he throw that back at her? "I still consider you my *friend*," she said severely, "but I've grown to believe you and I would never suit as a couple. Think about it. Do you really want someone who will always speak her mind, who loves to debate with you, whose strongest feeling for you is friendship?"

Calvin's demeanor had a tinge of pity to it. "If

you're counting on Noah, you should know he'll never appreciate you, never be concerned with your happiness. Never—"

She'd had enough. "Calvin, stop! Noah has nothing to do with this."

Calvin stiffened. "Noah did this, turned you against me."

She crossed her arms. "Do you really think me so weak willed that I can be so easily swayed?"

He pushed away from her buggy and straightened. "I apologize for bothering you," he said stiffly. "I'll let you go on your way." He turned back to his buggy but she called his name.

He turned and she saw a flicker of satisfaction.

A flicker she was about to snuff out. "Please don't string Wanda along. If you don't love her, let her go, but be kind."

With a curt nod he turned on his heel and climbed into his buggy.

Greta watched Calvin drive away, wondering how she had ever thought she wanted to marry him. Right now it was her fervent prayer that this seeming infatuation was just a passing fancy, that he would quickly realize Wanda was a much better match for him than she was.

But at the moment, Calvin and his yo-yo feelings were a distraction. Her real concern should be discussing what she'd just learned about Sara with Noah.

Part of her wanted to return to the mall. Noah would still be there and he'd want to hear how things went with Sara as soon as possible. But she was still a little on edge after her encounter with Calvin and needed time to collect herself. Besides, she wanted to wait to approach

Noah until she had some options for him, whether it be another woman's name to offer as a potential *fraa*, or something else.

Though what that something else might be she had no idea.

Chapter 16

By four o'clock, Noah had finished sanding the seats of the chairs he'd been working on all day. Stretching his back and shoulders, he decided it was time to take a break. Maybe some fresh air would help refresh him. He headed for the rear entrance of the workshop and paused when he stepped outside.

Rubbing his upper arms against the cold, he inhaled, drawing the crisp January air into his lungs. His gaze landed on the stable. It was a modest building, just large enough to provide shelter for his buggy horse and the horses of his employees and the other shopkeepers. There were ten stalls in all and a small paddock next to it. He headed inside, moving to Jericho's stall and adding a little grain to his feed bucket.

Velvet's stall was empty, which meant Greta had already headed out. Was she speaking to Sara right now?

Noah grabbed a curry comb and began to brush the

animal. The repetitive motions gave him time to think. And he had a lot of thinking to do.

But a moment later Paul Habegger entered the stable. With a nod of acknowledgment, Paul moved to the stall almost directly across from Jericho's. Holding a couple of apple slices in his palm, he extended his hand. "Here you go, Stucky."

From the moment he'd come into work this morning, Noah had sensed Paul had something weighty on his mind. He had the feeling his friend hadn't come out here merely to check on his horse.

Finally the man cleared his throat. "I need to speak to you about something, Noah."

Noah nodded and leaned back against the stall gate. Apparently his friend was ready to share whatever was bothering him.

"My *Onkel* Lazarus over in Sugarcreek is getting on in age and he needs some help," Paul said. "He and *Aenti* Margaret were never blessed with children and they've asked me to come live with them."

Noah stilled as the full implications of that declaration hit him. "And you want to do this?" he asked quietly.

Paul nodded. "He needs the help, and if I go I'd eventually inherit his farm." His words were rushed as if he knew how it would impact Noah. "Dinah and I would have a wonderful *gut* place to raise our *kinner*. And Dinah would be a big help to *Aenti* Margaret." Paul had a two-year-old son, and Dinah was carrying their second child.

"You would give up your woodworking to help with work on his farm?" Paul was such a skilled craftsman it would be a shame to see that talent go to waste.

Paul shuffled uncomfortably. "Not entirely, but yes, for the most part." He kept his gaze focused on his horse. "It's not as if I don't know what I'm getting myself into. I was raised on a farm and know what'll be required. I think it's a fair trade."

Apparently Paul's mind was made up. "Then of course you should go. How soon will you be moving?"

"I don't want to leave you in a bind. My *onkel*'s need isn't urgent, but I can't make him wait indefinitely. Does the end of the month sound fair to you?"

Noah nodded. "More than fair." He stepped forward and shook Paul's hand. "I appreciate you giving me so much notice and I wish you and Dinah well."

"*Danke.*"

Paul gave his horse a final pat and headed back to the shop. His step was considerably lighter than it had been when he walked in a few moments ago.

Noah stood where he was, trying to mentally adjust the delivery schedules for the projects he was already committed to.

He'd just won the bid on a major project that he'd hoped would lead to even more work. Being down one man was going to put his ability to deliver in jeopardy and be a blow to his business. Andrew was a hard worker and a skilled craftsman, but there was no way he could do the work of two men. Reuben had asked to apprentice with Noah, but though he showed a lot of promise, he was splitting his time between watching the sales floor and honing his skills, and he still had a long way to go.

No, he needed to hire an experienced craftsman if he was going to keep up with his orders, and the sooner the better.

The end of the month was just a little over two weeks away. It would be difficult to find a replacement in that space of time. Especially since he was trying to find a *fraa* as well.

The new year was definitely bringing with it lots of challenges.

Not the least of which was forcing himself to trust *Gotte* enough to leave it all in His hands.

* * *

Greta had been in her quilt room for over two hours but had gotten very little work done. She'd said a prayer for Calvin and Wanda, asking *Gotte* to help them both to discern His will. Then she'd resolutely pushed them out of her mind, concentrating instead on the situation with Noah.

She couldn't let go of the idea that there was something she could do, some way she could help him. She'd been alternately praying and wracking her brain for solutions all evening.

Even this room, which normally wrapped her in a sense of peace and well-being, failed to soothe her tonight.

She pricked her finger with her needle and brought it up to her lips. She studied her work, looking for signs she'd gotten blood droplets on it, but to her relief it looked unblemished.

It was time to put her needle away, however, before she did some real damage. She stood and eyed the quilt top again, this time studying the pattern. She had pieced about a third of the top, the clouds and some of the sunrise itself. Finding just the right combination of colors had been tricky—in fact she'd redone one whole section, but she was pleased with her progress.

Her Promise Quilt. Yes, her idea of what that promise encompassed had changed since she'd first conceived it, but it still held promise, *Gotte*'s promise that He had plans for her, plans to give her hope and a future. Jeremiah 29:11 was one of her favorite Bible verses.

Recollections of New Year's morning brought back thoughts of Calvin and how he'd approached her earlier today. Had her rebuff been enough to convince him she was no longer interested? She didn't know what she'd do if he persisted. The last thing she wanted was to be the cause of pain for Wanda, especially now that the girl was finally coming out of her shell.

Then she stilled as she had a sudden idea for both how to help Noah and how to ensure Calvin understood he really had no future pursuing her. It was unconventional, but isn't that what people expected from her?

No, it was too outrageous, even for her.

Yet the idea had taken root and wouldn't let go. Could she gather enough courage to suggest it? More to the point, would Noah even agree to it?

There was only one way to find out.

Chapter 17

Friday morning, Noah again left his home extra early, anxious to see Greta. Merely to find out what Sara had said to her, of course.

That question stayed with him all the way to the mall.

He entered the workshop and first checked the generator, then turned on the lights and raised the thermostat.

Once in the workshop, he glanced at the materials that were prepared and ready to install in the room upstairs. Unfortunately, they would have to wait. He needed to spend all of his available time working on client projects if he was to have any hope of meeting his deadlines.

With a sigh, he took off his coat and rolled up his sleeves, then went to work.

Around ten o'clock, Noah stood and stretched. Greta should be in by now. It was time to find out how things had gone with Sara.

He'd barely stepped out of the workshop and into the mall lobby when Greta exited the quilt shop.

Had she been watching for him? The fact that she made a beeline in his direction answered that question.

"*Gut matin,*" she greeted, her voice slightly breathless.

"*Gut matin.* I think we need to have a discussion, ain't so?" He motioned toward the stairs. "Would you like to join me in my office?"

"*Jah.*"

He waved a hand, indicating she should go first. When they reached the top of the stairs he saw Greta glance past his office to the new room. "I haven't done any additional work on it today," he said, forestalling her question.

"Of course. I mean, I know you have other work to do."

He preceded her into his office. "Unfortunately, I probably won't have time to get back to it for a while."

"Oh?" There was an obvious question embodied in that one word although to her credit she didn't press for details.

But he saw no point in withholding the information. "Paul Habegger is moving to Sugarcreek at the end of the month," he said as they both took their seats. "So I have about two weeks to find a replacement for him or I'm going to be very shorthanded."

She leaned forward. "Oh my goodness, I'm so sorry. I know that must be a blow coming on top of your other worries." Her brow wrinkled. "Do you know of anyone who can replace him?"

Noah shook his head. "Not at the moment, but I haven't started looking yet, he just told me yesterday."

"I take it you can't keep your business running short-term with just Andrew?"

"Not for very long, unless I cut back on my orders."
Which wasn't the way to grow his business.

"You'll figure this out. Just trust in *Gotte*."

Noah nodded, then straightened. "But that's not what
we came up here to discuss. Did you speak to Sara
yesterday?"

He saw the answer in her face before she said a word.

"I'm afraid things aren't going to work out with Sara
either. She wants to hold out for a love match."

He nodded, not really surprised. "That's it then."

Much as he hated to, it looked like it was time to
hire a nanny.

Greta saw his resigned look and her heart broke a little.
"I'm sorry none of the ladies I selected worked out. I
guess I'm not as good a matchmaker as I thought I was."
She chided herself for drawing this out, but she dreaded
his response to her confession.

His smile forgave her. "Don't be too hard on yourself,
they were all good candidates. I know you did your best,
it's just hard to tell if two people will be a good fit until
they actually spend time together."

His understanding made her feel even worse. She
forced herself to say what had to be said. "*Danke* for
your faith in me. But I have a confession to make." She
met his gaze, resisting the urge to look away. "Regardless of what you think, I didn't do my best for you."

"You're being too hard on—"

"*Nee!*" She inhaled a breath, then collected herself.
"Please let me get this out before you say anything."
He nodded and she continued. "I ignored what you said
about not wanting a love match and looked for a woman

I thought would make you happy. I should never have imposed my own ideas of what you needed on this project."

Noah's expression was unreadable. "Your intentions were *gut*. And it's likely the results would have been the same." Then he waved a hand. "What's done is done. Time to move on."

A better response than she deserved. "I actually have one more name for you to consider." She'd stayed awake most of the night trying to decide if she could really do this, if it was even the right thing to do.

But before she could continue, he shook his head. "There's really no time. I'll just have to hire a nanny to get me through the next few months. It's not ideal, but with Paul leaving I have a feeling I'll be working a lot of late hours."

"I'll do it." She hadn't intended to just blurt it out, but it was done now.

Noah's brow drew down in obvious confusion. "Be my nanny? That's very generous but—"

"*Nee*. I mean, *jah*, of course I'll take care of Anna and David for you. But I'm offering more." She wasn't normally so clumsy with her words. No wonder he looked confused. "What I'm trying to say is, what if I agree to be your *fraa*?"

There, she'd said it. Now it was up to him.

Unfortunately, he didn't respond immediately. As the seconds ticked away, Greta studied him anxiously, doing her best not to fidget. Trying to gauge his reaction, she saw flashes of confusion, hesitation, and perhaps just the tiniest flicker of interest? Then his expression shuttered completely.

She squeezed her hands tightly in her lap. Was he ever going to say something? Anything?

As the silence drew out, her heart sank.

Would even a man who wanted a loveless marriage reject her?

Chapter 18

Noah wasn't sure he'd heard right. He just sat there, staring at her, trying to read the intent behind her offer from the expression in her eyes.

Realizing he'd let the silence draw out much too long, he cleared his throat. "Let me make sure I understand. You want to make up for your mistake by offering yourself up to fill the role of my *fraa*?"

"*Nee*." She waved a hand helplessly. "*Jah*, a part of this is my wanting to make up for what I did. But that's just a very small part of it. I also want to do this because I'd benefit from this arrangement as well."

"How?" It would be interesting to hear her explanation.

She traced a design on the arm of her chair. "I've come to accept what people say, that unless I change my ways, no man will ever want to marry me."

Noah had to practically bite his tongue to keep from

protesting. Who had been so cruel, and so blind, as to tell her such a thing?

She lifted her chin and met his gaze again. "I don't want to change my ways, I like who I am."

Good for her. He rather liked who she was as well.

"But I do want to marry someday, to have *kinner* and a home of my own. Since you aren't looking for a love match, we can set that requirement behind us. Your main focus is to find someone who can take care of your home and your *kinner*. I believe I can do that quite well. So we can both get what we want out of a match between us."

"Are you sure you don't want to hold out for a love match?" Somehow it seemed wrong to rob her of that. He refused to look too closely at why that should be so.

But Greta gave him an assured smile. "I imagine every girl dreams of finding someone who will love her deeply and that she can love deeply in return. But I'm realistic enough to know that such a relationship isn't something that everyone can achieve."

Had Calvin's rejection led her into this fatalistic attitude? But there was no trace of self-pity or maudlin despair in her voice or demeanor, only calm acceptance.

She shifted in her seat. "I'd also like to think that you and I are friends and that we respect each other. That's an important part of any marriage." Then her smile warmed. "And of course I love Anna and David as if they were my own."

Looking at it objectively, Greta was the perfect candidate to become his *fraa*. No one knew better than she did what his expectations for the role were. The two of them got along well. And his *kinner* already knew and liked her. But he still had trouble accepting that she wasn't suggesting this out of a sense of obligation. "And you really want to do this?"

She nodded. "I wouldn't have offered if I didn't mean it."

"And what about your feelings for Calvin? I won't have a *fraa* who is pining for my *bruder*."

"That won't be an issue. Whatever I felt or thought I felt for your *bruder* is in the past. All that remains is friendship."

That was easy enough to say now, when Calvin's interest was focused elsewhere. But what if Calvin changed his mind and turned to her?

She shifted slightly as her shoulders went back. "However, I do have a few conditions."

He almost smiled at that—he should have expected as much. "I'm listening."

"I want to continue working in the quilt shop. And not just because I don't want to leave Esther in the lurch. I love the quilt shop and what we do there, as much, I imagine, as you love woodworking. But I'm willing to work an abbreviated schedule, say five hours a day rather than seven. I promise I'll work hard and neither the house nor the people will suffer."

He didn't doubt her intentions. "And who will care for Anna and David while you're working? Surely you don't intend to have them spend their days in the quilt shop on a regular basis."

"Of course not. But I've given that some thought. I know you said you didn't want to hire a nanny, but I think for the time that I'm working at the quilt shop, we can hire a sitter."

He frowned at that. "A sitter is almost the same as a nanny. If I'm going to end up putting them in the hands of a nanny, why do I need to get married?"

She stiffened and her lips compressed. "First, a sitter isn't the same as a nanny. Second, the sitter won't be Anna and David's main caregiver, you and I will have that pleasure. We'll be the ones to care for them, nurture them, tuck them in at night. We'll provide the stability and security that parents provide for their children. In fact, if you think about it, having a sitter watch over them several hours a day, five days a week, is almost like sending them to school, ain't so?"

He leaned back and nodded slowly. "I suppose that's true."

Her smile returned. "Then you agree?"

"That a sitter is a reasonable option? *Jah*. Do you have any other conditions?"

"This next is more a suggestion."

"Again, I'm listening." They were still talking around the whole marriage agreement issue.

"I'd like to have the sitter watch the children here. That way I can visit with them periodically during the day, and I'll be close by if I'm needed."

Now he was confused. "We already agreed you wouldn't take them to the quilt shop with you every day."

"No, of course not. I'm thinking of the new room you just built."

It was fascinating the way her mind worked. "I suppose that could work. And I do like the idea of them being close by."

"That's settled then." She leaned back in her chair.

"What about you? Do you have any conditions I should be aware of?"

Nice of her to ask. "I already told you my requirements when you agreed to be my matchmaker."

"*Jah*. But now that we're discussing my being your future *fraa*, is there anything more specific you want to add to the list?"

He had to make certain she had no illusions about exactly what she was getting into. "I want to be certain you understand that I'm serious about every one of those requirements, including the desire to keep things businesslike between us. That won't change just because we're friends."

Her expression flickered for just a heartbeat, so quickly he wasn't sure exactly what it signified.

But then she met his gaze with a steady one of her own. "I understand."

He hoped she really meant that. Because he was running out of reasons to say no to her offer.

She brushed at her skirt before meeting his gaze again. "Does this mean you agree to my proposal?"

The vulnerability in her expression surprised him. Was she expecting a rejection? He smiled, trying to offer reassurance. "I suppose it does."

Her relief was evident as she sat up straighter. "*Gut.*" Then she spread her hands. "So, what do we do now?"

His first thought was to wonder if she was expecting some show of affection, like a hug. Then he gave his head a mental shake. They'd both agreed to keep this businesslike. "I'll speak to the bishop tomorrow about an early wedding date. I know your idea to hire a sitter takes the pressure off for the most part, but I'd still like to have the wedding as soon as possible, so you can move in with us."

Her cheeks reddened, but she nodded.

He hid a smile. He found her flustered reaction very distracting. "That being said, I assume you have no objection to us having the ceremony in the next three or four weeks if we can make it work?"

"Of course. As you said, the sooner the better." She clasped her hands together tightly. "And given your situation with the *kinner*, I'm sure the bishop will be accommodating."

"Let's hope so. Maisie's birthday is Sunday and I'd like you to come to our celebration," he said. "If you're agreeable, I'll come by to pick you up, and while I'm there I'll speak to your *daed* and we can announce our engagement to your *shveshtra*. Then we'll go to my *mamm*'s home, where we'll make the announcement to my family."

She nodded. "That's a *gut* plan."

Greta's expressions were usually very easy for him to read, but not today. "I know this isn't the proper order of things," he said, trying to put her at ease, "but since we want to act quickly—"

She waved a hand. "Of course. It's the wedding itself, not the order of things, that matters here."

He still couldn't help the feeling that he was letting her down in some way. "I'm sorry. I know this isn't the engagement and wedding you pictured for yourself."

"No need to apologize. We've both agreed that we're entering into this marriage without any romantic pretense. Remember, it's a businesslike arrangement for both of us, not just you."

Was she really able to approach it that way? He

remembered how excited Patsy had been to plan their wedding, how she and her friends had giggled and carried on together, selecting dress fabrics, deciding on the menu, selecting token gifts for the guests.

Still, he pressed on. "After that we can begin planning the particulars of our life together."

She nodded again. "I know that with Paul leaving soon, you'll be very busy with your work, so I'll take care of looking for the sitter."

He stiffened. "I'll want to have a say in that." They were his *kinner* after all.

"Naturally. I'd never hire someone to look after Anna and David without your approval. I just meant that I'd find some good candidates for us to choose from."

He supposed he'd have to get used to there being an "us" and "we" in his life now. "*Danke*. That's something else that'll need to happen quickly. Sunday won't be a problem but starting on Monday—"

"I can take care of Monday—the quilt store is closed, remember? So we need to have someone by Tuesday. I think that's very doable. In fact I can already think of two girls who might be interested."

"*Gut*. The other pressing matter would be to get the loft room ready so there'll be a place for the sitter to care for Anna and David." Then he looked at her expectantly. "I assume I'll need to add some furnishings. Any suggestions?"

"I have a lot of ideas. Probably more than you want to hear."

He rolled his eyes, then smiled. "Let's have them."

She stood. "It'll be easier to explain if we're in the room."

Noah followed her, and a moment later they were standing in what was soon to be a nursery.

Greta pointed to the far corner. "I think we should put a couple of pallets there under the eaves for when they nap. Away from the windows so the light doesn't bother them. I have some old blankets that would serve the purpose."

"What else?"

Greta tapped her chin. "Maybe something to curtain off the sleeping area so they aren't disturbed by any activity or other light." She turned to the right. "A nice worktable with a couple of chairs over there against the wall would be useful. I imagine I might be watching them here myself from time to time, at least until we're married, and it would be nice if I had a place to work while they're napping."

"Is that it?"

She studied the adjoining wall. "We could also use a small chest, you know, to store extra bedding, clothing and towels. And a bin for toys. Oh, and a smaller table with chairs that your *kinner* can use to play and eat at. And maybe a cooler we can put ice in to store perishables."

He gave her a raised-brow look. "That's quite a list."

She appeared unrepentant. "It doesn't have to happen all at once. We can start with the nap area and some chairs for them to sit on."

"I think I can take care of most of your requests by Tuesday."

"*Gut.*" She gave him an apologetic look. "I know you'll need to get the children up and out of the house very early, but that's just temporary and they can nap when they get here. Once we're married and I can move into your home, we can set a more reasonable schedule."

He merely nodded, surprised that she felt the need to apologize for any of this.

She turned then and gave him a nervous bob of the head. "If that's all for now, I suppose I ought to head down to the quilt shop."

Noah watched her move toward the stairs, still processing what had just happened. She'd found a match for him, exactly as she'd promised. And she'd done it in the extremely tight time frame he'd given her. The fact that she herself was that match in no way diminished the impressiveness of her accomplishment.

He paused as it occurred to him for the first time since she'd made her offer just how much courage it must have taken for her to actually propose to him. True, she was bolder and more outspoken than the average Amish woman, but even so, it couldn't have been easy for her to admit her failing and then risk his rejection.

Greta was a woman of uncommon courage.

He just hoped she truly understood the limitations of the life he was offering her.

Chapter 19

Greta headed downstairs, her heart pounding. Had she really just done that—proposed to a man and had him accept her? She might have a reputation for being outspoken, but she'd never been quite that bold before.

Strange to think she'd gone up there as a single woman and she was descending as an engaged woman. He'd been right when he said this wasn't how she'd imagined her engagement going, but she wasn't going to let that aspect get her down.

This bargain she'd made would serve her well.

She was certain that Noah wouldn't try to change her. And in return she would make the best *fraa* for him that she possibly could. And the thought of being a *mamm* to Anna and David warmed her heart.

She was getting married—even now she was having trouble getting it to sink in.

But it was definitely real and she needed to stop mooning over what her future might hold and get practical. There was so much to do.

* * *

"Goodness, Greta, settle down. You're making me nervous with all your fluttering." Martha sat on the sofa, reading the latest copy of *Family Life*.

"Now Martha, be patient with her." Hannah, who was knitting, cast Greta an arch look. "I do believe our *shveshtah* is being courted."

"By Noah Stoll?" Martha stared at Greta in surprise. Then she leaned back and gave her a speculative smile. "Well now, isn't that interesting. I always figured it would be his *bruder* who would show an interest."

Greta cast a quick glance across the room to where *Daed* sat in his recliner, a copy of *The Budget* in his hands and the Bible on a table next to him. Satisfied he wasn't paying them any attention, she tried to ignore her *shveshtra* and their conjectures and instead focus on the important events to come.

Noah had spoken to the bishop Friday evening as he'd promised. He'd received permission to marry right away rather than waiting until November as was traditional. The bishop would publish their intentions next Sunday, and after that it would depend on how quickly they could pull everything together.

Now it was Sunday, Maisie's birthday, and she was waiting for Noah to arrive.

Skip's barking brought her to the window and sure enough, Noah's buggy was coming down the drive. She turned to Martha and Hannah. "If you don't mind waiting in the kitchen a few minutes, Noah and I would like to speak to *Daed* alone."

She ignored their wide-eyed looks, as well as the knowing glances they exchanged as she hurried to open the door and greet the object of their speculation.

Noah had told her yesterday that he'd drop off Anna and David with Maisie at his *mamm*'s house before coming to get her.

A few minutes later she was escorting him into the living room to speak to her *daed*.

After the two men exchanged greetings, Noah got right to the point. "Isaac, it's my pleasure to tell you that Greta has agreed to be my *fraa*."

Hearing him phrase it that way made her pulse flutter.

Her *daed* looked from one to the other of them, his surprise evident. "I wasn't aware that the two of you were courting."

"Noah and I have been spending a lot of time together these past few weeks," Greta said diplomatically. "We've formed a real attachment to each other, and since Noah's little ones need a *mamm* now, we've decided to get married right away."

Her *daed* stroked his beard. "I see." He met and held her gaze. "And this is what you want, Greta?"

"Very much."

He turned to Noah. "And you promise to provide well for my *dochder*."

"You have my word."

Her *daed* gave a decisive nod. "Then you have my blessing."

Greta leaned over and gave him a hug. "*Danke*."

Then she turned to Noah. "We'd better go tell Martha and Hannah before they burst with curiosity."

It took another ten minutes before they could extricate themselves from her *shveshtra*'s presence, but at last she and Noah were in his buggy, headed to his *mamm*'s home.

"I'm pleased that your family received the news so well."

Did he think they wouldn't? "I think Martha is actually excited to have a wedding to plan. She views it as a challenge to her homemaker skills."

"Your older *shveshtah* is a good cook and homemaker." His tone was strongly approving.

Best to make sure he had realistic expectations. "I should probably confess right now that while I'm adequate in the kitchen I don't live up to Martha's standard."

He smiled. "I'm sure you'll do quite well for us."

Noah noted how nervous Greta looked, fiddling with the wrapping on the gift she'd brought for Maisie. He put a hand over hers, halting her movements. "There's no need to worry. Everyone in my family likes you already. They'll be very pleased to have you join us."

She smiled, her expression grateful, but he could tell she was still nervous. Why would someone as brave as Greta worry about her reception?

Did this have something to do with Calvin?

Looking to distract her, he reached for something to talk about. "Have you given any more thought on a sitter for Anna and David?"

"*Jah*. I actually have two names for you to consider.

One is Eva Wagler, Andrew and Dorothy's niece. She's eighteen, has three younger siblings and is very conscientious."

Noah pulled up a vague image of the girl she was talking about—a tall girl with a serious demeanor.

"The other name is Naomi Petersheim. She's Mary and Leo's *dochder*, is fifteen years old and is looking for work to bring money into the family."

Noah nodded. Leo Petersheim had lost an arm in an accident three years ago and could no longer run his farrier business.

"I'd like to help the Petersheim family," he said slowly, "but fifteen seems young."

She gave him a challenging look. "You do realize Maisie just turned sixteen today and she's been watching Anna and David for over a year."

"Yes, but—"

"And the sitter will be right there in the mall where both you and I can check on her whenever we want to."

Noah accepted the logic of what she was saying, even if he still had reservations. "You're right, of course. But I was very familiar with Maisie and her capabilities. I can't say the same about Naomi." He cut her a probing look. "Do you really think she's capable of watching over them?"

"I wouldn't have mentioned her name if I didn't."

After a moment he nodded. "I trust your judgment. I think we should give Naomi a chance."

He was rewarded with a bright smile. He was growing quite fond of that dimple.

"*Gut*," she said. "I can speak to her this evening, unless you would prefer to do it yourself."

"Why don't you handle it?"

A few moments later they arrived at his *mamm*'s home and her smile dimmed and that worried look returned.

Greta stepped out of the buggy and took a deep breath as she faced the house. Part of her—the cowardly part—wished she had stayed with Noah as he parked the buggy and cared for his horse.

But he'd let her know not once but twice that he had faith in her, and that gave her the courage to shake off her hesitation and move to the house. Before she reached the door it was opened by Maisie, who greeted her with a smile.

"*Wilkom*, Greta. *Danke* for joining us to celebrate my birthday."

"It's my pleasure."

Maisie drew her into the house, where she was soon surrounded by Noah's family. Even his sister Faith and her husband Bryan and their new baby were there.

Greta felt suddenly shy as Noah finally joined them and stepped up beside her. As soon as there was a break in the conversation, he cleared his throat, claiming everyone's attention.

"Greta and I arrived early so we could speak to you before the other guests arrived." He took her hand and gave her a reassuring smile before turning back to his family. "We are engaged and plan to be married in the next few weeks."

There were general exclamations of surprise and congratulations.

Debra stood, with effort, and waved Greta to her. "I'm very pleased to welcome you to our family. I know you'll be good for my son and his *kinner*."

"I'll certainly do my best." Debra's genuinely warm reaction went a long way to setting her at ease.

Maisie came up next, a broad smile on her face. "This is *wunderbaar*!" She hugged Greta, then looked past her to Noah. "I didn't realize this is what you meant when you told me you had matters in hand. I know now that I'll be leaving the three of you in *gut* hands." She gave Greta's hands a squeeze. "It'll be nice to have you as a *shveshtah*."

Calvin shook his *bruder*'s hand, but Greta noticed his smile was merely lukewarm. Was he still upset over his supposed feelings for her? If so, she'd have to do what she could to set him straight as soon as possible.

Before she had a chance to speak to Calvin alone, however, Esther, her *mamm* and her younger *shveshtah* Bethany arrived. As soon as she heard the news, Esther rushed forward and gave Greta a hug. "*Ach*, I am so happy for you. You and Noah will be *gut* for each other."

"*Danke*. And I hope you'll be one of my attendants."

"Of course." She squeezed Greta's hand. "I know Noah was in a hurry. Have you decided when the marriage will take place?"

"It depends on how quickly we can pull everything together, but our hope is that it can take place within the next three or four weeks."

"*Ach*, that's not much time."

"Noah has already gotten permission from the bishop, and if anyone can pull everything together in that amount of time, it's Martha."

Esther dropped her hands. "I have to ask—will you

be giving up your work at the quilt shop now that you'll have a home and family to care for?"

"*Nee*, not altogether anyway. I've already discussed that with Noah. I'd like to work four or five hours a day, rather than the seven I do now."

"And who will be watching Anna and David while you're working?"

Greta explained about the sitter and the loft room. When Esther started to ask questions about wedding preparations, Greta laughed. "We'll have time to speak about all of that soon. But right now we're here to celebrate Maisie's birthday, ain't so?" And linking arms with her friend, she steered her back toward the main gathering.

Later, Greta managed to catch Maisie alone for a moment. "Anna and David are very happy, well-behaved *kinner*, and Noah said he has you to thank for that."

Maisie's cheeks pinkened at the compliment. "*Danke*."

"If I'm going to try to fill your shoes, I'd appreciate anything you can tell me about their routine, their likes and dislikes and anything else I need to be aware of."

"Let's see, I let them sleep most mornings until they wake up on their own, which is usually around seven thirty. David doesn't like to take naps, but if you'll settle him down with a story or lullaby he'll drift off eventually. And speaking of naps, I usually put them down right after lunch, and once they fall asleep they're good for an hour or so."

She brushed absently at her sleeve. "Anna is terrified of spiders. And she takes her cues from David. If David decides he likes or doesn't like something, she'll follow suit."

"That's good to know." She hoped she could do as good a job with them as Maisie had. "I'll be watching them at Noah's home tomorrow. Can you tell me what to expect?"

Maisie smiled. "I can do better than that. I'll spend one more night at Noah's tonight so I'll be there in the morning when you arrive. I'll stay a couple of hours, long enough to help you get the lay of the land and answer whatever questions you have."

"*Ach*, that's so generous of you, but I couldn't ask—"

"You're not asking, I offered." She waved a hand dismissively. "It's just one more night and I'll be back here to help *Mamm* before lunchtime tomorrow." And with another smile Maisie turned to greet some late arrivals.

Greta had to admit she was relieved to be able to ease into her new role with some hands-on help from Maisie. She looked around for Noah, but her gaze snagged on Calvin first.

And he seemed to be heading right for her with a very purposeful stride.

She smiled as he approached, though she kept her guard up. "Hello, Calvin. Isn't it nice that we'll soon be *bruder* and *shveshtah*?"

He nodded, but immediately changed the subject. "First I want to apologize for the other day by the schoolhouse. I realize now that Wanda is truly the girl for me. Approaching you that way was wrong, and just a temporary lapse on my part. I want you to know it won't happen again."

Some of her tension eased. "I'm glad. And you can count on my discretion. Wanda won't hear about any of it from me."

"*Danke*." Then he gave her a probing look. "I must say, Noah's announcement came as a surprise."

She nodded, glancing down as she brushed at her skirt. He had reason for his skepticism since she'd repeatedly told him there was nothing going on between her and Noah. "It all happened very suddenly."

"So it seems." Then he rubbed the back of his neck. "I'm worried about you."

What now? "Why?"

"I don't know how Noah convinced you to marry him, but you need to understand that he doesn't love you. I'm sorry to be blunt, but I care too much about you to sit back and say nothing. You need to know he's just using you."

She stiffened. This again. "How can you say such a thing?"

"Because Noah's not really capable of loving anyone or anything. It's just not in him."

"*Ach*, Calvin, he's your own *bruder*. You can't believe that of him."

But Calvin wasn't backing down. "It's true. I take no joy from this, but you have to remember I grew up with him."

Greta refused to let his words go unchallenged. "I don't know how Noah was as a *bruder*, but I do know who he is as a man, and you're wrong. Noah's not only capable of loving, but when he loves he loves deeply."

"I love and respect my older *bruder*, but I know his faults. I find it hard to believe he's made any declarations to you about—"

She wouldn't let him finish that statement. "What has

been said between your *bruder* and me is just that—
between him and me." She lifted her chin. "Noah is
a man of integrity and honor and he deserves your
support." And with that she turned on her heel and
walked away.

Chapter 20

Her *shveshtra* and *daed* were waiting for her when she returned home.

Hannah rushed over and embraced her. "It wasn't fair of you to deliver your news and then run off." Her light, happy tone held a teasing note.

Greta laughed. "We needed to tell his family too."

Hannah drew her by the hand to the sofa. "So come sit down and tell us all about it. How long have the two of you been courting? What plans have you made?"

She'd already thought out how she would answer that first question. "We haven't been dating very long at all, but we both knew within a short time that we were right for each other."

"Still, why the hurry?" Martha asked. Her tone was a bit less cheerful than Hannah's.

"Noah needs help with his *kinner*," she answered. "So we didn't see any need to draw this out."

Martha nodded solemnly. "*Kinner* need a *mamm*." Then she folded her hands in her lap. "So how much time do we actually have to plan this wedding?"

"That's a good question. We want to get married as soon as possible, of course, but I know it takes time to plan a wedding and I'm going to have to rely heavily on you. So, do you think it can be done in three or four weeks?"

"*Ach*, that's not much time at all."

At least that wasn't a no.

"Everyone will pitch in to help," Hannah interjected. "I'm sure *Aenti* Ruthanne will assist, as will *Aenti* Hilda."

"And every other aenti." Greta faced her older *shveshtah*. "But they'll be looking to someone for direction. Can I count on you for that?"

"February isn't a month where we can seat our guests under a tent." Martha turned to their *daed*. "We'll need the buggy shed and equipment barn for that week."

"*Jah*, we must do this right."

Martha nodded and Greta could see her mentally check one item off her list. "Since the quilt shop is closed tomorrow, we can spend some time planning everything."

"Actually, I told Noah I'd spend the day at his house watching his *kinner*."

Martha's lips thinned, but she nodded her acceptance. "Then we'll have to make do with whatever time you have before and after your work at the store this coming week."

"Again, I'll be watching his *kinner* while he works."

Martha's irritated look intensified. "Hannah and I will

do what we can to prepare for your wedding, but you'll need to do your part as well."

"*Jah*, of course." It appeared she wouldn't be getting much sleep between now and the wedding.

Hannah, ever the peacemaker, came to her rescue. "We can begin working on a list of what decisions need to be made and tasks that need to be accomplished. I'm sure there are things you can work on while you watch the little ones."

"And I can take care of making my wedding dress during slow times at the shop."

She turned to her *daed*. She knew the cost of things was always a concern for him. "We'll try to keep this as inexpensive as possible."

"There's no need to be concerned as long as you're reasonable. I have money put aside for the weddings of my *dechder*. After all, I can't have our family and friends think I'm stingy."

Was that his only reason? "*Danke*. I'll make sure we plan responsibly."

Her *daed* nodded, then chuckled. "Who would have thought that you would be the first of my *dechder* to get married."

Greta tried to swallow the hurt his words and tone inflicted. Then she realized her *daed*'s gaze had moved from her to Martha, and her own hurt took a back seat.

Martha had given up so much to take over as lady of the house after *Mamm* died. True, *Aenti* Hilda had stayed with them for the first six months, but even then Martha was preparing to take over, cutting her rumspringa short and getting baptized. She never allowed herself time to date, to attend the singings, to have any kind of fun normal for a *youngie*.

Even though she'd done all of this willingly and without complaint, it couldn't be easy to see her younger *shveshtah* get married first, and to know their *daed* had never displayed proper appreciation for her sacrifices.

Had she herself ever done so? And now Martha was taking on the burden of planning the wedding.

Greta leaned forward and touched Martha's hand. "It is truly good of you to step up to take this on. *Danke* for this and all the other times you quietly took care of what needed to be done. There's no one I'd trust with my wedding more than you."

Martha's eyes widened in surprise, then red splotches bloomed on her face. She gave a short nod as if not trusting her voice.

Had they taken Martha so much for granted that a simple thank-you could touch her that way?

She made a silent vow to remember this and to do better in the future.

* * *

"*Gut matin*." Maisie stepped outside as Greta pulled her horse up to Noah's house. "Noah left early this morning, said he had a lot to get done. I hope you don't mind tending to your own horse."

With a nod, Greta directed Velvet toward the stable. Twenty minutes later she was at the kitchen door.

Maisie stepped aside and waved Greta into the house. "*Wilkom*. Come on inside and get warm."

Greta stepped into the kitchen. "I wish Noah had said something yesterday about leaving early, I'd have tried to get here before he left."

Maisie smiled. "The two of you will work things out over time. Have you had breakfast yet?"

Greta looked around as she removed her coat. "*Jah*. But I wouldn't turn down a cup of that coffee I can smell."

Maisie nodded and went to a cupboard to fetch a cup.

"You have a very cozy kitchen here," Greta said as she hung her outer garb on a coat hook by the door. "Noah's been lucky to have you here to help him."

"*Danke*. But it's been my pleasure to help him and the little ones. I'll be sad to give this up."

Interesting. "So you're not eager to explore your rumspringa?"

"Of course. But I'll be giving up some freedoms as well."

Greta accepted the cup from Maisie and the two took seats at the table. "How so?"

Maisie waved a hand. "Here I was able to run the household as I saw fit, to prepare the meals I liked and set the schedule for chores as if this was my own household."

Greta nodded in understanding. "And once you move back home, you'll once again be the dutiful *dochder*, helping your *mamm* run her household."

Maisie gave a soft sigh. "But that's as it should be, I suppose, until I marry and have a home of my own. And *Mamm* needs me so I'll be there to help her and help care for her."

Maisie was a very mature young lady.

She took a final sip from her cup. "Where are Anna and David?"

"They're playing in the living room. I'll take you there in a minute. I thought I'd show you around the house first."

Greta stood. "Lead the way."

Maisie opened a door near the pantry that revealed cellar stairs. As she led the way down she continued talking over her shoulder. "If I understood what Noah told me last night, until the two of you marry you'll watch the children here on Mondays, he'll have them on his own on Sundays, and the rest of the week they'll be at the mall with you or a sitter."

Greta nodded. "*Jah*, that's the schedule we discussed. I know it's not ideal, but it's just for the month or so until we get married."

"Then I assume you'll want to do a thorough job of cleaning and laundry on the one day you're here." Maisie had reached the bottom of the stairs by this point. "There's a wringer washer down here and a set of clotheslines across the south end."

Greta nodded approval. It was a similar setup to what they had at the Eicher home.

Maisie pointed to a set of shelves lined up near the stairs. "Over here are all the jars of fruits, jellies, jams and vegetables that were put up last summer and fall."

"They're very well stocked." Greta gave Maisie an appreciative smile. "I see I'll have some big shoes to fill."

Maisie's cheeks pinkened in pleasure. "*Danke*." Then she moved back to the stairs. "Come. We can gather up the laundry while I show you the other rooms."

Maisie led the way into the living room, where David

and Anna sat on the floor, playing with a set of building blocks.

Anna spied her first. "Greta," she squealed as she pushed herself up from the floor and came running toward her, arms up in an obvious request to be lifted.

Greta complied, scooping her up and giving her a big hug.

"Story," the little girl demanded.

David merely looked up and greeted her with a smile. "I'm building a barn," he announced.

"I see that. It looks like a wonderful *gut* barn."

"Story," Anna said again, this time more forcefully.

"Right now your *Aenti* Maisie and I are going to gather up the laundry, but I promise to tell you a story a little later."

She looked around the room, studying the furnishings. "What a beautiful rocking chair."

"Noah made it." Maisie waved to the other side of the room. "He also made those two small tables and that bookcase."

It made sense that he would furnish his home with the labors of his hands.

"If you're ready, I'll show you the rest of the house."

Greta nodded and set Anna down, repeating her promise to tell her a story later, then followed Maisie from the room.

"You can start with the bed linens in Noah's room." Maisie pointed to a door to the left of the stairway. "I'll gather the laundry items from the *kinner*'s room."

With a nod, Greta moved to the door Maisie had pointed toward. She hesitated a moment before opening it—this felt almost like an invasion. Giving her head a mental shake, she pushed open the door and stepped over the threshold. She glanced around Noah's room as she gathered his bed linens, eager to learn what she could about her future husband.

The room was scrupulously neat and very masculine, right down to the stack of Zane Grey and Louis L'Amour volumes between the bookends on his dresser.

There were no touches of Patsy left in here that she could see.

She'd soon be sharing this room with her husband—the thought brought the heat to her cheeks. Then she paused. Would she be sharing this room? After all, he'd made it quite clear this was a businesslike arrangement. What were his expectations for their sleeping arrangements? Did he want additional *kinner*? She truly loved Anna and David, but she'd like to fill this house with little ones.

She couldn't believe he wouldn't want any more *kinner*. But what if he didn't, what if that was included in his definition of a businesslike marriage? Could she live with that?

As awkward as it would be to initiate a conversation on that topic, it was something they should definitely discuss before the wedding.

Chapter 21

Greta sat on the floor with Anna and David, playing a game she'd made up for them. Taking fabric scraps cut in simple shapes like squares, rectangles, diamonds and triangles, she was having them lay them out on the floor to design new quilt patterns.

"This one!" Anna said, handing her a bright yellow triangle.

"Lovely." Greta accepted the piece and then looked over the design-in-progress. She placed it next to a blue triangle, forming a square. "I think it would look nice right here, ain't so?"

Anna nodded enthusiastically. "Pretty!"

David, who was busy making a design of his own, set a red square down, forming a large finished rectangle. "Do you like mine?" he asked.

Greta nodded in approval. "That's perfect, David."

Then she studied the two large rectangles they'd

formed. "You two are wonderful *gut* quilt designers. I'm not sure which one I like better."

Anna clapped her hands. "Again!"

"What have we here?"

Greta looked up to see Noah, leaning against the doorjamb with an amused smile on his face.

"*Daed!*" David popped up and ran over to Noah. "We're designing quilt patterns for Greta." He tugged on his hand. "Want to see?"

"I certainly do." Noah allowed his son to lead him to where their handiwork was displayed.

Greta had taken out a roll of tape and was connecting the colorful pieces they'd grouped together in totally random designs. She glanced up at him as she tore off another length of tape. "You never told me these two were such great designers. Didn't they do a *gut* job?"

Noah stooped down next to her, examining the two makeshift rectangles with a critical eye. "Are you telling me these two monkeys created these great pieces?"

Greta smiled at his seemingly astonished demeanor. No wonder his *kinner* loved him so much. "*Jah.* They're beautiful, ain't so?" She finished taping Anna's patches and moved on to David's.

"Did you want to make one, *Daed?*" David asked. "It's fun, like making a puzzle."

"Fun," Anna agreed as she tried to climb up on Noah's knee.

"Perhaps another time," Noah said as he stood. "Greta needs to be heading on home before it gets too late."

Greta carefully folded the fabric creations, slipped them into her tote and accepted Noah's hand as she stood.

Noah released her hand and looked down at Anna and David. "Pick up your things while I walk Greta out."

As they entered the kitchen, Noah inhaled appreciatively. "Something smells *gut* in here."

"It's just a vegetable soup." Maisie had left the cooking, including the decision of what to cook, up to her.

"Soup's a nourishing meal, especially on cold evenings."

She appreciated that he was being encouraging. She just wished it didn't sound so stilted. Did he feel it too, this feeling that this was a dress rehearsal for how their life together would be after the wedding?

Trying to shake that off, she lifted her coat from the hook by the door. "Anna and David already ate. There's plenty left, simmering on the stove for you."

"*Danke*." He gave her a curious smile. "How was your day? Were you able to find everything you needed?"

"*Jah*. Maisie was very helpful, showing me around and filling me in on Anna and David's routines. After she left, David was able to help with the few questions I still had."

His smile warmed. "David likes to be helpful."

She nodded. "I do have a question for you. I saw a large loom and several skeins of yarn in the sewing room. Was that Patsy's or is it Maisie's?"

"It was Patsy's."

She'd figured as much. "I never knew she was a weaver."

"Do you weave?"

"No, but I'd like to learn."

He frowned. "I assure you, just because Patsy worked with a loom, I have no expectation that you—"

She held a hand up. "*Nee*, that's not why. I'm just thinking Anna might want to follow in her *mamm*'s footsteps someday and I want to be ready to teach her."

Noah realized Greta had managed to surprise him once again. "That's thoughtful of you."

Greta shrugged. "Anna deserves to feel a connection to her *mamm*, even if she never had a chance to know her." She reached for her bonnet. "I suppose I should go now."

"I've already hitched Velvet to your buggy." Noah helped her into her coat, fighting the urge to stroke the back of her neck. Clearing his throat, he took a step back. "I'll pick you up in the morning on my way to work."

She nodded as she tied the strings of her bonnet. "I'll be ready. Is there anything I should bring?"

"I have the furnishings set up in the loft room. But if you could bring meals..."

"Of course." She wound her scarf around her neck. "I told Naomi to come a little early tomorrow since it's her first day with the *kinner*. It'll give me a chance to answer any of her questions and give her instructions."

Once she'd gone, Noah looked around his kitchen. It had been strange seeing her here, at home in his kitchen. Strange, but at the same time right. He could already picture how it would be to come home every evening to her smiling presence.

And it was a picture he liked.

* * *

Tuesday morning, Noah picked Greta up on his way to work just as he'd promised. After she climbed into the buggy, she lifted a still drowsy Anna onto her lap and allowed David, who sat between her and Noah, to lean his head against her side.

Family. This was her family now. She allowed that thought to fill her and warm her to the core. She knew Noah had said he wasn't looking for a love match, but there was nothing that said she couldn't lavish her love on these two little ones.

When they arrived at the mall, Noah climbed down first and took Anna from her. "I'll help you get settled in upstairs then come back and tend to Jericho and the buggy."

They entered the mall through the workshop and Noah turned on the lights and raised the thermostat as they passed through.

Greta preceded him up the stairs and into the room that would now serve as a nursery. Then she paused, looking around at the changes he'd made.

"So, what do you think?" he asked. Was there the tiniest trace of smugness in his tone?

If so, he'd earned it. Everywhere she looked there was something new to delight her. Two small pallet beds were tucked into the far corner. A rod stretched just below the ceiling from wall to wall and held a curtain that, when unfurled, would cordon off the sleeping corner nicely. A sturdy worktable was built into the wall to her right with two adult-sized chairs tucked neatly under it.

A cupboard with cabinets on the bottom and open shelves on the top was set against the wall to the left of the sleeping area. There was even a small wastebasket and set of wall hooks nearby.

"I think you did a wonderful *gut* job. It's everything we discussed and more."

Noah seemed pleased by her response.

Then she noticed something odd on top of the cupboard. "What's that?"

"It's an air horn."

"Air horn?" What an odd item to include in a nursery.

But Noah was smiling. "It occurred to me that if there's any sort of emergency up here, it might be difficult for Naomi to get anyone's attention. This gives her a way."

"How clever! It seems you've thought of everything."

He shrugged away her compliment and changed the subject. "I know you want to work on your quilting as you can, so if you have a quilt frame you want to use up here, let me know and I'll have it brought up."

"That won't be necessary just yet. I'm working on piecing the top for my latest project, not the actual quilting. That'll come later."

"Is there anything else you need?"

"I'm sure other things will come up as we move forward, but I think this is a good start." Then she grinned as David yawned. "Perhaps we should let these two sleepyheads try out their pallets."

After they tucked Anna and David in, Greta motioned for Noah to join her near the door. "Do you have any rules for your *kinner* I should be aware of, something you'd like me to pass on to Naomi? For instance, is it all right if she takes them outside when the weather allows, or would you prefer they stay indoors all the time?"

He rubbed his jaw as he took a moment to think about

it. "I would prefer Naomi keep them up here, at least for now. When you're with them, though, I trust you to do what you think best."

Greta considered those words, and the sentiment they conveyed, to be a precious gift.

He straightened. "If you're settled in okay, I'll go down now and take care of Jericho and the buggy."

"Of course. We'll be fine." Then she remembered something. "Actually, if you don't mind waiting up here for a few minutes, I have something in the quilt shop I need to fetch."

"Of course."

Greta hurried down to the Stitched Heart and headed straight for the back. Last Saturday she'd brought over a braided rug from home. It was one she'd made several years ago, intending for it to be something she brought with her when she had a home of her own. But now she'd decided the nursery room would be a good place for it.

It was large and bulky, even when rolled up, but she hefted it up on her shoulder and stepped back in the mall lobby, locking the door behind her. It was only when she headed for the stairs that she wondered if she'd be able to carry it up to the loft on her own.

But she needn't have worried. Noah had been watching her from the loft.

"Hold a minute," he called down. "Leave it and come stay with the *kinner*. I'll bring it up for you."

With a nod she set her burden down on one of the mall benches and headed upstairs.

"What do we have here?" he asked as he returned to the nursery with his burden.

"A rug. I thought it would be nice to put it in here

so Anna and David would have something nice to sit on when they played on the floor."

Noah gave her an approving smile. "Very thoughtful." He set it down and unrolled it near the toy bin. He studied the floor covering, then met her gaze. "Did you make this?"

She nodded.

"It's nice, very colorful. It brightens up the whole room."

"It was for my hope chest." She shrugged self-consciously. "I figured this room will be an extension of our home."

He smiled at that and touched her arm briefly. Then he straightened. "I'd best get back downstairs and tend to Jericho and the buggy."

Once Noah made his exit, Greta looked around, taking it all in more slowly this time. It gave her a happy, just-want-to-hug-yourself kind of feeling. He really had done an amazing job, especially given his time constraints. And the fact that he'd let her have a small part in setting this up made her even happier.

Anna and David slept for nearly an hour, giving Greta plenty of time to explore the room in more detail, opening cabinets and digging through bins.

Once she'd explored to her fill, she set her tote bag on the worktable and pulled out her pattern pieces.

* * *

"Anna, David, this is Naomi, she's the lady I told you about who'll be staying with you."

Anna pasted herself against Greta's side, grabbing

her skirt with one hand and sticking her thumb in her mouth with the other. David wasn't so bashful, but still held back.

Greta resisted the urge to intervene, waiting to see how Naomi would handle things.

Naomi placed her bag on the table and pulled out a stack of very colorful books and held them out. "Would either of you like to look through these? They have some wonderful *gut* pictures in them."

David nodded and accepted the books from her. Then he turned to his *shveshtah.* "Come on, Anna." Within a few seconds the pair were seated on the floor looking through the books.

Greta showed Naomi where the spare linens and clothing were stored. Then she waved toward the cooler. "I've put the fixings for sandwiches in there, and you'll find some cookies in a bag in the cupboard." She met Naomi's gaze. "Do you have any questions?"

Naomi shook her head. "I have six nieces and nephews, several of them Anna and David's ages. We'll be fine."

"I'm right downstairs if you need anything. Oh, and Noah set an air horn up there for emergencies."

"We'll be fine," Naomi repeated.

With another mention that it was okay to fetch her if she should need help, Greta headed back downstairs.

She arrived at the quilt shop just as Esther was unlocking the door.

Once they were both inside, Esther gave her an eager smile. "We haven't really had a moment alone since you and Noah announced your engagement Sunday."

"I know. I've been busy."

"I imagine that's an understatement." Then she traced

a finger along the counter. "You can tell me this is none of my business but I have to ask. Does this mean Noah decided he wanted something more than the businesslike arrangement he started out asking for?"

Greta considered telling her friend the same as she'd told Calvin—that that was between her and Noah. But that in itself was an answer. "*Nee*. He and I are both agreed that this is the best arrangement for the two of us."

Esther's smile fell. "*Ach*, Greta, I know Noah wants to keep emotions out of it, and that's his business. But I know you, and I know this isn't the kind of marriage you really want."

Greta didn't bother denying it. Instead she did her best to explain. "But I do want a marriage and it looks like this is the only one I'm likely to have. Besides, I like Noah and his *kinner*, and I believe they like me too. Lots of marriages have been built on less."

Esther's sympathetic gaze was almost more than she could bear. She turned away, ostensibly to straighten a display of spools.

"Well, enough of that." Esther's brisk tone signaled she had read her mood. "How is your planning going? Have you selected your other attendants yet?"

Grateful for the change of subject, Greta smiled brightly. "Yes, Maisie, Rachel and Wanda. Maisie and Wanda are coming by tomorrow so we can pick out the fabric for your dresses." She'd spoken to Rachel using the cell phone in Noah's office this morning. Her friend had been delighted to be asked to serve as one of Greta's *newehocker*s. And though she couldn't join them tomorrow, she'd assured Greta she'd be happy with whatever fabric they picked out.

"Do you know what you want for your wedding dress?"

Greta nodded and went straight to a bolt of deep blue polished cotton fabric. It was her favorite color and she loved the soft feel of the cloth.

Later that day, when it came time to relieve Naomi, Greta was more than ready. She'd been very tempted to go upstairs and check on things at lunchtime, but she decided it would be best to let Naomi have her space. Before she headed upstairs, she made a detour through Noah's showroom. "Hello, Reuben, is Noah in the workshop?"

"*Jah*. Is there something I can help you with?"

"*Nee*. If it's okay I'll just step inside and have a quick word with him."

Reuben's brow furrowed uncertainly. "Noah doesn't like to have non-employees in the workshop," the youth said. "Too many sharp objects and chemicals lying around."

"He's taken me in there himself to show me the cats. And I just need a few minutes of his time, but if you prefer to check with him first..."

Reuben hesitated another moment, then nodded. He opened the adjoining door to the workshop. "Noah," he called out, "you have a visitor." Then he waved Greta through.

By the time Greta crossed the threshold, Noah had set aside his tools and stood. His look of inquiry turned to concern as soon as he recognized her. Not exactly the reaction she'd hoped for.

"What is it?" He moved quickly toward her. "Has something happened to Anna or David?"

"*Nee*," she said quickly. "Nothing like that."

He visibly relaxed as he closed the distance between them. "Then what can I do for you?"

"I want to borrow one of the kittens."

Noah's brows drew down in confusion. "Borrow a kitten? What for?"

"I thought Anna and David might like to have one for a playmate. If you think they're old enough to be handled."

Noah's expression cleared. "That's a *gut* idea. And *jah*, they should be old enough, as long as you keep an eye on the *kinner* to make sure they're gentle with it."

"Of course."

"Do you want to come pick one out?"

"Can I?"

With a wave of his hand, he led the way to the worktable where she'd first spotted the cats. Noah slid the box out and Greta saw all five kittens, but not the mother cat.

She knelt down beside the box. "Where's Sawdust?"

"Don't worry, she's around here somewhere. She never strays too far from her kittens." He stooped down and looked up at her. "Have you decided which one you want to bring upstairs?"

Greta was immediately drawn to one of the kittens, a curious, adventurous one that was climbing around on top of its siblings. She stooped down next to Noah and picked it up. "This one."

Noah stroked the feline's head with a forefinger. "Just out of curiosity, may I ask why this particular one?"

"This one seemed like it was eager to explore." Greta shrugged. "I figured it would react the best to being separated."

She thought he'd roll his eyes at that, but instead he nodded, then stood. "If you'll wait here just a minute, I'll find another crate and some rags you can use for bedding."

Greta set the kitten back in the crate and stood as well. "Actually, I need to relieve Naomi. Why don't you take care of that and bring the kitten upstairs when you're ready. I'm sure Anna and David would like to see you. If you can spare the time, that is."

"I think I can manage."

"Then I'll see you in a few minutes." And with a wave she headed for the exit.

Noah watched her leave and then turned to find a suitable crate. Greta was going to be a good influence on his *kinner*. She was thoughtful in how she approached their care, not only making sure they were safe and secure, but also finding ways to introduce fun into their lives.

He had the kitten's crate ready in short order and carefully transferred the animal to her makeshift carrier. He smiled as he remembered her explanation for why she'd picked this particular kitten. Had she identified with it?

He met Naomi at the foot of the stairs and paused to speak to her. "How was your first day?"

"Your *kinner* were very well behaved and didn't give me any trouble at all. We had a good time getting to know each other."

"That's *gut* to hear."

She peeked in the box he was carrying. "Oh, are you bringing that kitten upstairs? Anna and David will love playing with it."

"That's what we're hoping." And with a nod he headed upstairs.

Noah stepped inside the nursery, and as soon as Greta saw him her whole demeanor brightened. "And here is your *daed* bringing you two the surprise I promised you."

Anna and David ran up, clamoring to know what was in the crate.

Noah knelt and set the crate on the floor. "See for yourself."

"It's a kitten!" David knelt next to Noah. "Can I pick it up?"

"Let's give her time to get used to you first." He smiled at his son. "You can pet her, though, if you're gentle."

Both children stooped down, staring into the crate with rapt attention. David was the first to reach inside and pet the animal, but Anna copied him soon enough.

Her face split in a delighted grin. "Soft."

"What's its name?" David asked.

"She doesn't have a name yet." Noah kept a close eye, making sure neither of them got too rough.

"Naming an animal is a very important honor," Greta said. "Do you think you and Anna can come up with a name?"

David nodded solemnly. "It's a girl cat so we need a girl name." He turned to Anna. "She's mostly yellow. How about Lemon Drop?"

Anna nodded enthusiastically. "Lemon Drop!"

"I think that's the perfect name for her."

Noah stood. "I need to get back to work. Remember, be gentle with her, she's still just a baby."

Both children nodded, though their attention remained focused on the kitten.

* * *

It was nearing seven o'clock and the mall shops were closed when Noah finally came upstairs to fetch them. "I'm sorry for the late hour," he said before Greta could so much as greet him. "I'm trying to get as much accomplished as I can while Paul is still here, and I can't ask my men to stay late if I don't stay with them."

"I understand." She put away the quilted place mat she'd been working on while Anna and David played with their building blocks. How could she tell him all the work she had on her plate when he was under such pressure? "I take it this means you haven't found a replacement for Paul yet."

He shook his head, and though his expression remained calm, she could tell he was troubled.

"Not yet. But Paul did say he'd check with his *onkel* in Sugarcreek to see if there's anyone there who has the right skills and who'd be willing to move here. He sent the letter Saturday."

"Then perhaps you'll have some good news soon."

Rather than respond, he straightened. "I've already hitched Jericho to the buggy." Then he turned to his *kinner*. "It's time to go. Let's gather up everything."

Greta scooped up Lemon Drop and wrapped her in a towel before setting the kitten gently in her sewing bag. That would keep her hands free so she could help Noah get the children down the stairs.

As they headed out, the children chattered about Lemon Drop and Naomi and her books.

All in all, it sounded like the day had been a success.

* * *

Wednesday passed in similar fashion. Noah picked Greta up in the morning and she stayed with Anna and David until Naomi arrived. Then Greta went down to the quilt shop, where she split her free time between working on quilts for customers and her wedding dress.

Right after lunch, Maisie and Wanda came by, and after some discussion they settled on a light purple fabric for their dresses. Though it was tradition in their community for the bride to make the dresses for her *newehocker*s, at Esther's suggestion the ladies all agreed to make their own.

To her relief, Noah came to fetch her and his *kinner* around six o'clock that evening. Maybe she'd have time to sit down with Martha and Hannah when she got home and go over the wedding checklist to see how things stood.

As they headed down the stairs, she holding David's hand and Noah carrying Anna, she remembered something she'd meant to ask earlier. "Have you found a replacement for Paul yet?"

He shook his head. "*Nee*. But I figured I owed it to you to get you home at a decent hour."

She'd noted the shadows under his eyes earlier. Was he getting much sleep at all? "Has Paul heard from his *onkel* yet?"

Noah nodded, but his furrowed brow indicated it wasn't good news. "It doesn't look as if I'll be getting any help from that direction after all."

They'd reached the exit by then and she placed a hand lightly on his arm. Stoically ignoring the little spark that was becoming more common when they happened to touch, she pressed on. "I'm sorry. I know you were counting on that."

His gaze flickered briefly to her hand but he didn't pull away. "I just have to have faith that this will work out as it should."

She nodded, then took firmer hold of David's hand as they stepped out into the cold. A few minutes later they were settled snugly in the buggy with the doors closed.

She turned to Noah, eager to offer what she thought was a possible solution to his problem. "Something occurred to me last night. Have you given any thought to Gideon?"

He cut his gaze her way before focusing back on his horse. "Gideon Chupp? The man I apprenticed with?"

"*Jah*. If he taught you how to work with wood, then he must be very talented. And when you spoke of him it sounded as if you were *gut* friends."

Noah nodded. "He is and we are, at least we were back when I last worked with him." He smiled as if remembering that time. "He's an amazing craftsman. But he wouldn't be interested in working in a shop like mine."

Greta grimaced. "Sorry. I should have realized that you would've checked with him already." Another instance when her pride had gotten ahead of her.

But Noah was frowning. "Well, no, I haven't. But there's no need, I already know what he'll say."

Anna shifted on her lap and Greta adjusted her hold. "And just how would you know his answer if you didn't ask? Are you a mind reader?"

"He told me." He cut her a look and must have realized

he needed to elaborate. "Back when I apprenticed with him he said he preferred to work alone because that allowed him to take on whatever projects caught his interest and to pass on the ones that didn't."

She waved a hand, trying hard not to roll her eyes. "That was, what, a dozen years ago? Gideon may have changed his way of thinking by now. If not, maybe you could find a way to make both of you happy."

"What do you mean?"

If the *kinner* hadn't been around she might have been tempted to stamp her foot at him. "You need to start looking for solutions that are unconventional. Perhaps Gideon would be willing to come in a couple of days a week, or full-time for a few months, just to tide you over until you can find a permanent solution."

Noah stroked his beard. "I don't know..."

Why was he being so stubborn about this? "That's just it. You won't know until you ask."

"I'll think about it."

There was such a thing as being too analytical. "What is there to think about? After all, what can it hurt? The worst Gideon can do is refuse. And he might just agree."

Noah's face remained set in stubborn lines for another moment, then a crooked smile curved his lips. "You're right. I'll contact him tomorrow."

"*Gut*! And while we're exploring ideas—"

"Don't tell me—you've thought of yet another way to help me."

Was he actually teasing her? Smiling, she pushed ahead. "I don't know if you remember, but when I first mentioned Rachel to you I told you her *daed* is a cabinetmaker."

"I'd forgotten that, but *jah*."

"If you like, I can write to her and ask if her *daed* knows of anyone with the right skills who would be willing to move here. You can include a note with any particulars you're looking for if you like."

He nodded. "Another *gut* idea."

"Don't sound so surprised," she said in mock annoyance. "I do have those from time to time."

"I'm beginning to discover that for myself."

Pleased with his response and the approving look in his eye, she settled back against the buggy seat. Perhaps their marriage partnership would allow for more mutual appreciation than she'd first dared hope.

Noah was still smiling as he put Anna and David to bed that evening. Greta definitely wasn't one to let go of an idea easily. If it had been Patsy who'd made a suggestion that he brushed aside, she would have immediately let it drop. This tendency of Greta's to debate how best to approach a problem was an indication that his second marriage would be very different from his first.

And he found himself actually looking forward to the experience.

The next day, when eleven thirty rolled around, Noah looked at his lunch pail for a moment, then pushed it aside and headed across the mall lobby to the quilt shop. When he stepped inside he saw Greta at the counter serving an English customer who was paying for a purchase. Esther was with an Amish woman discussing what looked like fabric for a dress.

He waited until Greta's customer was finished and had walked away before he approached her.

"Hello," she greeted. "Is there something I can do for you?"

He liked the way her expression brightened when she spotted him. "I plan to walk down to Rosie's for lunch today and wondered if you'd like to join me." Rosie's was a small café across the highway from the mall. It was owned and operated by Norman and Rosalind Rodgers, an English couple who employed two Amish women as waitresses.

"*Jah*. Let me just let Esther know I'm taking first lunch today."

Ten minutes later they were stepping out of the mall into the brisk air. There had been a light dusting of snow the night before but the sunny morning had quickly turned what little had stuck to the ground to slush.

Noah took her arm, wanting to help her with her footing. And it was a good thing he did. As they were crossing the highway, her foot slid on a wayward patch of ice and she would have fallen hard if he hadn't had a firm grip on her arm.

She ended up tight against his side for a few moments, and it was just like when she tripped in the workshop. Her wide-eyed, startled gaze drew him in, and the urge to protect her, to pull her tighter to him, was almost overwhelming. Then someone blared a horn, bringing him back to himself.

"Are you okay?" he asked as he put more space between them without letting go of her arm.

She swallowed, nodded, and without another word they continued on their way.

By the time they entered Rosie's, Noah had himself back under control. They were greeted by Patience Lantz, the waitress, and she led them to a booth next to a window. They remained silent as Patience filled their water glasses and handed them each a menu.

Once she'd bustled off to seat another customer, Noah leaned back in his seat. Time to set things back on course. He met Greta's gaze with what he hoped was an easy smile. "You were right."

"About what?"

"Gideon has agreed to come to work for me four days a week starting on Monday."

She reached across the table and put her hands on his. "Oh, Noah, I'm so happy for you." She gave his hand a squeeze. "So that means he's starting before Paul even leaves. I know that's a relief."

Noah did his best to ignore the spark of awareness brought on by her hand touching his. That seemed to be happening to him a lot lately. Must be the lack of sleep making him so susceptible.

The reappearance of Patience interrupted them, and he wasn't sure if he was pleased or not. They quickly placed their orders—he ordered pot roast and she ordered chicken pot pie.

Trying to focus back on her words, he nodded. "Having him four days a week won't completely replace Paul, but it'll go a long way towards helping me keep up with the majority of my orders until I can find a more permanent solution."

"That may happen sooner rather than later. I sent the letter off to Rachel this morning. Perhaps we'll get some *gut* news from her as well."

He liked the way she said "we." Already she was acting like they were a family.

"Now that I have this commitment from Gideon, I have a little more time to focus on the wedding. Are there things you need me to take care of?"

"You're the one who's been through this before. Perhaps you can help me go over my list to make sure I've included everything."

"Of course. In fact, I think it would be *gut* for us to have lunch together every day—just the two of us. That way we can discuss the upcoming wedding and our plans for afterwards. And, since we bypassed the courting process, it'll give us an opportunity to get to know each other better before the wedding." He figured he owed her that much.

Greta smiled at his offer. "I'd like that." Both the chance to have lunch with him every day and the chance for them to get to know each other better. He'd meant it in the most platonic sense, she was sure. But it still made her happy to learn he wanted to know her better.

Then a sobering thought intruded. Once he got to know her better, would he begin to think less of her, the way her other suitors had?

Patience returned with their orders just then, giving her a chance to pull herself together. By the time she left them, the moment had passed. Noah already knew she was more forward than other ladies—if nothing else, the fact that she'd proposed to him would have driven that home.

Noah picked up his fork. "I thought I might start moving some of your things to my house. If there are items you won't need between now and the wedding, that is."

"*Jah*, of course. I'll start organizing my belongings so

I'll be ready for you whenever you want to stop by. And if you let me know ahead of time, I'll ask Amos to stay after the evening milking to help you."

After that, they focused on their meals, and the conversation was made up of mostly small talk about the weather and the *kinner*.

Truth to tell, Greta was having a little trouble concentrating. She was trying to gather her courage to speak to him about that sensitive matter she'd been putting off since Monday.

Finally, when the meal was over and they stepped out of the café, she decided it was time. "If you don't mind, I'd like to take the long way back to the mall."

"The long way?"

"Rather than going in the front entrance, perhaps we can walk around to the back." She looked down, pretending to avoid the patches of ice. "I have something of a delicate nature to discuss with you."

"Of course." To his credit he didn't press her for additional details. He took her elbow and slowed his steps, no doubt attempting to give her the additional time she asked for.

She took a deep breath, still not meeting his gaze. "I know we agreed that this marriage would be based on a businesslike arrangement."

Noah nodded but didn't respond otherwise.

"And I'm not asking to change that," she said quickly. "But I need to make sure I understand exactly what that means."

"It means just what we discussed—neither of us is to expect any warmer feelings than respect and friendship from the other." His words were clipped, matter-of-fact.

She mentally winced. That aspect of their arrangement was getting less palatable by the day. "I understand that part. But what I need to know is, does it also mean we won't be sharing a bedroom?" Even though her cheeks heated, she managed to look up and finally meet his gaze.

She saw the startled spark in his expression just before his guard went up. A moment later it was his turn to shift his gaze to some point ahead of them. He was silent for a long moment and she began to wonder if she'd gone too far this time.

Finally he spoke up. "It's my wish that we'll do so, but if you're uncomfortable with that, we can ease into it."

She let out a breath she wasn't aware she'd been holding. "That's not necessary." Her cheeks grew warmer as she realized how that had sounded. But she pressed on. "I just wanted to make sure I understood your expectations." She shifted her gaze again as they reached the mall door. "I would love to have some additional *kinner* to fill your house with."

Noah was surprised by the jolt of pure pleasure that surged through him at those shyly uttered words. The idea of a house full of little ones, with a *fraa* who would stand by his side and love them, was something he wanted with a sharp yearning that stabbed right through him.

But he had to keep his guard up, had to steel himself against the pull of what was, for him at least, a mirage.

Chapter 22

Noah stepped into the Eicher kitchen Sunday morning, stamping his boots on the mat. "Something smells *gut* in here."

Greta rewarded him with a pleased smile. "It's a pot roast with root vegetables. Martha shared *Mamm*'s recipe with me."

"I look forward to tasting it." This was the Sunday their marriage plans were to be published to the congregation at the church service. As was traditional, he and Greta were not attending the service. Instead Greta was cooking a lunch for the two of them. He'd dropped Anna and David off with Maisie and his *mamm* so he and Greta would have this special time alone.

"It'll be a little while before the food is ready."

There was that nervous undertone in her voice. He remembered she'd also sounded unsure when she'd cooked for him on Monday. And he realized he hadn't given her any feedback on that meal. He kept forgetting she wasn't as immune to criticism as she appeared. Time to be more supportive. "If it's as *gut* as that soup you cooked for us on Monday, then it'll be well worth the wait."

He was rewarded with a surprised but happy smile.

Looking for a safe topic to distract her, he decided the wedding would serve the purpose. "What's the latest on the wedding plans?"

"Martha's working on the menu and she plans to talk to our *aentis* after the church service today to recruit their help. And we're planning to use the buggy shed and equipment barn to seat our guests. They'll still have to eat in shifts, but we should be able to accommodate everyone."

"That sounds *gut*. Let me know when cleaning day is and I'll be here."

Greta nodded, then straightened. "While we're waiting for the food to be ready, why don't I show you what items of mine can be transferred to your house anytime you're ready and which ones should wait until I move in?"

"Lead the way."

Greta ushered him upstairs to her room. "My hope chest is there at the foot of my bed."

He glanced around her room, deciding it suited her. The quilt on the bed was a bold pattern of squares and triangles in shades of green, red and cream. There was a sketchbook and a mason jar of colored pencils on her bedside table. Her hope chest guarded the foot of her bed, and everything else was put away, hidden in the closet, dresser or chest. "Is there anything else from this room that you plan to bring with you?"

"Only my clothing and my books." She waved a hand

toward her bed. "And the quilt on my bed—it's one *Mamm* and I made together."

"That'll be easy enough. Anything else?"

"*Jah*. Follow me." She led him back downstairs and into her sewing room. Once they were inside she waved a hand. "Some of this will come with me when I move to your house."

"Some?"

"It depends. I saw that there was a sewing machine in the sewing room at your place, but I didn't see a quilt frame anywhere."

"*Nee*, Patsy didn't quilt. She preferred to focus on weaving."

Greta bit her lower lip thoughtfully. "I'll definitely need a quilting frame for my projects."

"If you want to leave this quilt frame behind for your *shveshtra*'s use, I can build you a new one."

"*Ach*, that would be *wunderbaar*. This frame was my *mamm*'s, and while neither Hannah nor Martha do much quilting, it should stay here in case they want to make use of it."

"That won't be a problem. I'll have it constructed and in place before the wedding." He was happy to be able to provide that for her.

"*Danke*."

Greta watched as he moved closer and studied the quilt currently stretched in the frame. She had finally finished piecing the top of her Promise Quilt yesterday and it was awaiting her quilting needle. She studied it right alongside him.

The sky and shards of sunlight fractured into a myriad of colors as it spilled down from the heavens and across the horizon. It was lovely, if she did say so herself, but she had a niggling feeling that something wasn't quite right, though she couldn't say what that something was. Proportion, colors, perspective all seemed right.

"I don't think I've ever seen this pattern before."

She couldn't tell from his tone what he thought of it. "That's because it's a new design."

"Well, you've done a *gut* job of bringing the design to life. I can almost feel the warmth of dawn's rays coming from it."

"*Danke*. It's actually my own design."

She saw something akin to respect in his gaze. "You designed this?"

She nodded. "I told you, I enjoy designing new patterns. Every bit as much as the quilting itself." She gazed back down at the quilt top. "But I have to admit, this is the most intricate one I've done to date. I call it my Promise Quilt."

He studied it again. "I can see that, the promise of a new day, ain't so?"

"Among other things."

"Is it for a customer?"

"*Nee*. This one is intended for my hope chest."

"*Gut*."

For some reason she felt her cheeks warm. Then it hit her what was missing from her quilt design—a personal touch. Like the hearts and homes her mother had added to her own quilt, this needed something to anchor what the quilt's promise meant to her. And that would require a bit of thought.

Turning, she quickly changed the subject. "These will go with me," she said, waving toward the quilt stands.

He moved closer to study them. "Did you make those quilts as well?"

"*Nee*. One is the wedding quilt *Mamm*'s friends made for her when she got engaged. The other is one she made herself for her hope chest."

She stroked the older quilt, wondering how her *mamm* would feel about this unorthodox marriage arrangement she was entering into.

"It appears that quilt means a great deal to you."

Greta nodded, surprised by his perceptiveness. "And not just because *Mamm* made it, though that alone would make it special to me." She smiled as the memories swirled around her. "When me and my *shveshtra* were little girls and something scared or troubled us, *Mamm* used to wrap all three of us up in that quilt and tell us silly stories. Sometimes we would play a game she made up—she'd describe one of the patches and then we'd try to be the first one to find it. Before long we forgot that we'd been afraid."

She gave it a final pat. "Nothing makes me feel closer to her than wrapping myself up in that faded quilt. It's as if she's wrapping me up in a big warm hug once more."

Then she shook her head and gave him a sheepish grin. "I suppose that sounds pretty silly."

But his gaze was warm rather than amused. "Not at all. It sounds like a nice memory."

Then, as if realizing he'd let down his guard, he straightened and changed the subject. "Do you want to wait until closer to the wedding to move these to my house?"

Greta hesitated. "Maybe we can wait and take this one when it's a little closer to our wedding date." She touched her throat self-consciously. "It's my most cherished possession and I admit it's hard to part with it. Again, I know it's silly, but as long as I have it nearby, I feel I have a bit of my *mamm* with me."

He touched her arm briefly. "Of course we can wait. Keep it with you as long as you want, until you move if you like."

Giving him a shy smile, she nodded and moved toward the door. "I'd better check on the food—I don't want to be serving a burnt roast."

Noah followed her from the room and in a matter of minutes they were seated at the table with Greta's meal before them.

Once they had offered thanks and served their plates, Greta cleared her throat. "I have a question for you, and you don't have to answer if you don't want to."

His lips quirked up at that. "That's always an option, ain't so?"

She returned his smile. "For sure and for certain." Then her smile faded and she pushed the food around on her plate with her fork. "Is there some sort of problem between you and Calvin?"

His expression sobered and he took a sip from his glass. "Why do you ask? Did Calvin say something?"

She decided not to answer that directly. "I sense a kind of tension when the two of you are together." The kind of tension she could sense in him now. "I'm not asking for the sake of gossip. I want to know because I'll be part of your family soon. And that means your joy is my joy and your pain is my pain."

He rubbed the side of his glass with his thumb for a moment, his expression thoughtful. "You're very observant."

"So there is something there."

He nodded, taking a bite of the roast.

She held her tongue, leaving it up to him to either explain or change the subject. To her relief, he decided to explain.

"When we were kids, Calvin used to follow me around like Anna does David. It was irritating at times, but I liked it too."

She smiled, picturing the two of them as little boys.

But Noah wasn't smiling. "Then, when I was twelve years old and Calvin was about six, that all changed. We'd brought home an injured fox that Calvin grew to really love. When it came time to set it free, *Daed* left it to me to take care of. Calvin pleaded with me to help him hide it, but I refused. Because I didn't listen to him and didn't get upset over it, Calvin considered me heartless." His jaw worked. "He hasn't looked at me quite the same way since."

She reached over and placed her hand on his. "I remember that day, and you weren't quite as unemotional as you'd have everyone believe."

He drew his hand back. "I was a boy back then. I've changed."

Greta doubted that, but instead of saying so, she responded to his previous statement. "As for Calvin's reaction, he was too young to understand that you were just doing what had to be done. Surely he understands that now."

Noah gave her a cryptic look. "That wasn't the only time I disappointed him. There were several times over the years where difficult decisions had to be made and it was left to me to make them. The last time, for Calvin at least, was when *Daed* died."

Greta knew what was coming. She remembered Calvin complaining about it. But she'd only heard his side of it.

"There were some outstanding bills that came due, some major purchases *Daed* had made that he hadn't had time to repay before he died. Calvin wanted to appeal to the community for assistance, but I disagreed since we had the means to pay."

Of course he would take that stand, he was too honorable to do otherwise.

"I discussed it with *Mamm* and we decided to sell ten acres in the northeast corner of our property along with the small barn that was there. Calvin considered that a betrayal of *Daed*. He also thinks that I somehow coerced our *mamm*, and that it was easy for me to sell off a piece of our farm because I didn't consider myself a farmer."

"That was unfair of him."

"Calvin can't help it that he feels things deeply. While I obviously don't."

"Says who?"

He shrugged. "Just ask anyone who knows me." He took a sip from his glass. "I'm the one the family comes to when there are difficult decisions to be made, because everyone knows I can take care of things without letting emotions get in the way."

"Nonsense."

He raised a brow at that. "I assure you they do," he said mildly.

"I meant it's nonsense about you not feeling things. You absolutely feel and I'd guess you feel deeply. You just don't show it the way Calvin does."

He stared at her a moment, his expression unreadable.

Then his expression hardened. "If you're marrying me with the idea that you're going to change me, that I'll grow to love you—"

She lifted a hand, palm forward. "I assure you that's not the case." So why had those words cut so deep?

Neither said anything for the next few minutes, concentrating instead on their food.

When Noah finally did speak again, it was to discuss the invitations that would go out, since that was traditionally the groom's responsibility.

But for Greta, much as she smiled and discussed wedding plans with him, there was an undercurrent of somberness to the day that hadn't been there before.

Was this a preview of how their married life would be?

Chapter 23

Tuesday, Greta found herself watching the clock. The lunches she shared with Noah at Rosie's were something she looked forward to more and more.

Yesterday he'd moved several of her items to his house. Her hope chest now sat under the window in his bedroom. It had looked unexpectedly at home there.

He'd also transported the two quilt stands she'd pointed out to him on Sunday and placed them in the sewing room at his house. She was surprised and warmed to see he'd given them a place of honor by moving the loom against the far wall.

As soon as the clock hands reached eleven thirty, she put her sewing away. A moment later she saw Noah crossing the mall, heading for the quilt shop. Giving Esther a wave, she met him just outside the shop door.

As they stepped outside in the cold, he took her elbow to help her navigate the wet sidewalk, just as he had every time they'd taken this walk. She was used to it now, that and the little tingle of awareness it always gave her.

"How are things working out with Gideon?" she asked.

"He's really jumped right in to help. Having him in the workshop will make a big difference when Paul leaves at the end of the week."

"And I have some more *gut* news for you. I received a response today from Rachel. She says her *daed* has found someone with an interest in woodworking who'd be willing to move here and work with you." It felt *gut* to be able to bring him this news.

"Did she tell you anything about him?"

"His name is Hiram Detweiler and he's only nineteen years old. Rachel's *daed* feels he's talented, but he wants you to know Hiram is still inexperienced. If you gave him the job, Hiram would also need to find a place to stay, preferably with a family who'd be willing to lease him a room until he could save up and find a more permanent accommodation."

"That sounds promising, especially since Gideon will be around to help get the big projects out."

"So you are interested then?"

Noah nodded. "I'd definitely like to speak to him."

"I'll ask Rachel to give him your contact information and the two of you can take it from there."

"*Gut.*" Their conversation paused as they reached Rosie's.

Once they were seated and had placed their orders, Noah leaned forward. "I have a favor to ask of you."

"Of course. What do you need?"

"Mrs. McAllen asked if I could get her china cabinet finished two days early. I can tell her no if I need to, but

I think I can get it taken care of if I stay an extra hour or so this afternoon. Would you mind staying a little late this evening? I can ask Patience to fix some sandwiches for us to take back with us so you and the *kinner* will have something to eat for supper."

"Of course. When we get back to the mall I'll stop in the bakery and tell Hannah so my family will know I'll be late."

"*Danke*."

Patience brought their food just then, and as she laid the plates in front of them, she smiled. "I understand congratulations are in order." She gave them an arch look. "I knew something was up, the way you two have been coming in for lunch every day and smiling at each other as if you think the other one hung the moon."

Greta felt the heat crawl up her neck into her cheeks. How did they respond to that? Patience had obviously misread their relationship but she couldn't very well say so.

Keeping her head down as she put the napkin in her lap, she glanced up through her lashes at Noah. To her surprise, he seemed to take the comments in stride.

He smiled at Patience as he picked up his fork. "*Danke*. And of course you're invited to the wedding."

"I'll be there. And Greta, if you and your family need help with the preparations, let me know."

After Patience bustled off to take care of another table, Greta met Noah's gaze.

Apparently he could read the question in her expression without her saying a word. "There's no need to share our private business with the world," he said quietly. "You and I know the truth of the matter and that's enough."

She nodded and then focused on her meal, feeling oddly deflated. How was it that this man could rattle her so much with just a few words or a look? Or was it just that she'd grown moody?

Whatever the case, she didn't like this unsettled feeling.

She'd better find a way to keep her guard up or she'd be a mess by the day of the wedding.

Chapter 24

Greta was getting worried. What was taking Noah so long? Had he just got caught up and lost track of time? Or had something happened to him?

After another thirty minutes she decided it was time to go check things out for herself.

"All right you two, what do you say we bring Lemon Drop back downstairs to be with her *mamm* and find your *daed*?"

"Is *Daed* hiding?" asked David. His tone made it clear he was ready to play.

"Maybe." She carefully placed the kitten in her tote, grabbed her charges' coats and scarfs, then turned to David. "Hold tight to your *shveshtah*'s other hand."

Greta set a slow and careful pace as they navigated the stairs. A few minutes later they were at the entrance to the woodworking shop. Setting their winter gear on one of the benches, she tested the door and was relieved to find it unlocked.

Standing in the open doorway, she called out Noah's name several times, with no response.

Something was definitely wrong.

The feeling that Noah was in trouble intensified and she had the urge to rush inside and find him.

But she held back, trying to decide what to do with Anna and David. She didn't like the idea of leaving them alone in the lobby, but the workshop could be a dangerous place for little ones. And she was growing increasingly worried about what state she would find Noah in.

"Do we go find *Daed* now?" David asked hopefully.

Deciding on a compromise, Greta chose her words carefully.

"I'm worried that it might be too dangerous for Anna to be around all the sharp tools in the workshop. You're a big boy now, so I'm going to leave you in charge of keeping her safe while I look for your *daed*. Can you do that?"

His lower lip jutted out rebelliously and she thought he was going to be stubborn about this.

"I tell you what, since you can't play hide-and-seek with your *daed* this evening, we'll have our own little treasure hunt tomorrow. Doesn't that sound fun?"

His eyes had widened at the words "treasure hunt," and he nodded readily this time.

She ruffled his hair. "*Danke*. Now I'm going to leave this door open so you can call me if you need me for anything, but you must make sure that you stay with Anna and under no circumstances let her go inside."

"I won't."

"You're a very *gut* big *bruder*." She set her tote down in front of them. "And make sure Lemon Drop doesn't get out."

That would give them something else to focus on. She found a thin piece of wood she could use as a doorstop—added insurance the door would stay open—and with one last reassuring smile David's way, she headed inside.

She quickly lost her smile as she looked around the large, much-too-quiet workshop. "Noah? Noah, are you in here?"

A low moan coming from somewhere on the left had her rushing forward in that direction. She turned a corner and found her worst fears confirmed.

A heavy shelving unit pinned Noah down on his back. There were paint cans and other items scattered all around. Her heart was pounding now, and silent, disjointed prayers were running through her mind.

Struggling to keep her voice low enough not to worry her two charges, she called his name again, making her way around the scattered cans and other debris with more speed than care until she could kneel next to him. "Noah, are you all right? Please be all right." How long had he been pinned down? She touched his head, and his face turned in her direction.

"Greta?"

Almost sobbing with relief, she stroked his cheek.

His eyes cleared, focused on her. His hand lifted and a finger brushed her cheek. It was only then that she realized there were tears there.

"Sorry to worry you. I think I must have passed out for a moment."

"Are you hurt?" Silly question, his pallor and pinched face were indications enough.

"My left foot is pinned and I think it might be broken." He shifted, and a wince spasmed across his face. "Where are Anna and David?" His voice was strained.

"They're sitting right outside in the lobby. I left the door open so I can hear if they call."

"*Gut*. Don't let them come in."

"They won't. Now we need to get you free. Let me see if I can move the shelf enough for you to—"

"*Nee!*" He took her hand to prevent her from rising. "It's too dangerous."

She tried to focus on the situation instead of the feel of his hand holding hers. "I can't just leave you—"

"Yes you can. I want you to use the cell phone in the showroom to call for help."

"Of course." Why hadn't she thought of that herself? "I'll be right back."

But again he held her back. "*Nee*. Anna and David need you right now more than I do. Stay with them and wait for help to arrive."

"But—"

"Greta, you can't do anything to help me. But it'll set my mind at ease to know you're watching over Anna and David."

Touching his cheek, she nodded and quickly stood. She hurried to the showroom, pausing only long enough to reassure the *kinner* that she'd be right back out. She wasted a few moments fumbling around behind the counter before she located the phone, then quickly dialed 911 and reported what had happened.

That done, she headed back to check on Anna and David.

"Did you find *Daed*?" David looked close to tears.

Greta stooped down, careful to erase signs of worry from her own face. "*Jah*. But he hurt his foot so he can't come out right now. He's going to be all right, though, we just need to get a little help."

"I want *Daed*," Anna added plaintively.

Greta took one of the little girl's hands and gave it a squeeze. "I know, sweetie, but he can't come out right now."

"I can help," David said, puffing his chest out and tugging on his suspenders in a little-boy show of bravado.

"That's very generous of you to offer. But I already called for some help. There are some men coming who know the best way to help your *daed* without hurting him further. Besides, I still need you to help me keep an eye on Anna and Lemon Drop. Will you do that?"

He nodded, though he looked back through the open doorway as if trying to see Noah.

She stood. "Right now we need to unlock the door so the men can get in when they get here. But first..." She lifted the tote with the kitten and hung the straps over her shoulder. "There, she'll be out of the way and safe." Then she picked Anna up and took David's hand and headed for the mall's front entrance.

Unlocking the main door, she fought the urge to go back to Noah. But the sensible part of her knew she couldn't take Anna and David in there and she couldn't leave them alone again. Thankfully she heard the sirens almost immediately.

"Here they come," she said, adopting a cheery tone. She gave Anna a squeeze and smiled down at David, trying to allay their fears. "You are both being so brave. Your *daed* is going to be so proud of you." She moved to the bench nearest the door, sitting with a child on either side of her so she could wrap an arm around them both.

Within minutes, the firemen and EMT crews were on-site. Standing, but remaining by the bench, she directed them to the workshop and told them how to find Noah.

The emergency responders were followed by some familiar faces.

Daniel Mast, Esther's *bruder*, was the first to reach her.

"We were at Rosie's and saw the emergency vehicles. What's happened? Is there anything we can do to help?" Marylou Stolzfus was at his side and was apparently part of the "we."

"Noah's been hurt." She tried to keep the worry out of her voice for the *kinner*'s sake. Before saying more, she turned to her charges. "David, did you know Marylou really likes kittens?" She handed David the tote. "Why don't you and Anna show her Lemon Drop?"

For a moment David looked as if he would refuse. But Marylou stepped forward with a smile. "Lemon Drop is a great name for a kitten. I'd love to see him. Would you please show him to me?"

David finally nodded reluctantly and took Anna's hand. "It's a her not a him," he said as Marylou led the way to one of the benches a short distance away.

Once they were out of earshot, Greta turned back to Daniel. "A large shelving unit fell over and pinned him down. He thinks his foot may be broken."

"What can I do to help?"

"Anna and David probably shouldn't be here when

they bring their *daed* out, especially if it's on a stretcher."
She turned to make sure they were still distracted. "The
best way you can help is to take them to his *mamm*'s
house and to let his family know what's happened."

"Of course. Let Marylou know and I'll go get my
buggy now."

"And Daniel, one other thing if you don't mind."

"Yes?"

"Stop in at my house and let my family know what's
happened and that I plan to stay with Noah until I'm sure
he's going to be okay."

Karl Schmucker, who'd been standing behind Daniel,
stepped forward. "I can take care of that. Daniel will
have his hands full with the *kinner*."

"*Danke*. And if you don't mind, would you hitch
Noah's horse to his buggy for me? It's around back."

"Will do. I'll bring it around front so it'll be ready
whenever you are."

She'd already decided she would either take Noah
home if the EMTs released him or follow the ambulance
to the hospital if they decided he needed to be checked
out there.

As soon as Karl headed around back to take care
of the buggy, Greta turned to the trio currently playing with the kitten. "David, Anna, let's get your coats
on. Marylou and Daniel are going to take you to your
grossmammi's house."

David's lips set in a stubborn line. "I want to see
Daed first."

Greta was itching to see what was going on in the
workshop, but she had the *kinner* to take care of. "All
those men you saw go inside your *daed*'s workshop are

there to help him. But they can't do their job if any of us get in their way." She stooped down so that her face was on the same level as David's. "If you want to help your *daed*, I know it'll make him feel better if he knows Anna is safe at home with your *Aenti* Maisie. And it will be a lot easier on her if she has her big *bruder* with her. Can you do that for him?"

David nodded reluctantly. With an approving smile, Greta stood. "I tell you what," she said impulsively, "if you're very careful with her, you two can take Lemon Drop with you and show her to your *grossmammi*, *Aenti* Maisie and your *onkel*s. Would you like that?"

Both of them nodded.

"All right, but remember, she's just a baby so you need to treat her gently."

"I'll make sure everyone at *Grossmammi*'s knows." David's earnest assurance brought a smile to her lips.

Marylou had already started helping Anna into her coat, so Greta helped David.

As soon as they were ready, Marylou picked Anna up and with her free hand took hold of David's. Greta took the tote and followed them to the door. Daniel was already there with his buggy, so everyone was loaded up in record time.

Before closing the buggy door, Greta smiled at both Anna and David. "Don't worry. Your *daed* is going to be just fine. And I'm sure he's going to be happy when he hears you're both being so brave."

With that she stepped back so the buggy could pull out. Then she turned and all but ran back into the mall lobby and over to the workshop.

One of the firemen stopped her at the threshold,

holding an arm out to bar her way. "Sorry ma'am, but it's too dangerous for you to go inside."

"How is he? Is he going to be all right?"

Rather than answering, he asked a question of his own. "May I ask what your relationship is to Mr. Stoll?"

"We're engaged." That still sounded a little strange to say out loud. Before she could say more, she saw two men rolling out a stretcher bearing Noah.

She moved back to give them room to maneuver, but as soon as they cleared the door she rushed forward and grabbed Noah's hand. Before she could ask how he was doing, though, he spoke up. "Anna and David?"

She walked alongside the moving stretcher. "Daniel Mast was at Rosie's with Marylou and came by to offer help when he saw the emergency vehicles. They're bringing them to your *mamm*'s place."

"*Gut*."

She noticed he was being more succinct than usual. "How are you feeling?"

"I'll be okay."

That wasn't really an answer.

He nodded toward the men propelling the stretcher. "They want to bring me to the hospital for tests and X-rays, just to make sure there's nothing wrong besides my foot."

"*Gut* idea." She took his hand. "I'm going to follow in your buggy."

"That's not necessary."

A not unexpected response, but she wasn't going to let that stop her. "Maybe not necessary, but it's what my heart needs."

He seemed startled by her words, but before he could respond, they reached the ambulance.

One of the men handling the stretcher turned to Greta. "Sorry, ma'am, time for us to load him up."

Giving Noah's hand a final squeeze, she stepped back.

Noah tried to relax as the ambulance sped away from the mall.

Away from Greta.

The way she'd kept her head throughout this whole ordeal was impressive. She'd called for help, taken care of Anna and David and directed the emergency responders.

He could still feel the strength of her grasp as she held on to his hand, see the concern in her eyes.

Her parting words had him concerned. Was she starting to feel something warmer than friendship? Had she forgotten so soon what he'd said about their relationship remaining strictly businesslike? They weren't even married yet.

This didn't bode well for their future life together.

So why did he feel this warm glow inside?

It took Greta some time to get to the hospital. Before she could even set out she had to make sure all the people had exited the mall, then she had to take care of the lights and thermostat and lock the place up.

The trip from the mall to the hospital by buggy took nearly thirty minutes. Thank goodness Jericho was used to icy conditions and light traffic. He negotiated the trip without problem. Still, it was a long time to be alone with her own thoughts.

And her thoughts kept jumping back to that horrible moment when she'd first seen Noah there in the workshop, flat on his back under the heavy shelf, eyes closed, unmoving, unresponsive. Her heart had seemed to stop altogether for a moment before it stuttered back to life and set her pulse racing.

It was in that instant, when she thought she might have lost him, that she'd had an epiphany, a flash of absolute clarity.

She'd realized she was impossibly, deeply, irrevocably, in love with her fiancé.

Chapter 25

When Greta finally made it inside the hospital she rushed over to the reception desk. "Can you tell me where I can find Noah Stoll?" Her voice sounded breathless, even to her own ears.

The dark-haired receptionist looked up from her paperwork with a sympathetic smile. "Is he a patient here?"

"*Jah*. An ambulance would have brought him in sometime in the last hour."

The woman was already typing something into her computer. "Yes, here he is. Mr. Stoll is with a doctor right now." She waved to an area on her left. "If you'll have a seat in the waiting room I'll make certain you're notified as soon as it's okay to go back. Just leave your name on this sign-in sheet."

"*Danke*." Greta wrote her name, then took a seat as she'd been instructed. There were three other people seated there as well—a few chairs over, a woman sat with a weeping toddler in her lap. She gave Greta an apologetic smile, then went back to comforting her little boy. Across the way an older man sat staring down at his hands clasped between his knees, his expression drawn.

It was a good reminder that she wasn't the only one with cares weighing on her.

She bowed her head and closed her eyes in silent prayer, giving thanks for all the people who'd helped them this evening and asking for healing grace for Noah and the others in the facility.

When she was done, she shifted in her seat, staring straight ahead without seeing anything. What did she do with the knowledge that she loved him? Her first instinct, when she'd realized Noah was still breathing, was to blurt the news out to him.

She had no illusions that he reciprocated those feelings. He'd warned her that he didn't want her love and that he absolutely would not love her in return if she made the mistake of falling for him. Did she keep her feelings to herself, hold them close to her chest and go on as if nothing had changed? Could she even pull that off?

"Miss Eicher. Miss Eicher?"

Greta looked up to see the woman manning the front desk waving her over.

"You can go back to see him now," the woman told her as she approached the desk. "He's in room 225. Take the elevator to the second floor and then turn down the corridor to your right."

A few minutes later, Greta stood outside Noah's room.

She hesitated a heartbeat. Would he see a difference in her? There was only one way to find out.

Pasting a smile on her face, she knocked.

Noah's gruff "Come in" invited her to step inside.

She found him stretched out on a hospital bed with his injured left foot wrapped, iced and elevated.

As soon as he saw her, he grabbed the controls to adjust his bed into a seated position and his frown relaxed into something more welcoming. "I thought you were another nurse."

"Not a nurse." She moved closer. "I see they decided to keep you here rather than send you home. Were there more injuries than your foot?"

Noah grimaced. "A bruised rib, nothing serious. But since I was trapped for over two hours and passed out for an undetermined amount of time, they wanted to hold me overnight for observation."

That sounded like a *gut* idea to her, but from the look on Noah's face it was probably better she didn't say so. "What did they have to say about your foot?"

"It's my ankle and it's only bruised and sprained. I'll have to wear a special boot and stay off of it for about a week."

"I'm so sorry, I know that's going to be hard for you."

He shrugged, then winced. Was his bruised rib more painful than he'd let on?

"Since it's just my ankle," he said, "I'll still be able to work."

Of course that would be his main concern. "I took care of shutting things down and locking up the mall, so you don't have to worry about any of that—just concentrate on resting up and getting better."

"*Danke*."

She placed a hand on the bed rail. "Is there anything you need or that I can get for you?"

"*Nee*."

"How about something to eat?"

He spread his hands and gave her a look that seemed almost patronizing. "Greta, I'm fine, there's no need for you to worry over me."

All the worries, fears and emotions of the evening suddenly hit her, washing over her in a forceful wave that made her heart feel like it would pound right out of her chest.

"No need!" She used her index finger to jab his shoulder. "First I find you unconscious under a pile of metal. Then you come to, but I have to leave you there while I call for help. Then I have to keep up a calm front for your *kinner* when all the while I have no idea how you're doing. Then I have to watch while you're carted off in an ambulance, with sirens blaring no less, while I stay behind to lock up."

She'd punctuated each point with another finger jab, and Noah finally took her hand to stop her.

"I'm sorry," he said gently, the regret etched deeply in the lines of his face. "My words were thought-less."

Greta shook her head, not trusting herself to speak. She had to get herself back under control—and quick. The tears were just below the surface, and she'd leave the room before she'd add to her unseemly display by crying in front of him.

"Do you need something?" He reached for the call button. "Should I call for a nurse?"

She placed her free hand on his to stop him, and again she shook her head.

Poor man, he looked really alarmed now. She had to swallow her emotions and speak up, had to allay his concerns. "It's me who should apologize." Hearing the hitch in her own voice, she paused a minute to compose herself. "I shouldn't have said all of that. It's just that I feel like what happened is partly my fault. I knew something was wrong. If I'd just gone downstairs to check on you sooner—"

His alarmed look softened into something more akin to sympathy. "Nonsense. None of this is your fault."

"But—"

"Greta, you had Anna and David to think of. You did everything just as you should."

"But you were trapped. If I'd found you sooner I could have saved you some pain."

He placed his other hand on top of hers. "Listen to me, none of that is your fault. In fact you were remarkable. The fact that you didn't panic, you kept your head and got help and managed to take care of my *kinner* all at the same time is impressive."

Greta was mesmerized by the warmth of his voice, by what she saw in his eyes, by the feel of his hand on hers. Was it possible he returned, even in the smallest bit, the emotion she felt for him?

The air around them thickened, formed a bubble of sorts that seemed to shut out everything but the two of them. Noah saw the vulnerability in her expression, the unshed tears in her eyes, and it tugged at him in a way he'd never felt before.

If she'd actually shed those tears, which she'd seemed very close to doing, he wasn't sure what he'd have done. Patsy had always wept easily, whenever anything hurt her or affected her emotionally. After a while the tears had been more or less expected.

Seeing Greta so vulnerable was an entirely different matter, especially since she'd been trying so hard to hide it. Not that she didn't have a valid reason to get emotional, given what he'd put her through.

Almost of its own volition his upper hand lifted, trying to satisfy the need to offer comfort, to feel the softness of her cheek.

A knock snapped Noah out of his momentary weakness, cleared his muddled mind of the emotional fog.

Thank goodness, the nurse was back to save him from himself.

But when he looked past Greta to the doorway, he saw not a nurse but Calvin. And his *bruder* was staring at their clasped hands with a frown.

Calvin finally looked up and nodded to Greta first. "Hello. I wasn't expecting to find you here."

Noah felt the loss as she released his hand and took a small step back. "I wanted to make sure Noah was okay."

"Of course."

The smile Calvin gave Greta irritated Noah for some reason. He cleared his throat, claiming Calvin's attention.

"I hear you got yourself in a bit of trouble." Calvin's tone held a hint of smugness.

"I've faced worse." He tried to temper his irritation. "But it was *gut* of you to come check on me."

"Actually, *Mamm* sent me to find out how you were

doing and to see if you needed a ride home." He studied Noah critically. "But it looks like you're settled in for the night."

Noah grimaced. "Not my idea. The doctor insisted I stay overnight for observation." He shifted to a more comfortable position. "How are Anna and David?"

"Maisie was putting them to bed when I left. Though she was having trouble separating Anna from that kitten."

"Kitten?" He turned to Greta.

Her cheeks pinkened. "Did I forget to mention that I sent Lemon Drop home with them?"

A laugh escaped him before he could stop himself. She looked so much like a little girl caught with her hand in the cookie jar.

Greta gave him an exasperated look and then turned to Calvin. "Was your *mamm* upset about the kitten?"

"Not at all." His smile was almost intimate. "It was a *gut* way to keep them occupied so they wouldn't worry about their *daed*."

Noah tried to recapture Greta's attention. "It seems I owe you yet another thank-you."

She waved a hand dismissively. "Sending Lemon Drop with them made it easier to convince them to go with Daniel and Marylou."

There was another knock at the door and this time it did herald the arrival of a nurse.

"I see you have some visitors." Her voice was cheery rather than chiding. "My name is Rita and I'll be checking in on you from time to time this evening. Don't let me interrupt your visit, I'm just here to take a few readings." She reached for the blood pressure cuff near his bed.

"We need to be going anyway," Calvin said. "Greta, I can give you a ride home."

"*Danke*. But I drove Noah's buggy here so I'll drive it home when I leave."

But Calvin didn't let it drop. "It's getting late. Noah needs his rest after the day he's had, and you shouldn't be on the road alone at this hour." Calvin glanced his way. "Ain't so?"

What could he say to that? "*Jah*. Greta, you should go while Calvin can follow you. I'm fine, I don't need anyone watching over me."

Was that hurt that flashed across Greta's expression? It was there and gone so quickly he couldn't be sure. But there was nothing he could do about that now.

"Very well." Greta straightened. "I'll come back tomorrow to give you a ride home."

"That's not necessary, I can—"

She interrupted him, her gaze stern. "We've had this discussion before. We don't always deal in what's necessary, we sometimes deal in what our heart tells us we need." Her expression softened. "It'll also give us time to discuss how you'll be getting around for the next few weeks." And with that she squeezed his hand and turned to follow Calvin from the room.

Noah settled back, allowing his bed to unfold into a flatter line as Nurse Rita finished taking her readings.

A few minutes later he was once again alone with only the hum of the medical equipment for company.

Greta had definitely regained her feisty spirit before she'd made her exit just now. Was it in reaction to Calvin's presence? Or something else?

Had she really been as emotionally vulnerable as he'd

thought? Or had he confused what was merely reaction to the evening's excitement and a touch of exhaustion for something else?

She'd certainly run the gamut this evening—displaying everything from anger to guilt to vulnerability to that bright spirit he found so endearing.

He might not want a love match, but there was nothing that said he couldn't enjoy having her in his life.

"Noah is lucky you were around to call for help."

Greta stopped in her tracks right in the middle of the hospital lobby, trying hard to curb her irritation. "It wasn't luck, Calvin, it was *Gotte*'s will."

"Of course. I just meant this could have gone much worse if he'd been alone tonight." He brushed at his sleeve. "I just hope my *bruder* appreciates you as you deserve."

She decided it was time to clear the air a bit. "I asked Noah why there was this tension between the two of you."

Calvin stiffened but didn't immediately respond.

"As his future *fraa* I wanted to understand your relationship."

"And what did he say?"

"He told me what happened with the fox when you were both just boys, and about the decision to sell a portion of your land after your *daed* passed. He also said there were other incidents as well where he had to make unpopular decisions."

"And I suppose you took his side."

In a little one, his tone would have been considered pouty. "It's not a matter of taking sides." How could she make him see what she saw? "I understand why you resent some of the things your *bruder* did. But I want you to try to look at this from his standpoint."

"I have." Calvin waved a hand angrily. "He carries out all these decisions without taking anyone else's feelings into account and without any signs of regret or hesitation."

She crossed her arms over her chest. "You keep implying that Noah is unemotional, that he doesn't feel things the way you and I do. What if I told you that you're wrong, that he actually feels things very deeply, but that he's good at hiding it? That it takes a whole lot of courage for him to make those hard decisions that no one else wants to make, and that it wounds him deeply when those close to him get angry or upset with him for doing what must be done."

Calvin didn't seem ready to relent. "I'd say that I know Noah a lot better and for a whole lot longer than you. And I've never seen any hint of this so-called wounding."

"Perhaps it's because you've never looked closely enough." She held his gaze with her own. "Here's one other thing to think about. Ever since Noah started noticing me you've seemed to see me in a different light and tried to discredit his intentions. Why do you think that is?"

Calvin dropped his gaze as he rubbed the back of his neck. "I told you that my discussion with you by the schoolhouse was a mistake, that I was momentarily confused. I truly love Wanda."

"And I believe you. But again, why did you do it in the first place? And why do you always see your *bruder* in such a negative light when you must know in your heart what a *gut* man he is?" Greta let that sink in.

Then she straightened. She'd said enough for today. "Now, it's time we get on the road." And without waiting for a response, she headed out of the hospital door.

Chapter 26

I hope I didn't keep you waiting too long." Greta picked up the reins and set the buggy in motion.

"*Nee*." Noah shifted, carefully stretching out his left leg, which sported a medical boot. "Dr. Mitchem had just signed off on my release when you arrived. I'm actually glad you were able to sleep in late after the day you had yesterday."

Did he truly think she was late because she'd over-slept? "I spoke to your *mamm*. She said if you'd like to stay at her house with your *kinner* for the next few days that you're welcome to do so."

He moved his crutches to rest against the seat between them. "I gave that some thought last night and came to the same conclusion."

It was a relief to know she wouldn't have to argue with him on that point. "*Gut*. Then that's where I'll drop you off."

"Actually, I planned to stop in at the workshop."

"I've already told everyone what happened and that you won't be in today. Paul took charge of cleaning everything up from the accident and offered to take care of locking up this evening."

"And when did you talk to Paul?"

"Someone had to open up this morning."

She felt his gaze on her, studying her closely. "And when did you talk to my *mamm*?"

"This morning before I went to the mall."

"So you didn't sleep in this morning, did you?"

She shrugged. His question didn't really require an answer.

"What else did you take care of before you came to the hospital?"

"I left a note for Esther explaining what had happened and that I'd be late getting in this morning, and then I stopped by Naomi's to let her know Anna and David wouldn't need her today."

"Sounds like you thought of everything."

He grimaced and shifted again. Was he in pain?

But before she could comment, he continued. "I'd still like to stop by the workshop and make sure the men don't have any questions about what projects have priority."

"Noah, I know being idle is difficult for you. But the nurse told me what the doctor said. You need to take it easy for a few days."

"I didn't say I wanted to get right to work. I just want to check in on things."

The slightly petulant note in his voice had her swallowing a grin. "Your men are all experienced and capable of carrying on without you for one day, ain't so? It's going to take you some time to get used to those crutches anyway. You'll be in better condition to go into work if you wait a day. Or even two."

"Direct and to the point, as usual."

Did he mean that as a compliment or insult? Not something to worry about right now. "Besides, Anna and David are anxious to see you. The chaos when the emergency responders arrived last night and the fact that I rushed them off with your cousin before they could see you was very scary for them."

He rolled his eyes. "You win. Bring me to *Mamm*'s."

She smiled. Did he realize she hadn't intended to give him a choice?

Before she could claim victory, however, he cut her a challenging look. "But I make no promises about tomorrow."

She wisely decided to change the subject. "Now that that's settled, we need to discuss whether this changes anything."

"What do you mean?"

"If you have to use those crutches for more than a couple of weeks, do you want to delay the wedding until you can walk on your own?"

"According to Dr. Mitchem I should be able to put away the crutches by the end of next week. But if I'm not, will it bother you if I'm still using them on our wedding day?"

"Not at all."

"Then I see no reason to postpone anything."

"*Gut.*" She turned the buggy into a left turn. "I want to get back to what I said about how scary last night was for Anna and David. They were both very brave, but they had a lot to deal with. All they knew was that you were hurt and they couldn't go in the workshop to see you. Then these vehicles with loud sirens and flashing lights pulled up and uniformed responders rushed in with strange equipment."

"So you're saying they've been through a lot." There was a lot of self-recrimination in his tone and expression.

"*Jah*, they have. But I didn't tell you this to make you feel bad, it was so you can keep it in mind when you see them. They're likely to be very clingy for the next few days."

He nodded.

She changed the topic to the wedding, giving Noah an update on what had been done and what was still left to do. It seemed to serve her purpose in keeping his mind distracted from his workshop until they finally turned onto the lane that led to his *mamm*'s house.

Noah shifted in his seat as Greta pulled the buggy to a stop and set the brake.

"We're here," she said unnecessarily. "Should I get one of your *brieder* to help you?"

"I can manage." He tried to rein in his frustration, none of this was her fault. He just wasn't used to requiring assistance for something as simple as driving a buggy or climbing in and out of one.

True to form, Greta made it around to his side of the buggy in record time. While she didn't out-and-out offer to assist him, she obviously stood ready to do so.

He managed to get out on his own but it required some less-than-graceful sliding onto his uninjured foot. Before he'd quite gotten his balance, the front door swung open and David came racing outside.

"*Daed*!"

Greta intervened before his son could barrel into him. "Easy, David. Your *daed*'s a little shaky right now."

David held back and studied the bulky gear on his foot. "Does it hurt?"

Noah gave him a reassuring smile. "Only a little. But I'm not supposed to walk on it for a while. That's why I have these." He lifted one of his crutches.

By this time Maisie had come out as well, with Anna resting securely on her hip. "*Daed*." She raised her arms, an obvious plea to be transferred to his hold.

"Let's go inside where it's warmer," he said diplomatically. "We can have a seat on the sofa, and you can tell me all about how Lemon Drop is doing."

He turned to Greta. "You can join us, of course."

But she shook her head. "I need to get back to the quilt shop. I have a special-order project I want to finish up." She turned, then paused and faced him again. "I'll come by and check on you in the morning before I head for the quilt shop in case you decide you want to go in." Her expression said she hoped he wouldn't. "I'll speak to Paul about closing up tonight and opening back up in the morning, so don't look for me before eight thirty."

"You don't need—"

She didn't let him finish. "I have your horse and buggy, remember?" And before he could form another protest, she turned and climbed back into the buggy.

When he turned back he saw Maisie grinning at him. "The more I'm around Greta," she said, "the more I like her."

Deciding that didn't require a response, Noah headed for the house. Once he'd greeted his *mamm* and let her fuss over him for a bit, Noah eased himself down on the couch, doing his best not to jostle his bruised rib. As soon as he was settled, Anna and David scrambled to sit on either side of him.

Trying to take their attention away from his injury, Noah steered the conversation elsewhere. "How is Lemon Drop doing?"

"*Grossmammi* let us feed her," David said proudly. "Anna filled her water bowl and I gave her some bread soaked in broth."

"Those are both very important jobs." Then he squeezed both their hands. "I'm sorry you two were so worried about me. But Greta said you were both very brave and went with Cousin Daniel without any fussing at all."

David nodded. "Greta said it would make you feel better if you knew we were with *Grossmammi* and *Aenti* Maisie." His little face gazed up earnestly. "Did it truly make you feel better?"

Noah nodded, thankful for the way Greta had handled the whole situation. She was a woman of uncommon compassion and sense. "It most certainly did."

"What's that on your foot?" David asked.

With a sigh, Noah resigned himself to answering their questions about his injury, his mobility and his boot and crutches.

Finally his *mamm* came in the room and interrupted their barrage of questions. "All right, you two need to let your *daed* get some rest. He'll visit with you some more after lunch."

Noah brushed aside the idea that he was tired. "I'm fine. I thought I'd take a walk out to the barn and—"

"Nonsense. Greta told me the doctor prescribed lots of rest for you."

He grimaced. No doubt Greta thought she was helping, but he was able to gauge his own limits.

Getting to his feet with some effort, he followed his *mamm* down the hall. "I thought it would be better if we set up a room for you downstairs, so I asked Calvin and Benjamin to move the bed from your old room down to my sewing room."

Noah nodded. "*Danke*. That'll work just fine for the few days I'll be here."

"Maisie went to your place this morning and collected a few of your things. But if there's anything she missed I'm sure you can borrow from Calvin or Benjamin."

She opened the door and stepped aside for him to enter first.

Noah had a quick glimpse of her quilt frame shoved near the far wall and a bed squeezed in between it and her sewing machine. Then she reclaimed his attention.

"From what I understand of what happened yesterday, Greta seems to be a very level-headed, sensible woman."

Noah couldn't tell whether she thought that was a good or bad thing. But he was ready to defend her. "I agree. And I'm grateful she was there."

"As am I." She turned the bed down. "You have found yourself a *gut* woman, one you can trust with your *kinner*." She gave him a probing look. "And with your heart."

That set him back a moment. For a heartbeat he

wondered if she knew what had happened between him and Patsy. Then he dismissed the thought. She was just being a typical soft-hearted mother.

She plumped the pillow, then straightened. "I hope you'll appreciate her as she deserves."

With that she moved to the door. "Lunch will be ready in about an hour. Until then, try to rest."

Noah sat on the bed, mulling over her words. He shouldn't have been surprised that she thought so highly of Greta, it hadn't been that long ago when she'd put Greta's name forward as a possible *fraa* for him, calling her a sensible, intelligent girl.

Her admonition that he appreciate Greta, however, was dangerously close to interference. He did appreciate her, of course. Still he had a feeling his *mamm* placed a deeper layer of meaning to her words than what he was capable of fulfilling. But in any case, that was between him and Greta.

He leaned his crutches against the wall and swung his legs onto the mattress. Placing an arm behind his head, he stared up at the ceiling.

Instead of the ceiling, though, he again saw Greta's vulnerable expression when she was in his hospital room yesterday evening. It wasn't just that she'd been close to tears, it was that she'd been close to tears because she thought she'd let him down.

No one had ever made him feel so valued before, at least not since a gap-toothed six-year-old girl had told him she was proud of him seventeen years ago.

Keeping things businesslike between them was becoming increasingly difficult the more time he spent with her.

Chapter 27

"How's Noah?" Esther had her hands clasped tightly in front of her. "Is he going to be all right?"

Greta had barely walked in the door of the quilt shop when Esther had pounced with her questions. "*Jah*, didn't I say so in my note?"

"You did, but I heard about all the emergency vehicles that were here last night, and when I went over to his workshop to find out what the men knew, they told me what a mess they found everything in when they arrived this morning."

Greta unbuttoned her coat and hung it on the hook behind the counter. "He hurt his ankle, so he'll be on crutches for the next several days. And he bruised a couple of ribs, so he needs to take things easy for a while. Otherwise he's fine." She turned back to her friend. "He and his *kinner* will be staying at his *mamm*'s place for now."

"*Ach*, that's *gut* to hear." Esther studied Greta a moment. "And what about you? That couldn't have been easy to deal with."

Greta pasted on a bright smile and moved toward her quilt frame. "I'm just happy it didn't turn out any worse than it did." Other than discovering I'm in love with a man who'll never love me back.

Greta spent most of the morning working on the baby quilt a client had ordered from her. She barely paused at lunchtime to eat a sandwich she'd brought with her. She had no interest in going to Rosie's without Noah for company.

When three o'clock came, rather than heading home, Greta walked over to the woodworking salesroom.

"Hello, Reuben, I'd like to speak to Paul for a few minutes. Can you let me into the workshop?"

This time Reuben didn't protest but nodded and went to the workshop door and opened it for her.

She found Paul rubbing sandpaper over a chair leg.

As soon as he saw her, he paused and set aside his work. "Greta, hello. Is there any new word on how Noah's doing?"

"He's doing well, but the doctor has said he should take it easy for the next few days."

Paul smiled. "I can imagine how he took that."

Greta returned his smile. "And you would be right. But I stopped by because I'd like your help with something."

"I'll do what I can. What do you need?"

"Despite what I just said, I'm pretty sure Noah plans to come into work tomorrow."

"I'm not surprised."

"I can't really stop him from coming in, but I hope to limit his work hours to the ones I work in my quilt shop, at least for the remainder of this week."

Paul looked skeptical. "Have you discussed that with Noah?"

"Not yet. But the favor I want to ask of you is something that will make Noah's life easier when he does come in."

"Of course. What did you have in mind?"

* * *

Noah followed Greta to the rear door of the mall. It was frustrating to try to cover ground with the crutches—they definitely slowed him down. But that wasn't all that had slowed him down this morning. He'd been ready to head to work at his regular time and had tried to persuade Benjamin to give him a ride to the mall. But *Mamm* had forbidden it and so he'd had to wait for Greta. It seemed he was going to slow down for a day or two, whether he wanted to or not.

Anna and David were going to stay at his *mamm*'s place with Maisie for another day.

Greta opened the mall door and stepped aside for him to pass through. "I'll take care of Jericho and the buggy and then be right in."

Noah shook his head. "Don't worry about the buggy, I'll send Reuben out to unhitch Jericho and tend to him."

Greta hesitated a moment, as if she wanted to protest, but then she nodded and stepped inside. "Would you like me to get the workshop door for you?"

"*Nee*. I'll go in through the sales floor."

She bit her lower lip, then with a nod turned to the quilt shop.

Noah studied her retreating back for a moment. Had he upset her, been less than gracious?

He slowly turned and moved to the woodworking sales floor.

Reuben looked up and a wide grin split his face. "*Gut matin*, I'm glad to see you back."

"It's *gut* to be back." He looked past Reuben and saw what appeared to be a room divider. "What's that?"

"It's a temporary office we set up for you. Actually it was Greta's idea, but we all worked on getting it set up."

"I see." It seemed Greta was one step ahead of him yet again. He walked around the temporary wall to find a small but efficiently set up office. A small worktable had been drafted to serve as a desk, and on the wall behind it someone had fashioned or found a three-shelf bookcase. His ledgers, stationery and files, along with miscellaneous office supplies, were neatly arranged on the table or bookshelves.

"*Danke*. This will work wonderful *gut* until I can climb the stairs again."

"We had orders from two new clients yesterday. I left the information on your desk and told them they'd need to speak to you for specifics on schedule and cost."

"*Gut*. While I look over your notes, would you head out back to unhitch the buggy and take care of Jericho for me? I'll keep an eye on things out here until you get back."

With a nod, Reuben made his exit.

Noah found the notes front and center on the makeshift

desk. Reuben had done a *gut* job taking notes. The first order was for a small dresser, a simple project they would be able to work into their schedule with little trouble. The second one was more complex. It was for a large, elaborate desk with a matching bookcase and side table. There was a requested delivery date of the end of March. Noah started mentally reviewing the other orders they had on the schedule, trying to figure out how these could be worked in.

Before he'd gotten it figured out, Reuben returned and Noah put away the paperwork to head into the workshop.

As soon as he stepped through the door, all three men put aside their work. They met him before he'd taken two steps inside, and welcomed him back with wide grins.

Once the greetings were done, Noah was ready to get down to business. "Where do we stand on the Richardson project?"

"Everything's on schedule to deliver next week," Paul responded. "We're on schedule with the table and chairs for the Perrys as well."

"*Gut.*"

Gideon spoke up before Noah could ask another question. "Andrew and I are headed out to the Haskell place this afternoon to install their cabinets."

"It sounds like you all did just fine without me."

Gideon stuck his thumbs through his suspenders with a grin. "You were just out for one day."

Noah returned his grin—he was right. But it definitely felt like a lot longer.

Then Gideon turned to the others. "Time to get back to work."

Paul waved them on. "I need to speak to Noah for a minute."

Once Gideon and Andrew had moved away, Paul turned to Noah. "I know tomorrow is supposed to be my last day, but with your accident and the upcoming wedding, I figured I could delay that. So I sent word to my *onkel* that I'll need an extra two weeks."

"I appreciate that, but I don't want to cause any problems with your *onkel*."

Paul waved away his objections. "Another two weeks isn't going to make a big difference. Besides, I should be here to see you get married, ain't so?" And with a wave, Paul headed back to his workbench.

Noah turned and slowly returned to his makeshift office. He'd been truly blessed to be surrounded by such good, caring people.

And he included Greta at the forefront of that number.

* * *

Greta wasn't sure how to take Noah's gruff dismissal this morning. Was it because he was in pain? Or frustration with his crutches? Or was he upset with her for some reason?

Surely he hadn't guessed about her feelings for him.

The morning passed slowly. Only four customers came in. Two were just browsers who spent time looking over the items for sale and asking Greta about the piece she was working on. They, of course, ultimately left without purchasing or ordering anything.

The third lady, an English woman who'd purchased some of their work in the past, bought the latest piece from their quilting circle. She was delighted to learn that a portion of her payment would be going to charity. The last of them, a grandmother-to-be, placed an order with Esther for a baby quilt.

By eleven thirty Greta was ready to get up from her quilting and walk around a bit. Would Noah keep their lunch date today or would he decide not to brave the weather with his crutches? Should she walk over to his workshop and check in with him?

Before she could make a decision, she saw Noah exit his showroom. After only a moment's hesitation, she stepped out of the shop to meet him.

"Are you ready for lunch?" he asked.

"I wasn't sure you'd want to go out and brave the slushy sidewalks with your crutches."

He gave a twisted smile. "I think I'll chance it."

As they stepped outside he cut her a sideways glance. "I understand I have you to thank for my temporary office."

"I merely suggested it. It was your workers who set it all up."

"Still, I appreciate your thoughtfulness. It'll definitely make life easier for the next several days."

She was pleased that he appreciated her efforts. But she missed having his hand protectively cradling her elbow as they walked.

"Hiram came by this morning to discuss the opening I have for another craftsman." Noah had managed to master a smooth rhythm with his crutches. "With all that's happened the last two days, I'd forgotten we had an appointment."

"And how did that go?"

"He seems like a bright, well-motivated young man."

They stepped into the crosswalk. "So are you going to hire him?"

Noah nodded. "I agreed to give him a one-month trial. He'll start next week and Gideon has already agreed to let Hiram board with him."

"That's *gut* news. I know he won't replace Paul from a productivity standpoint, but between him and Gideon perhaps you'll be able to keep up with your orders."

Noah let her hold the door for him as they entered Rosie's. "And Paul told me this morning he plans to stay until the wedding, so he won't be leaving this week after all."

"*Ach*, Noah, that's so *gut* of him."

Patience pointed them to a table with a hurried "I'll be right with you."

Noah led the way. "I know I owe a lot of this to you," he said over his shoulder. "You recommended I contact Gideon and you contacted Rachel's *daed* on my behalf."

She was surprised by his acknowledgment. "Those were small things and I was happy to do them."

He met her gaze as she took her seat, his smile warm. "Nevertheless, I can see already that we'll make *gut* partners."

Greta returned his smile, but this time his words didn't provide her the satisfaction they obviously did him. Because she longed to be so much more to him than a *gut* partner. Still, holding the precious knowledge of the love she felt for him close in her heart gave her a quiet joy nothing could extinguish.

Nevertheless, she was happy when Patience came up

and asked for details of what had happened to Noah and
wanted to rehash the excitement from Tuesday night.

Later, when she returned to the quilt shop, Esther
gave her a searching look. Wanting to avoid any probing
questions, Greta went straight to her quilting frame and
set to work.

"Something's changed."

Greta didn't look up. "What do you mean?"

"You've changed since Noah's accident, you're more
subdued. And there's a peace about you that wasn't
there before."

"Noah's accident was very sobering," Greta said,
trying to deflect Esther's curiosity. "It could have been
much more serious than it was."

"There's more to it than that." Esther suddenly straightened. "You've fallen in love with him, haven't you?"

Greta stifled a groan. "That's something between me
and Noah."

"You have!" Esther clasped her hands together as if
trying to contain her excitement. "And Noah, have his
feelings changed as well?"

"*Nee*, he's gone to great pains to let me know that
wasn't possible. He obviously loved Patsy very much."

"What makes you say that?"

What an odd question. "Why else would he be so
insistent that his second marriage be a businesslike arrangement? Patsy's death must have pained him so much
he's decided he doesn't want to go through that again."

Something about the way Esther averted her eyes and
ran a hand across her own quilt frame alerted Greta that
something was off. "What is it?"

Esther still didn't look up. "Ever since you and Noah

announced you were engaged I've been wondering if I should share a bit of history with you."

"If it's something that will help me understand Noah better..."

Esther nodded but didn't say anything right away. Greta held her peace, letting her friend decide on her own whether to proceed or not.

Finally, Esther broke her silence. "Do you remember when Patsy's *daed* had his accident?"

Greta thought back and slowly nodded. "*Jah*. A truck collided with his buggy, ain't so?"

Esther nodded. "Do you remember any of the details?"

"Just that he died without ever regaining consciousness. It was such a sad time for their family."

"That's right. He was immediately taken to the hospital in critical condition and put on life support. Patsy's *mamm* was nearly hysterical with grief and Patsy was the oldest of the children. Her only *bruder* was ten years old at the time. So when the doctor asked for someone to be the decision maker for the family, Patsy's *mamm* asked Noah to stand in."

Greta's hand went to her throat as she tried to swallow a protest. That would have been a terrible burden to carry, but she knew Noah would have accepted it without protest or hesitation.

Esther brushed at her skirt. "When the time came, it was Noah who gave permission to take Patsy's *daed* off of life support."

"How awful for him. He must have loved Patsy very much to take on that responsibility."

Esther's jaw clenched. "The thing is, Patsy never forgave him for doing it. She convinced herself that Noah acted prematurely, that her *daed* could have been saved if he had just waited a little longer."

Greta remembered what Noah had told her about the trouble that lay between him and Calvin, the difficult decisions he'd had to make and his family's belief that he could make those decisions because he didn't feel things as deeply as others, that he didn't let emotions get in the way.

Apparently, in the end, Patsy had shared those sentiments.

And suddenly she understood what Esther was trying to tell her. Noah didn't want a loveless marriage because he felt he couldn't love anyone else the way he'd loved Patsy.

It was because he couldn't stand to be betrayed yet again by someone he should be able to count on.

That explained so much.

So, what was she going to do about it?

Chapter 28

Greta had originally planned to keep her epiphany about falling in love with Noah to herself. After all, he'd repeatedly told her he didn't want any romantic entanglements and wouldn't reciprocate any emotions deeper than friendship.

After what Esther had told her about his relationship with Patsy, though, she'd been feeling more and more compelled to tell him. Not in the hopes that he would return her feelings, but because someone who had been wounded as deeply as he had deserved to know he was loved.

She knew telling him wasn't going to be easy. It would mean baring her soul to him in the knowledge that he wouldn't be happy with her declaration. Proposing to him had been easy compared to this.

Still, she couldn't let that stop her, that was just cowardly. And it would be even worse to wait until after they were married. Which meant the sooner she spoke to him the better. So on Sunday, after she visited with him and his *kinner*, who were still at his *mamm*'s, she asked him to walk her to her buggy. "There's something I need to discuss with you."

"Something about the wedding?"

"*Nee*. Something about me."

She saw the slight stiffening of his features, the wary look that tinged his expression. Had he guessed what she had to say?

Noah had a feeling he knew what was coming. But, much as he wanted to, he couldn't very well stop her. "What's that?"

"That day you had your accident, when I saw you laying there, trapped under that heavy shelf and so still— I thought for just a heartbeat that I'd lost you."

If only he could have spared her that. "I'm sorry. I didn't mean to scare you like that."

She waved aside his apology. "Please, let me say this. The thing is, it was an instant of time that seemed to span an eternity. And in that frozen heartbeat, I realized that somewhere along the way I'd fallen deeply and inescapably in love with you."

He swallowed a groan. He'd been afraid of this. "Greta—"

"No, hear me out. You owe me that much."

He snapped his mouth shut. Everything in him screamed to put an end to this, but she was right, he did owe her.

She took a deep breath. "I know you didn't ask me to love you and I'm not expecting you to love me in return. And that's okay." She touched her throat, then dropped her hand. "It's just that, when you truly love someone, it's not something you should hide away. You want that person to know it because to be loved is a wonderful gift. So it's important to me that you know you are wholly and unequivocally loved just for who you are, and that includes your faults as well as your strengths."

"I told you that I can't—"

She touched his arm, a soft gesture that stopped him as effectively as a left hook. "I know. As I said, I don't expect you to reciprocate. And I won't speak of it again if you don't want me to. I just didn't want to start our marriage with any secrets between us."

He met her gaze and felt impelled to say something kind. "I know you believe what you're saying."

She smiled, a sweet, warm, vulnerable smile. "And you don't. At least not yet. But I've said my piece, and I'll bid you good-bye."

And with that she turned and headed to her buggy.

Noah watched her go and felt a sudden yearning to call her back, to throw caution to the wind and let himself believe her declaration. She'd been so earnest, so sweet. But she'd also said her realization of those tender feelings had come on the heels of his accident. What was much more likely than a sudden blossoming of love was that she'd been caught up in the heightened emotions of the moment. Feelings born of such an event didn't last.

Remembering Patsy had also said she loved him snapped his guard back in place. Her feelings had been too shallow to survive when she felt he'd let her down.

As he'd undoubtedly let Greta down someday.

He'd much rather never have had her love than have it and then watch it turn to ashes at the first sign of trouble. Should he call things off now, before this went any further? Then he thought about how much Anna and David loved her, and he couldn't do that to them. He'd just have to remember not to give her any encouragement on that front.

But the yearning she'd awakened with her declaration had already taken root.

*   *   *

On Monday, Benjamin transported Noah to and from the mall. Maisie had volunteered to watch Anna and David so Greta could take care of some wedding preparations. Greta took advantage of the time to put the finishing touches on her wedding dress and to answer Martha's many questions about the menu and the setup for the meal.

She also slipped in some time to work on her Promise Quilt. She could already picture it spread out on Noah's bed. It would bring a much-needed feminine touch to the room and make it feel more like theirs rather than his. As for that special something that would personalize it, she still hadn't figured that out.

All this busyness kept her mind occupied during the day. But at night, when she stared at the ceiling trying to drift off to sleep, she could still see Noah's face when she'd confessed her feelings, see his struggle to let her down easy. It only made her love him more. He was such a *gut* man. How could his family members not see how deeply he felt things?

Would she ever be able to get through to him?

On Tuesday, Greta drove Noah to his follow-up appointment with the doctor. There was a bit of awkwardness between them when he first climbed in the buggy. It was the first time they'd been together since she'd professed her love, and he obviously wasn't sure how she was going to act today. Did he think she would bring it up again after she'd said she wouldn't?

It appeared it was going to be up to her to set him at ease. "Hiram's first day was yesterday, ain't so?"

"*Jah*. From what I could see of his work yesterday, he has a way to go but he has talent and he seems to be a hard worker."

"Are you going to be training him yourself?"

He smiled. "I'd planned to, but Gideon's taken a liking to him and has agreed to be his mentor."

"That's *gut*, ain't so?"

Noah nodded. The tension she'd sensed in him earlier seemed to evaporate as he leaned back. The rest of the drive passed in inconsequential small talk.

She waited in the clinic lobby while Noah went in to see the doctor. When he finally came back out she was surprised to see he had his crutches under his arm.

Before she could ask, he explained. "Dr. Mitchem said I could put weight on it to whatever extent I could bear." This statement was delivered with a challenging tone, as if he expected her to protest.

Greta had a feeling there had been additional restrictions put on him, but she figured it wouldn't do any good to say so. "I'm glad to hear you're healing well." She waved a hand toward the door and felt a guilty twinge of satisfaction at his surprised look.

They reached the buggy, and he stopped her when she tried to climb in on the right-hand side. "I think I'll drive today."

Resisting the urge to argue, she capitulated with a nod. "Of course."

A few minutes later, Noah had the buggy headed toward the mall. He cut a glance her way. "So it appears I'll be able to stand on my own two feet for the wedding after all." Then he grimaced as he looked down. "Though I may still be in this oversized boot."

She grinned. "I've sort of gotten used to seeing you in it now."

"I'm not sure if that's a *gut* thing or a bad thing."

She laughed. "Me either." Then she sobered. "Promise me one thing."

He shot her a cautious look. "What's that?"

"That you won't try to climb those stairs to the loft until after the wedding." She figured that would give his foot time to heal properly.

He didn't answer right away and she thought he might actually refuse.

"Consider it a wedding gift," she added quickly.

At last he nodded. "All right, I agree."

Satisfied that she'd won the bigger battle, Greta settled back in her seat. As for the rest, she'd just have to trust Noah to be sensible.

When they arrived back at the mall, Greta came around to help Noah climb down. But before she reached him he was already standing on the ground. He had one hand on the buggy, as if to steady himself, and his face was pale. Was his ankle bothering him?

"Why don't you let me take care of Jericho?" she offered. "I'm sure you're anxious to get back to your workshop."

Noah's face was drawn tight in an irritated frown.

"Greta, I'm perfectly capable of unhitching the buggy and taking care of my horse." His voice had a hard edge to it. "If you think mothering me will make me return your self-professed feelings, you are mistaken."

Greta drew back as if he'd slapped her. "I'm sorry you feel that way," she said stiffly. "If you're sure you don't need my help, I'll head inside. Esther has had to cover too many of my hours as it is."

And with that she spun on her heels and marched toward the door.

* * *

Noah tried to focus on the tabletop he was sanding, but all he could see was the hurt look on Greta's face when he'd snapped at her earlier. Truth to tell, when he exited the buggy he'd stepped wrong on his good foot and the pain had shot up through his leg. This sign that he wasn't as ready to get back to normal as he'd thought had been hard to take.

So he'd taken it out on Greta.

He'd regretted it almost immediately, had wanted to call her back and apologize, but somehow he hadn't been able to form the words.

His leg was back to normal now, it had just been a temporary spasm. Still, he'd have to find a way to make it up to Greta, to let her know how much he regretted the tone he'd taken. Perhaps over lunch . . .

The workshop door opened and he looked up to see Esther approaching. He straightened. Something was wrong. The frown she was wearing was fierce.

He stood, placing his hands on the table to aid in his balance. "What's happened?"

She stopped in front of him and crossed her arms over her chest. "You happened."

He sat back down. "What do you mean?"

"I never thought of you as deliberately cruel, Noah, but it appears I was wrong."

"If I've offended you—"

"Not me. Greta."

He frowned. "Let's find a more private place to talk."

He grabbed one of his crutches and led the way out to the mall lobby. When they reached the far end, which was unoccupied, he turned back to Esther and went on the offensive. "First off, Greta shouldn't be discussing what goes on between the two of us with anyone else, even her best friend. If she sent you—"

Esther tilted her chin up as she interrupted him. "You should know the woman you're going to marry better than that."

He swallowed the rest of his indignation. She was right and he did know Greta better than that.

"She didn't discuss it with me," Esther continued, "and she didn't send me. Just the opposite, she all but told me it was none of my business."

"*Gut* advice."

She gave an exasperated sigh. "Noah, I love you but you can be so stubborn sometimes. Greta might not have wanted to discuss it with me but I could tell she was hurting."

Noah tried not to wince. "I warned her what she was getting herself into. I can't help it if she didn't believe me."

"Of all the stubborn, self-righteous, addlepated men, you take the prize. I hope you're pleased with yourself.

You've wounded her more deeply than Calvin ever did or could hope to do."

Noah stiffened. Surely she was exaggerating. "I find that hard to believe."

"Well it's true. Don't you understand that a person can't hurt you unless you care about them?" She gave him a challenging look. "You of all people should know something about that."

He refused to be sidetracked. "And a month ago she thought she was in love with Calvin."

Esther waved her hand in a dismissive gesture. "Greta was never in love with Calvin, she was in love with the idea of what Calvin represented."

"And who's to say that's not what she feels for me? The first time I disappoint her she's going to realize I'm not lovable."

"In case you haven't noticed, Greta isn't Patsy." She sighed and some of the starch went out of her. "There's something you need to know about Greta, something she'd never tell you herself."

Noah wasn't sure he wanted to hear whatever it was Esther had to say. "If it's something she doesn't want to share—"

"You need to hear this. Greta's *mamm* passed away when she was thirteen. She was devastated. The whole family was, of course, but Greta and her *mamm* were especially close. Her *Aenti* Hilda moved in to help out afterwards. Unfortunately, Hilda didn't understand or approve of Greta's outspoken ways. Instead of the loving support she'd gotten from her *mamm*, Greta's *aenti* tried to impress on her the virtues of being meek and biddable. She told Greta, over and over, that if she ever wanted a man to court her, she needed to be more like other girls."

He was glad Greta had managed to hold firm to who she was.

"Hilda was only with them for about six months," Esther continued, "and then Martha took over as lady of the house. But by then the damage was done—Greta had learned she was different from other girls and that different wasn't a *gut* thing."

Is that where the vulnerability he occasionally saw in her came from?

"The two young men who did show an interest in courting her both ended things quickly. One said she was too spirited and the other never gave an explanation. In her mind, that just proved what Hilda said was true— no man would find her lovable unless she changed who she was."

Noah had a very strong urge to find out who these two men were and throttle them.

"But I've known Greta a long time and I understand things about her she may not even know herself. I think she was able to bear the rejections and remain whole because her heart wasn't truly engaged with either of them. Even with Calvin, why do you think she got over him so quickly? She never once made herself vulnerable to him, never once told him she loved him."

Unaccountably, Noah felt a fierce surge of elation at the thought that he was the only one she'd ever said that to. Then he realized Esther was waiting for him to respond.

"I'm sorry that happened to her, but she seems to

have grown into a confident woman who's not afraid to be herself."

Esther shook her head. "She's more fragile than she lets on."

"I'll keep that in mind. But beyond that, the rest has to be between me and Greta."

Esther pursed her lips, her eyes glaring at him. Then she threw up her hands. "You're right. I need to stay out of the middle of this and trust in *Gotte* to bring the two of you to your senses." And with that she stalked off.

Noah watched her leave and found himself unwilling to return to the workshop just yet. He moved to take a seat on the loft stairs.

Esther's tirade had added to his feelings that he owed Greta an apology. As for Greta loving him, he believed she was sincere, he just didn't believe it would last.

Greta stood behind the counter with her sketchbook. She'd had a customer come in and ask if she could design an original quilt for someone who loved to go bicycling. Working on her pattern sketches helped calm her, gave her time to think through what had happened this morning.

Yes, Noah had been short and rude and her feelings had gotten hurt. So much so that Esther had figured out something was wrong. But she'd settled down now and had gotten past her hurt. The lashing out had just been so uncharacteristic of Noah. Remembering how he'd leaned against the buggy and the pinched look on his face, she now suspected that it had had something to do with pain he was experiencing but didn't want to admit to. Men could be so vain when it came to showing weakness. He was also likely a little edgy still over her admission that she loved him.

Esther came back in the shop, a bag from Hannah's bakery in hand.

Greta smiled. "So that's where you disappeared to."

Her friend nodded and set the bag on the counter. "You looked like you could use a treat."

Greta grimaced. "I'm sorry I was such a mess earlier. I'm fine now."

Esther shrugged. "We all have our moments. And you have a lot on your mind right now, what with the wedding and taking on the care of Noah's *kinner* and trying to keep up with your quilt orders."

Greta opened the bag and smiled in delight. "Cinnamon shortbread—my favorite."

"That was the idea." Esther's smile held a touch of smugness. Then she held out her hand. "But I made sure to get enough for two."

Later, when lunchtime rolled around, Greta was in a much cheerier mood.

When she saw Noah exit his workshop she immediately grabbed her coat and went out to meet him halfway.

Noah greeted her with an apologetic smile. "I wasn't sure if you'd want to go to lunch with me today after the way I treated you this morning."

It was a promising opening. "I'll admit I was upset when I left you, for sure and for certain. But it didn't last. You've had a lot to deal with lately, so you can be forgiven that show of temper." Then she gave him a mock-stern look. "This one time anyway."

Noah's attentive look quickly turned to a startled blink

at her last statement. Then he grinned and gave a tip of the head. "Understood."

Figuring they'd said enough on that topic, she changed the subject. "I see you're still not using your crutches."

He waited until they'd stepped out on the sidewalk to respond. "I've been sitting most of the morning, so my foot isn't tired out yet."

Knowing it wouldn't do any good to press him on the matter, she merely nodded.

As they crossed the highway, Noah was still trying to get his balance—not physically but mentally. He'd expected to have to eat some humble pie along with his lunch today. Having her let him off the hook before he'd even gotten a formal apology out should have been a relief. Instead it made him feel even more of an oaf.

Then he almost stopped in his tracks as he replayed those thoughts in his mind. Just because she'd let him off the hook didn't mean he didn't owe her an apology.

She looked at him in concern. "Are you okay? Should we go back and get your crutches?"

"No, I'm fine. But I just wanted to officially say I'm sorry for the way I acted this morning. You didn't deserve that, especially after all you've done for me."

Her cheeks pinkened in pleasure. "*Danke.*"

They reached Rosie's and Noah opened the door, letting her enter first. One thing that was for certain sure, life with Greta was never going to be predictable.

Chapter 29

Greta spent most of Thursday evening working on her Promise Quilt. When she tied off the final stitch and leaned back, she looked at her work with approval. True, most of the quilt was hidden within the folds of the roller, but what she could see of it brought her joy.

She'd finally found her missing element—it wasn't a patch or appliqué, it was some white-on-white embroidery. There, in one corner of the snow-covered ground, she'd stitched an intricate pattern of vines that formed the shape of a heart. And in the center of the heart was an open area that formed the shape of a dove. Together they symbolized love and faithfulness.

It transformed the meaning of what she'd dubbed her Promise Quilt. It was no longer a nebulous promise of a new beginning, it was now a symbol of her promise to Noah, the promise to love him no matter what the future might bring. Even if Noah never saw or understood the meaning of this small element of the quilt, she would know it was there. This was her true wedding quilt, her wedding gift to him. And she'd managed to finish it with little time to spare, the wedding would happen one week from today. Rather than waiting, she'd bring it to his home tomorrow. She'd place it on his bed, on the bed they would share, as a surprise for him.

Feeling her cheeks heat, Greta stood, twisting and stretching in an attempt to ease her muscles. She'd remove the quilt from the frame shortly, but for now she needed to find a little something to snack on.

She padded barefoot down the hall to the kitchen, using a flashlight and trying not to make any noise. The house was quiet and dark—apparently the rest of her family had retired for the night.

Serving herself a slice of the cherry pie left over from dinner, she pondered the fact that her wedding would be happening one week from today.

Would she be a *gut fraa*? Would she ever be able to get past Noah's guard, show him it was safe for him to love again? And even if she did, would he ever think of her that way, or was he like every other man in her life, drawn to a less bold woman? She took a deep breath and reminded herself of what *Mamm* used to say at times like this, that worrying served no purpose.

Even after all these years, she still missed having *Mamm* around to talk to, especially when she was feeling so insecure.

She rinsed off her saucer and fork, then made her way back to the quilt room. Rather than going to her newly finished Promise Quilt, she went straight to the stand supporting the quilt her *mamm* had poured so much of herself into. As precious as this was to her, was she really doing it justice by letting it just sit here?

She lifted it and carried it upstairs. Fifteen minutes later she slid into bed and snuggled under the quilt, feeling like it was the next best thing to being in her mother's arms.

She sighed contentedly, knowing she'd have sweet dreams tonight.

Chapter 30

Calvin, what are you doing here?" Greta slid her hand over Skip's head, scratching him behind the ears, quieting his barking.

It was three days before the wedding and she was expecting Noah to arrive soon so together they could pick up some serving platters from one of his *aenti*s and some candlesticks from another. The last thing she needed was another dose of Calvin's moodiness.

His smile had a wry twist to it. "Is that any way to greet your *gut* friend?"

"I'm sorry." She regretted her tone, this was Noah's *bruder* and her friend. "It's *gut* to see you. Is there something I can do for you?"

"Do you have a few minutes? I'd like to talk to you."

"Of course." There was something different about him today, though she couldn't put her finger on just what that something was.

"I've been doing a lot of thinking about what you told me the other day at the hospital."

"Oh?" She wasn't sure where he was going with this.

"You were right. I've been acting like a spoiled *kinner*. It wasn't fair to you or to Wanda." His lips twisted in a half smile. "Or Noah."

Greta felt an enormous sense of relief. "*Ach*, Calvin, I'm so glad to hear this. And I'm sure Noah will be too." She tapped her chin. "Have you spoken to him yet?"

Calvin shook his head. "Not yet."

"It'll be the best wedding gift he could receive."

He gave her that wry smile again. "Is that your way of telling me I need to have that discussion before the wedding?"

She held his gaze. "The sooner you do, the sooner the two of you can repair your relationship." And it would be one less layer of tension as they prepared for the wedding.

Noah guided the buggy down the lane toward the Eicher home. The wedding was only three days away and he'd decided he would make things as easy on her as possible.

But when he pulled up at her house, he received a shock. Calvin was there, speaking to Greta. And she was looking up at him with a warm, glowing smile on her face and a hand resting on his arm.

What was going on?

She noticed his arrival just then, and the smile on her face as she moved toward the buggy put his mind at ease.

And perhaps his pulse to racing.

He set the brake and climbed down, still careful not to put all of his weight on his left foot. Before he could say anything to Greta, Calvin approached him. "Would you mind if we take a little walk," his *bruder* asked. "There's something I want to discuss with you."

Wary but curious, Noah nodded. "Lead the way."

Noah walked beside his *bruder*, noticing that Calvin was adjusting his pace to match his limping progress. Neither said anything for several minutes until Noah finally cleared his throat. "So what is it you wanted to discuss with me?"

"I've been doing some thinking about how things are between us. You're going to be married soon, and things are going well between me and Wanda. Perhaps it's time we put old feelings behind us."

"Old feelings?"

"*Jah*." Calvin rubbed the back of his neck. "It started with what happened with Kit all those years ago. And we never really got back on a *gut* footing after that."

Noah nodded, waiting for what his *bruder* would say next. Was Calvin actually going to finally apologize?

Calvin gave him a steady, unflinching look. "Granted, I didn't react well, either then or later."

His *bruder*'s admission was a *gut* start. He could meet him halfway. "I only did what I felt had to be done, but I know I disappointed you."

Calvin shook his head. "You still don't understand. And I admit I didn't either, not for a long time. But, thanks to Greta's insistence that I take a *gut* look at why I insisted on seeing you in a negative light, I've been doing a lot of soul-searching recently. And what I've come to understand is that I wasn't upset all this time because of what you did. I could have gotten over that eventually."

So he had Greta to thank for this conversation. He should have realized that from the outset. "Then what? Is it because I don't get visibly upset when bad things happen? Because you know that's not the way I handle situations like that."

Calvin waved a hand dismissively. "It's not that. Though I guess if you'd shown a little more emotion it might have made things easier. But no, it's more because you were trying to be *Daed*."

That last statement took Noah completely by surprise. "I don't understand."

"When I needed you to just be my big *bruder*, you were more interested in being a copy of *Daed*."

"And what's wrong with that? *Daed* was a fine man."

"He was." Calvin stopped walking and met his gaze directly. "But I already had a father. What I needed was my big *bruder*."

Noah shook his head, still trying to make sense of what Calvin was saying. "I don't understand. I'm here. I've always been right here."

"Not really. I wanted the *bruder* who helped me teach Kit tricks, who would take me walking in the woods just to explore, who helped me catch tadpoles, who taught me how to make a slingshot." Calvin started walking again. "That person disappeared along with Kit in the woods that day."

Noah was stunned by his *bruder*'s words. "But you said you hated me."

"I was six years old. I didn't really mean it." Then he waved a hand. "Or maybe I did in that moment. But it didn't last." He cut Noah a sideways look. "The thing is, I was just six years old, but what I'm coming to terms with is you were just twelve."

Before Noah could respond, Calvin swallowed, and spoke up again. "While I'm being honest, I might as well admit that as I got older, I grew jealous."

"Jealous? Of me?"

"Of the relationship you had with *Daed*. You were apprenticing with Gideon and it was obvious you weren't going to be a farmer. Yet *Daed* always discussed his plans with you, debated issues with you over those chess games you played most evenings, looked to you when he had important decisions to be made. If I was included at all, it seemed almost an afterthought." He swallowed again. "Then *Daed* passed just as I was coming into my own, and any chance I had of impressing him was gone."

Regret and guilt weighed down on Noah. "I'm sorry," he said quietly. All these years he'd been waiting and hoping for an apology from Calvin, figuring himself to be the injured party. How could he have ignored the sinful pride in that attitude? "I don't know what to say. I didn't know." So much time wasted. So much needless strain between them.

Calvin halted again to face Noah fully. "I want to apologize for the grudge I held against you for so long." He held out his hand. "But more than that, I'd like to see if we can make a fresh start, see if we can be *gut brieder* again."

Noah reached out and took his hand with a firm grasp. "I'd like that, for sure and for certain."

*   *   *

When the two men had walked away, Greta had returned to work getting the house ready for the upcoming nuptials. It was nearly thirty minutes later before Noah rejoined her.

"Where's Calvin?" she asked as she handed him a cup of hot coffee.

"He had to return home to take care of some chores."

"Did you two have a *gut* talk?"

He nodded and she noticed a new openness in his demeanor. "I think Calvin and I have made a start to being friends again." He gave her a probing look. "Something tells me we have you to thank for this."

Greta spread her hands. "Only the two of you can heal your relationship."

He set his now empty cup aside. "True. But perhaps it needed a little nudge to get us started." Then he straightened. "Are you ready to go?"

"Just let me get my coat and bonnet." She nodded toward the hallway. "And you can get my *mamm*'s quilt from the quilt room. We can drop it off at your place when we pass by on the way back."

"Are you sure?"

She nodded. "*Jah*. As your *fraa*, I will be trusting my heart and my future to you. This quilt is part of both of those. I know I'm placing it in good hands."

The smile he gave her told her she'd made the right choice. She got the impression when he'd moved her other things that he saw her desire to hold on to it as a reluctance to totally commit to him.

Or maybe she'd just been imagining things. He'd

certainly been pleased to find her Promise Quilt on his bed Friday.

When they stepped outside, a few flakes had begun to fall. Noah paused. "We can put this off if you don't want to get out in this weather."

Greta pursed her lips as she considered. "I promised Martha we'd take care of getting those items for her today. And it's just a light dusting—with your closed buggy we should be fine."

An hour and a half later, Greta was reconsidering her decision. They'd collected the loaner items from both homes, and visited with the *aenti*s and assorted cousins long enough to be polite. But now the gently falling snow had suddenly changed into something much more hazardous.

She stared out the front of the buggy, chewing on her lower lip. Even the headlights were proving inadequate. "The snow's getting heavier and it's getting harder to see the road." Then she winced, knowing she'd only stated the obvious.

"That's for sure and for certain." Noah's voice was tight. "Don't worry, though, Jericho will get us home."

She squinted, trying to make out something up ahead to their right. "What's that?"

Noah slowed the buggy even more. "Looks like there's been an accident." He pulled the buggy to a stop as they came abreast of it. "Wait here. I want to make sure no one's hurt."

She reached for the door handle. "You might need some help." Had he forgotten it had been less than two weeks since he'd injured his ankle?

She pushed open the door and was startled when the

wind pushed back. Pulling her scarf up over her mouth and nose, she stepped out. Barely correcting herself after a near fall, Greta carefully picked her way through the patches of slush toward the wreckage. Noah's hat was already turning white from the snow.

From what she was able to see, the car had slid off the road and hit a tree. Before she'd made it across the street, she could see Noah had pried open the driver's-side door and was bent over with his head inside.

Then she reached his side and inhaled sharply. There was a woman slumped over the steering wheel, unmoving. "Is she—"

"She's unconscious but still breathing."

Greta tried to see past him to the woman. The windshield had shattered and the woman was covered in broken glass and snow. "Do you see any injuries?"

Noah straightened. "Her right leg is bleeding and her arm is twisted—I think she may have a broken wrist. I need to get her out of the vehicle to tend to her, but she's wedged in." He was pulling his scarf off as he talked, and now he reached inside, holding the folded cloth over the injured driver's leg.

"Let me try the other side." Greta made her way around the vehicle, only to see it was useless. "The tree's blocking the door, I won't be able to budge it."

"I was afraid of that."

She headed back around, but just as she neared Noah she slid on a patch of frost. Landing on her backside in an icy puddle, she sucked in a startled breath as the frigid water quickly soaked through all the layers of her garments.

Noah's head shot up as his gaze met hers in concern. "Are you okay? Do you need—"

"Stay where you are." Greta waved him off and stood with the aid of a hand to the car's wheel well. "She needs your help more than I do."

Noah gave her an assessing look, then turned his attention back to the injured driver. "If I could just shift the steering wheel a few inches..." His frustration added an edge to his voice.

"We need help." She tried to unobtrusively pull her wet garments away from her skin.

Noah, who thankfully wasn't paying her any attention, nodded. "I agree. The community call box isn't too far from here." He glanced up at her. "If you'll take my place—"

She put a hand up, halting his words. "I'll go. You stay here and keep working on getting her free."

He grimaced. "No, it should be me." He nodded toward the buggy. "It's not a matter of just driving it down the road. It'll be impossible to turn it around on this narrow slushy road. That means unhitching Jericho and riding him bareback. I can't ask you to do that."

Greta glanced at the buggy. He was right. "You didn't ask, I offered. And I've ridden Velvet bareback before, so I'm pretty sure I can manage it with Jericho." She met his gaze again. "I know you want to take care of both of us, but that's not an option. Right now she needs you more than I do. You're the one with first aid training, ain't so?"

"Greta—"

She didn't let him finish the protest she could see coming. "I'm not even sure my arms can reach in as far as yours can, and we both know you have a better chance of getting her out of there than I do." She stepped back.

"You'll be a lot more help to this woman than I ever could be. So let me go for help."

Noah's lips pinched as she watched him battle with himself. Then he gave a resigned nod. "Okay. Unhitch Jericho and then lead him beside the buggy so you can use the buggy as a mounting block."

He held her gaze. "You might be tempted to take a shortcut through the fields but don't or you run the danger of Jericho stepping in a hole or stepping on rocks hidden by the snow. Just stick to the road."

Greta nodded and hurried back to the buggy. Her uncomfortable wet coat and skirt weighed her down and it seemed to take forever to get the horse unhitched. Finally it was done and she led the animal next to the buggy, just as Noah had instructed. Her teeth were chattering and she eyed Jericho's wet coat with something less than enthusiasm. Perhaps she could use the buggy blanket to sit on. She quickly grabbed it from the buggy seat and threw it over Jericho's back. It took two tries but at last, propelled by a sense of urgency, she was sitting atop the horse with a handful of mane in her grasp. "I'll be as quick as I can," she called out, and then with a squeeze of her legs headed for the phone box.

Noah kept one hand on the makeshift bandage over the woman's wound, his thoughts divided between worry over the injured driver and Greta. He kept telling himself she was a strong, competent woman, but there were so many things that could go wrong and she was on her own.

A low moan brought his thoughts back to the woman he could help. "Miss, miss, can you hear me?"

Her eyes fluttered open, but her gaze was glassy, unfocused.

"Wake up. Come on, speak to me."

If he could get her to come fully awake, she could help set herself free.

After several more interminable minutes she finally seemed to focus on him. "What happened?"

"You've been in an accident. Your leg is bleeding so I've applied a bandage of sorts. I need to know if you're hurt anywhere else."

"My wrist hurts."

"Anything else?"

"I don't think so."

"What's your name?"

"Stephanie Little." Her voice was strained and her teeth had started chattering.

"Hello, Stephanie. I'm Noah. My friend has gone for help. In the meantime I'm going to try to make you as comfortable as possible."

"Okay."

"All right. Now, the first thing we need to do is try to warm you up. We have to get you out of this front seat where the snow keeps blowing in. But your hip is trapped by the steering wheel. I need you to try to shift your weight so I can slide you out. Do you think you can do that?"

"I'll try."

Then he realized her clothes were soaking wet and she was shivering badly. He had to make a slight plan adjustment. "I've got a blanket in my buggy I want to get so we can warm you up, but to do that I need you to keep the pressure on the cloth over your injury, holding it as firmly as you can. Are you able to do that?"

She nodded and moved her hand to her leg.

He took her hand and repositioned it. "There. Nice and firm now. We don't want it to start bleeding again."

She nodded, and he stayed where he was a moment, making certain she could maintain the required pressure.

Then he straightened. "I'm going to grab a blanket from my buggy, and I'll be right back."

He raced to the buggy, ignoring the residual pain in his left foot. He yanked open the buggy door, looking for the buggy blanket he and Greta had used earlier. It was only after searching under the seat that he realized Greta must have taken it.

He had to find a way to warm her up. Glancing in the back of the buggy, he stilled. There was Greta's *mamm*'s quilt, the one that was so dear to her, the one she'd trustingly placed in his charge.

And there was the rub. It was happening again. Just like all those times before when others had placed their trust in him—whether it involved a cherished pet, a family debt or someone's final breath—the choice he had to make was going to turn someone against him. For a heartbeat he rebelled.

Then he shook his head, clearing it of all but his *daed*'s words on the measure of a man—the choice between duty and desire. There was no time to waste on anger at the unfairness of it all—a woman's life was at stake.

Trying not to think about the consequences, Noah grabbed Greta's cherished quilt and hurried back to the vehicle. He opened the rear door and laid the quilt on the seat. Then he went around to the front. "Do you think you can swing your legs around so your feet are on the ground?"

"I think so."

She still sounded groggy, unfocused. "Keep the pressure on the cloth. Slow and easy. There you go."

"Now just sit there a minute, I'm going to take your scarf, okay?"

She nodded and he gently unwrapped it from around her neck. Using it as a bandage, he wrapped it tightly around the wound, cloth and all. "Now, that ought to hold for a little while. Place your good arm around my neck and we're going to move you to the back seat where you can be drier and more comfortable." He helped guide her arms as her shivering escalated. "Careful of the glass."

A few minutes later she was seated on the quilt, her feet on the ground. "Let's get your wet coat off of you." He helped her slip out of it. "Now lay back and I'll wrap you in this quilt so you can stay cozy and warm until help arrives." He helped her wrap her shoulders and chest, then he checked her leg. The bleeding had slowed considerably. He adjusted the cloth bandage and then wrapped the rest of her as snugly as he could in the quilt.

Had Greta made it to the phone yet? Had she run into any problems?

He kept up a silent litany of prayers for both women. A moment later he noticed his patient was growing drowsy. "Stephanie, talk to me. What were you doing out here?"

"I think I must have taken a wrong turn." Her words were slurred. "I was trying to find a place where I could either get directions or turn around. A dog ran across the road in my path and I slammed on the brakes, only the car went into a skid." Her eyes fluttered closed. "I don't remember much after that."

Were those sirens? Thank goodness, Greta must have gotten through. But where was she? She wouldn't have gone home. Could the EMTs have beaten her here?

Three vehicles were speeding toward them. What appeared to be a county deputy and a fire truck arrived first, followed closely by the ambulance. To his relief, Greta climbed out of the lead vehicle and came rushing forward. Her feet skidded on the ice, but this time she was able to regain her balance before she fell.

The deputy reached him first.

"Her name is Stephanie Little," Noah said as he backed away. "She has a leg wound and her right wrist is injured."

Time to let the emergency responders do their jobs. His focus needed to be on Greta now.

He moved to her side but she spoke before he could say anything.

"I see you managed to move her. How is she?" Greta linked her arm with his. Was it for support?

"She's conscious. I think she's going to be all right."

"I left Jericho tied up by the phone shack. The deputies wanted me to show them the way."

"That's fine." She obviously hadn't seen the quilt yet. How would she react? She'd said she trusted him, but would she second-guess his decision, regret she'd placed that trust in him? Would she reject him, give him the cold shoulder the way Patsy had?

Whatever the case, he was certain he'd no longer have to worry about her making additional professions of love.

Best to get it over with. "Greta, there's something I need to tell you."

"What—" Her gaze moved to something behind him, and the color drained from her face. She met his gaze, a bruised look in her eyes.

She must have seen the quilt. "I'm sorry." That sounded so inadequate.

She swallowed and nodded.

At least she hadn't jerked away from him.

Then he saw the quilt, lying discarded in the dirty slush near the car. By this time the EMTs had loaded Stephanie onto a stretcher and were wheeling her to the ambulance. Noah quickly gathered up the quilt, but even he could see it was ruined. Not only was it wet and dirty, he saw large blotchy bloodstains and at least two rips.

The ambulance sped off, closely followed by the firemen. The deputy remained behind, however, and now approached them. "I have a few questions for you two. Would you like to sit in my car to get out of this weather?"

"*Jah*." Noah took Greta's elbow with his free hand and led her toward the car. She didn't pull away from him, but neither did she lean into him.

He opened the front door for her and waited until she'd slid in. He closed the door behind her and climbed in the back. He answered all the deputy's questions about what they'd witnessed and how to get hold of them for followups if needed. Then the officer closed his notebook. "Do you folks need a lift back to your horse?"

"*Jah*." Noah studied Greta's white face and willed her to say something. But she stared straight ahead without saying a word.

The fifteen-minute ride was conducted almost entirely in silence. From where he sat in the back seat Noah couldn't tell anything of Greta's mood.

When they pulled up at the phone shack, Noah leaned forward. "I'll ride Jericho back to the buggy. Officer, if you don't mind taking Greta back home I'd appreciate it. It's nearby."

"I'll be glad to."

Noah had carefully folded the quilt during the ride, and now he passed it over the seat to her. She accepted it without comment.

As he stepped out of the vehicle, she rolled down the window. "I'll see you tomorrow."

At least she was still speaking to him. Which hopefully meant she also still planned to marry him. But it was probable that she'd no longer look at him with the same affection or even friendship.

Would she want her own room as Patsy had?

Could he bear that?

Greta thanked the deputy for the ride and stepped out of the vehicle. She paused to give Skip a few pats but her heart wasn't in it and she quickly headed for the house. As soon as she stepped inside, her *shveshtra* wanted to know why she was arriving home in a deputy's vehicle when she'd left in Noah's buggy. After giving them a quick explanation, she headed up to her bedroom and gently unfolded the quilt, laying it across her bed.

It was ruined, that much was obvious. But she couldn't bear the thought of throwing it out.

Surely she could find another option.

Chapter 31

Greta headed for Noah's place the next morning in a better frame of mind than when she'd last seen him. Yes, she was going to miss having her *mamm*'s quilt around—it still hurt to think about it—but she would salvage what she could of it, perhaps make a lap quilt or even a baby blanket out of it.

The more important thing was she was starting a new life with a husband and two sweet *kinner*. *Mamm* would tell her to count her blessings and that her new family was worth much more than any object, no matter how dear.

And speaking of lap quilts...

She glanced over at the neatly folded items beside her. She wanted to do what she could to keep Anna and David from feeling left out on their wedding day, to feel like they were part of the festivities. So she'd made them a wedding gift of their own. She'd taken the quilt patches they'd laid out for her that first afternoon she'd spent in their home and created a quilt around each. Noah was supposed to come by their place later this morning to help with the clearing out of the buggy shed and equipment barn, but she wanted to deliver this in person.

She hoped Noah didn't mind the surprise visit.

Noah looked out the kitchen window and was surprised to see Greta trudging through the snowy yard to his side door. What was she carrying and why was she here? Surely she wasn't so upset over yesterday that she was ready to call things off.

No, she wouldn't do that to Anna and David. At least he wouldn't have to wait all day to show her the change he'd made.

He opened the door without waiting for her to knock. "This is a nice surprise. I hope your unexpected arrival doesn't mean there's something wrong."

"Not at all." She looked past him. "Where are Anna and David? I have a surprise for them."

"They're playing in the living room."

She set the bundle on the table and slipped off her coat and removed her bonnet. "Do you mind if I go on in?"

"Of course not. But first, can we talk?"

Her brow drew down in a puzzled expression. "*Jah*. What did you want to talk about?"

"Were you able to repair your quilt?"

She shook her head, some of her warmth dimming. "The blood wouldn't wash out and some of the patches were ripped beyond repair."

He heard the loss in her voice. "And there's no replacing those patches?"

She shook her head. "Some of those patches were from *Grossmammi*'s and *Grossdaadi*'s clothing. It wouldn't be the same." She kept her gaze focused downward as she picked at something on her skirt. "But I'll rescue the undamaged piece of it and that will be enough."

He heard the hopeful note in her voice, but he found her refusal to meet his gaze telling. Time to get this over with.

"Come with me—I want to show you something."

Noah led her through the house, past his bedroom door to another room two doors down.

He opened the door, then ushered her inside. "Is this agreeable?" He'd set this room up as soon as he returned home yesterday evening. Better for him to take the initiative than to wait for her to demand it.

He watched Greta closely, waiting for her reaction, hoping she'd like it, hoping it was enough to make her want to stay.

As she looked around, taking everything in, she smiled. "I think it'll make a fine guest room."

He swallowed a groan at her obvious misunderstanding. "I didn't mean it as a guest room. How do you like it as your own bedroom?"

Greta went very still. "My room?"

Chapter 32

Noah tried to read her expression. "What's wrong? Is it too small? Would you prefer something upstairs?"

"No. I mean, I thought we agreed to share a room. Have I done something—"

"No. I just thought, after yesterday..."

"What about yesterday?"

Why was she making him say it? "I ruined your *mamm*'s quilt."

"And you thought—" She took a deep breath. "How dare you!"

Now he was truly confused. "I don't—"

But she powered through as if he hadn't spoken. "How dare you call me a liar. Do you think me so shallow that I would put my *mamm*'s quilt above what I assured you I felt for you?"

"No, but, I mean, you told me how much that quilt means to you."

"And I still have the quilt, can still cherish it as it is."

She jabbed a finger at his chest, her eyes blazing. "But even if it had been burned to ashes, it is a *thing*. The memories of my *mamm* are still safe within me."

She looked magnificent. But he still wasn't sure he understood her response.

She fisted her hands on her hips. "Did you set out to deliberately ruin that quilt?"

"No, of course not."

"And did you feel it was necessary to help that woman?"

"She was soaked through and shivering badly. I was worried for her well-being."

"And you think I'm so unfeeling that I would prefer to keep that quilt safe rather than use it to help someone in need?"

"No, of course not." She was confusing him, firing questions at him that way. "But you were devastated. I could see it in your face when you saw what had happened."

"Of course I was upset. That quilt meant a lot to me and I hated to see it ruined. But I wasn't upset with you. Even my *mamm* wouldn't have begrudged you what you did."

She dropped her hands, and her expression took on a sadness that was like a knife to his heart.

"You obviously don't know or understand me at all." She waved a hand toward the bed. "So *jah*, this room will work for me." Then she straightened. "Please give Anna and David the gifts I brought them." And with that she stalked past him and out the door.

Noah stood rooted to the floor, stunned, trying to process what had just happened. She said she hadn't blamed him. But Patsy had said that at first too. Things had quickly changed with her. They undoubtedly would with Greta as well.

Still, a stubborn little nagging voice from deep inside told him Greta was different.

"*Daed.*"

David's call and the sound of Anna's weeping shook him out of his uncomfortable thoughts. "Coming," he called as he hurried to the living room. When he reached the living room he found Anna sitting on the floor, crying, with David hovering over her with a worried look on his face.

As soon as he saw Noah, David burst into explanation. "She fell while she was trying to reach for the storybook."

Noah scooped up his daughter and sat on the sofa with her on his lap. "Where does it hurt, pumpkin?"

Anna sniffled and pointed to her elbow.

Noah studied the affected area and couldn't see so much as a scrape. Maisie was much better at this than he was.

As was Greta.

He solemnly kissed it, then looked at his daughter. "How's that? Is it better?"

She nodded, maneuvering her arm to try, unsuccessfully, to see her elbow. But at least the crying had stopped.

Remembering Greta's parting words, he looked at both his *kinner*. "Greta brought a little gift for each of you and left it in the kitchen. Would you like to see?"

"*Jah!*" they said almost in unison as Anna, hurt elbow forgotten, squirmed from his lap.

He let the pair rush ahead of him to the kitchen while his thoughts turned back to Greta.

He'd never doubted her love for Anna and David. Still, Greta had surprised him yet again—she'd taken time out of what had already been a busy schedule to make gifts for his *kinner*.

He showed the pieces to Anna and David, surprised to see she'd made child-sized quilts for them. And right in the center of each was the large block they'd designed themselves. He was impressed by her craftsmanship, it was obvious she'd taken time and care in the making of them. She would undoubtedly make a great *mamm*.

Even if he'd pushed her too far away for her to want to be a good *fraa*.

Shaking off the thought that he'd made a terrible mistake, he turned to his *kinner*. Both were excited by the gift, remembering when they'd pieced the blocks together.

He admired the quilts with them, then straightened. "You'll be spending the day with *Aenti* Maisie and *Grossmammi* while I help with some work. Pick up your playthings and fetch your coats while I hitch the buggy."

"Can we bring our quilts to show them?" David asked.

"*Jah*, but leave them here for now while you get ready."

While they headed to the living room to do as he'd asked, he went to his room to fetch a pair of work gloves. He paused, as he had every time he'd walked into this room since she'd delivered her Promise Quilt. It still had the power to capture his attention. Every time he studied it he saw something new.

Greta really was an artist. He turned toward his dresser,

then paused and moved closer to the bed. What was that in the corner? He bent down to study it closer and made out the intricate stitching of foliage, vines shaped into the pattern of a heart with a dove inside.

Symbols of love and fidelity.

Thirty minutes later, Noah had said good-bye to Anna and David and was headed back toward his buggy when Calvin called out to him from the stable.

He turned and waited for his *bruder* to catch up to him.

As soon as Calvin was in comfortable speaking distance, he launched into him. "Noah, what is the matter with you? Are you *verrict*?"

The question caught Noah off guard. Why would his brother call him crazy? Had the new peace between them disappeared already? "What—"

But before he could get his question out, Calvin pressed on. "I just got back from delivering some chairs to the Eicher place. Greta arrived just as I was leaving and I've never seen her so upset. What did you say to her?"

Noah stiffened while guilt ate at his gut. "That's between Greta and me."

"Don't give me that. You felt it was within your rights to call my hand on the way I treated her New Year's Day. So now I'm calling you out on your behavior. You clearly hurt her."

"That wasn't my intention."

Calvin stared at him for a long moment and it was all Noah could do not to squirm.

Finally Calvin shook his head. "I know I was stubborn and childish in the way I blamed you for all the bad things that happened in the past. And I'm beginning to see what it did to your ability to trust. But surely you can see that Greta isn't me and she's not Patsy. She's someone worth investing your trust in."

"Are you done?"

"Look, it's obvious you love her."

Noah was caught off guard by his *bruder*'s matter-of-fact statement. He wanted to deny it but the words wouldn't come.

And Calvin had more to say. "Just please tell me you haven't done something to push her away, just because you wanted to do it before she pushed you away. Because Greta would never do that." He placed a hand on Noah's shoulder. "And I'll never do that again either."

Noah felt a tightness inside of him loosen, as if a weight he'd carried around for so long it had become part of him suddenly rolled away. Mimicking Calvin, he placed a hand on his *bruder*'s shoulder. "*Danke*. Knowing I can count on you means a lot to me."

"And Greta?"

Noah grimaced as he dropped his hand. "It may be too late."

Calvin grinned. "You'll never know if you don't try."

He was right. Noah nodded, gave his brother a smile and marched to his buggy. As he set Jericho in motion, he tried to make sense of things, to view what had happened through the lens of what he knew to be true of Greta.

She was outspoken, letting you know what she was thinking, but never in a mean or spiteful way. She was honest almost to a fault.

She'd said she didn't hold the destruction of her *mamm*'s quilt against him.

She'd said she loved him and always would.

She'd written him a love letter in her Promise Quilt.

Suddenly his whole world shifted on its axis and he got a sick feeling in the pit of his stomach.

She'd managed to get through to Calvin, had made his *bruder* see the need to take that difficult first step.

She'd seen him ruin a precious, irreplaceable memento and hadn't held it against him.

Greta had opened up to him, made herself vulnerable, and he'd repaid her with a cowardly show of distrust.

He didn't deserve another chance, but he planned to fight for it nonetheless.

Because he finally realized he had been in love with Greta for a very long time. And she was a woman he could trust with his heart.

Chapter 33

When Noah arrived at the Eicher home he immediately went in search of Greta. He looked first in the equipment shed, where her *daed* and several men were busy clearing it out. They pointed him back toward the house. There he found her in the kitchen with her *shveshtra*. Martha and Hannah were cooking and she seemed to be inventorying stacks and stacks of dishes.

He greeted the three of them but his gaze was focused strictly on Greta. She glanced up, then tilted her chin defiantly and went back to work.

He took his hat off and approached her purposefully. "Can we speak?" He glanced toward her *shveshtra*. "Privately."

She didn't answer right away and he was prepared to press her, but then she nodded and stiffly led the way from the room.

Time to do some groveling.

She sat primly on the sofa with her hands in her lap. Her eyes looked suspiciously moist, and that pierced him like a dagger.

He remained standing, positioning himself directly in front of her. "Greta Eicher, you are a remarkable woman."

Her lips tightened in obvious irritation. "Something you seem to forget periodically." She wouldn't meet his gaze. "Now, if that's all—"

He gently touched her arm. "Not just yet. Would you please look at me?"

"Why should I?"

He couldn't blame her for that lack of trust. He just prayed he could regain it. "Because it's my turn to say I have something to tell you."

She hesitated a moment, then looked up. She crossed her arms over her chest. "Now, what?"

"Do you know when I first took notice of you?"

"When?"

"That day at the pond."

Her expression softened. "You looked so sad and when I asked you why, you told me your *bruder* hated you."

"When I explained to you why it was my fault, do you remember what you told me?"

"Not specifically. Just something about how brave you were."

He nodded. "I remember it like it was yesterday. You told me obedience makes *Gotte* smile and that you were proud of me."

He sat beside her, set his hat down and took her hands.

"It was something I really needed to hear on a very dark day. It stuck with me."

He took it as a good sign that she didn't try to draw her hands away. "You were so young, but even then you had a bold, generous spirit that I admired."

Her gaze searched his face. "Why are you telling me all of this now?"

"A wise woman once said to me that when you love someone, you shouldn't hide that information. You should make sure that person knows they are loved."

Her eyes grew wide and her breath seemed to catch in her throat.

"Greta Eicher, despite all of my foolish attempts to deny it, I find I've fallen very deeply in love with you. I don't want a businesslike relationship and I'm through guarding my heart against rejection. I want to take chances and open up my life to possibilities." He gave her hands a squeeze. "In other words, I don't want to just do what's necessary any longer, I also want to do what my heart tells me I need. And for me that means a true, loving marriage. If you'll have me."

Greta could hardly believe she'd heard correctly. Noah, who'd professed to be done with love, had said he loved her!

"*Jah*! Oh, Noah, *jah*! I will absolutely have you." Then she threw herself at him, wrapping her arms around his neck.

Realizing what she'd done, Greta tried to pull back but she was too late, he'd already caught her to him.

"Don't ever try to suppress your exuberance for me," he said softly. "When I said I love you, I meant I love all of you." He leaned back just enough to look into her eyes and gently brush the hair from her brow with his fingers. "Especially that fierce, joyful spirit that is so much a part of you."

Her heart felt like it would burst from her chest. At last she had found a man who wouldn't try to change her.

Epilogue

Greta glanced out the kitchen window as she prepared breakfast. The first rays of dawn were already coloring the sky, reminding her of the quilt that graced her and Noah's bed.

They'd been married for nearly six months now and she'd never been happier. Anna and David were thriving. Noah was smiling more freely. And she was gradually putting her own mark on this home.

Lemon Drop stropped herself against Greta's leg, looking for some attention. Answering the feline's unvoiced request, Greta bent down and gave the cat a quick scratch behind its ear. "*Gut matin* to you too."

Humming, she straightened and went back to preparing breakfast. She'd gotten up a little early this morning so she could take extra care preparing their meal. It was a special day and she couldn't wait to have it start.

Instead of the usual oatmeal and fruit, she had maple rolls in the oven, knowing they were a favorite of Noah's. There was also a platter of fluffy scrambled eggs on the counter and a dozen strips of bacon sizzling in the skillet.

Ten minutes later she stood back and looked around the kitchen. The table was set and all the food platters were placed near the head. The coffee had finished brewing and was on the back of the stove where it would be kept warm. She nodded in satisfaction and, as if on cue, Noah stepped into the room. He had that easy smile and a rested, early morning look to him that brought her such sweet joy.

"*Gut matin*, sleepyhead," she teased.

He crossed the room and gave her a hug and a kiss on the cheek. "*Gut matin*. You're up early." Then he looked at the table. "What's all this? Is there a special occasion I've forgotten?"

She moved to the cupboard and grabbed a mug. "Can't I cook a special meal once in a while just for the joy of it?" she asked as she poured him some coffee.

He raised his hands in mock surrender. "Of course. And far be it from me to complain. Do you want me to wake Anna and David?"

She shook her head, setting his coffee mug next to his plate. "Not just yet." Then she turned to him, leaning back against the table. "I visited with Wanda yesterday and I noticed there was a large quantity of celery planted in her family's garden."

Noah grinned at this sign that a wedding was imminent. "That doesn't surprise me. Calvin has been strutting around with a wide smile on his face lately."

That was another thing that brought a quiet joy to Greta—Noah and Calvin had grown close over the months since the wedding. It hadn't happened all at once but it had grown steadily. Now one could see a genuine friendship drawing them together.

But now it was time to share her good news. "Actually, there is a reason for the special meal. I have something to tell you."

He smiled. "Something other than my *bruder*'s upcoming nuptials?"

She nodded. "It's much better news." She straightened and placed her hands on his broad chest. "It appears we'll be adding another little one to our family come February."

His face lit up as he understood her meaning, and he gave a whoop of pure joy. A heartbeat later, he grabbed her around the waist and spun her around. Then he stopped abruptly and gently set her down. "I'm sorry. I shouldn't have—"

She laughed. "Don't worry, I'm not fragile. And I won't have you treating me like an invalid."

He pulled out a chair and sat, tugging her gently onto his lap, and wrapped his arms around her. "Very well, not like an invalid. But rather as the precious treasure you are to me."

She leaned her head against his chest, reveling in the feeling of being cherished and protected. "So I take it you're happy with the news."

Noah kissed her forehead. And just as he had every day since they'd pledged their mutual love, he silently thanked *Gotte* that Greta had come into his life. Thanks to her he had learned to trust again, had regained a *bruder*, and he had love and laughter in his life. It was so much more than he'd ever hoped for.

And now their family was growing. He gave her a squeeze.

"*Jah*. I am very happy, for sure and for certain."

Debra Stoll's Special Rhubarb Pie

INGREDIENTS

- Pastry for a 9-inch double-crust pie
- 1 cup white sugar
- ⅓ cup light brown sugar
- 5 tablespoons all-purpose flour
- ¼ teaspoon salt
- 4 cups chopped rhubarb
- ½ cup pulped blueberries or blueberry juice
- 1 tablespoon butter

DIRECTIONS

1. Preheat oven to 425 degrees F.
2. Prepare pastry for pie shell and roll into 2 nine-inch circles. Line bottom of pie pan with 1 of the rounds.
3. Mix together the sugar, flour and salt.
4. Add rhubarb and toss until evenly coated.
5. Spoon rhubarb mixture into pie shell.
6. Pour blueberries evenly over top. Dot with butter.
7. Cover with second pastry round, crimp edges to seal, and cut a few decorative vents to allow steam to escape.
8. Cover fluted edges with aluminum foil to prevent excessive browning.

9. Set pie plate on baking sheet in oven and bake for twenty minutes.

10. Reduce heat to 375 degrees and bake for an additional 15 minutes.

11. Remove foil and continue baking another 10–15 minutes, until crust is golden brown and the filling bubbles.

12. Remove from oven and allow to cool before serving.

Don't miss the next heartwarming story in
the Hope's Haven series

Her Amish Christmas Miracle
Available Winter 2021

ABOUT THE AUTHOR

Winnie Griggs is the multi-published, award-winning author of romances that focus on small towns, big hearts, and amazing grace. Her work has won a number of regional and national awards, including the Romantic Times Reviewers' Choice Award. Winnie grew up in southeast Louisiana in an undeveloped area her friends thought of as the back of beyond. Eventually she found her own Prince Charming, and together they built a storybook happily-ever-after, one that includes four now-grown children who are all happily pursuing adventures of their own.

When not busy writing, she enjoys cooking, browsing estate sales and solving puzzles. She is also a list maker, a lover of exotic teas, and holds an advanced degree in the art of procrastination.

You can learn more at:

WinnieGriggs.com
Twitter @GriggsWinnie
Facebook.com/WinnieGriggs.Author
Pinterest.com/WDGriggs

Fall in love with these charming contemporary romances!

A VERY MERRY MATCH
by Melinda Curtis

Mary Margaret Sneed usually spends her holiday baking and caroling with her students. But this year, she's swapped shortbread and sleigh bells to take a second job—one she can never admit to when the town mayor starts courting her. Only the town's meddling matchmakers have determined there's nothing a little mistletoe can't fix...and if the Widows Club has its way, Mary Margaret and the mayor may just get the best Christmas gift of all this year. Includes a bonus story by Hope Ramsay!

THE TWELVE DOGS OF CHRISTMAS
by Lizzie Shane

Ally Gilmore has only four weeks to find homes for a dozen dogs in her family's rescue shelter. But when she confronts the Scroogey councilman who pulled their funding, Ally finds he's far more reasonable—and handsome—than she ever expected...especially after he promises to help her. As they spend more time together, the Pine Hollow gossip mill is convinced that the Grinch might show Ally that Pine Hollow is her home for more than just the holidays.

CHRISTMAS ON REINDEER ROAD
by Debbie Mason

After his wife died, Gabriel Buchanan left his job as a New York City homicide detective to focus on raising his three sons. But back in Highland Falls, he doesn't have to go looking for trouble. It finds him—in the form of Mallory Maitland, a beautiful neighbor struggling to raise her misbehaving stepsons. When they must work together to give their boys the Christmas their hearts desire, they may find that the best gift they can give them is a family together.

SEASON OF JOY
by Annie Rains

For single father Granger Fields, Christmas is his busiest—and most profitable—time of the year. But when a fire devastates his tree farm, Granger convinces free spirit Joy Benson to care for his daughters while he focuses on saving his business. Soon Joy's festive ideas and merrymaking convince Granger he needs a business partner. As crowds return to the farm, life with Joy begins to feel like home. Can Granger convince Joy that this is where she belongs? Includes a bonus story by Melinda Curtis!

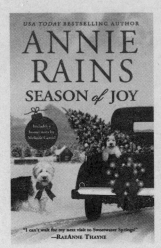

HER AMISH WEDDING QUILT
by Winnie Griggs

When the man she thought she would wed chooses another woman, Greta Eicher pours her energy into crafting beautiful quilts at her shop and helping widower Noah Stoll care for his adorable young children. But when her feelings for Noah grow into something even deeper, will she be able to convince him to have enough faith to give love another chance?

THE AMISH MIDWIFE'S HOPE
by Barbara Cameron

Widow Rebecca Zook adores her work, but the young midwife secretly wonders if she'll ever find love again or have a family of her own. When she meets handsome newcomer Samuel Miller, her connection with the single father is immediate—Rebecca even bonds with his sweet little girl. It feels like a perfect match, and Rebecca is ready to embrace the future...if only Samuel can open his heart once more.

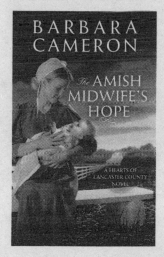

Discover bonus content and more on
read-forever.com

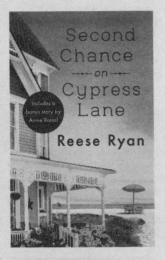

SECOND CHANCE ON CYPRESS LANE
by Reese Ryan

Rising-star reporter Dakota Jones is used to breaking the news, not making it. When a scandal costs her her job, there's only one place she can go to regroup. But her small South Carolina hometown comes with a major catch: Dexter Roberts. The first man to break Dakota's heart is suddenly back in her life. She won't give him another chance to hurt her, but she can't help wondering what might have been. Includes a bonus story by Annie Rains!

FOREVER WITH YOU
by Barb Curtis

Leyna Milan knows family legacies come with strings attached, but she's determined to prove that she can run her family's restaurant. Of course, Leyna never expected that honoring her grandfather's wishes meant opening a second location on her ex's winery—or having to ignore Jay's sexy grin and guard the heart he shattered years before. But as they work closely together, she begins to discover that maybe first love deserves a second chance...